Trusting
the
Cat Burglar

ALSO BY PAMELA GOSSIAUX

Mrs. Chartwell and the Cat Burglar (A Russo Romantic Mystery: Book 1)

Trusting the Cat Burglar (A Russo Romantic Mystery: Book 2)

Romancing the Cat Burglar (A Russo Romantic Mystery: Book 3)

Good Enough

Why Is There a Lemon in My Fruit Salad? How to Stay Sweet When Life Turns Sour

A Kid at Heart: Becoming a Child of Our Heavenly Father

Six Steps to Successful Publication: Your Guide to Getting Published

Trusting
the
Cat Burglar

pamela
gossiaux

Tri-Cat Publishing

Scripture quotations are taken from The Holy Bible, New International Version, copyright 1973, 1978, 1984 by International Bible Society.

Visit the author's website at: www.PamelaGossiaux.com

First Printing, May 2018
Library of Congress Control Number: 2018903198

ISBN 978-0-9976387-7-6 (paperback)
ISBN 978-0-9976387-8-3 (ebook)

Cover Design: Llewellen Designs
Editor: Erin Wolfe, WordWolfe Copy Editing
Formatting: Dallas Hodge, www.ebeetbee.com
Author Photo: Vera Davis Photography

Published in the United States by Tri-Cat Publishing

Tri-Cat Publishing

For she had eyes and chose me.

— William Shakespeare, *Othello*

Chapter One

Tony Russo gripped his rope in his gloved hands and lowered himself quietly down through the darkness toward the vase. The university's Museum of Art had low auxiliary lighting when it was closed, and it gave him enough light to see by without using his penlight, for which he was grateful. Five stories was a long way down, and he preferred both hands on the rope.

His entrance had been uneventful. His dark bodysuit and experience at his craft had taught him how to get into places that people wanted you to stay out of. The schematics he hacked in to earlier on his computer showed the peripheral alarm systems as well as the laser beams that could trip internal systems. He had easily overridden the peripherals, but the only way to avoid the lasers was to come in from the ceiling. Which is what he was doing now.

He could see it below. A fifth-century Grecian vase. It sat on a pedestal surrounded only by light—light that would trigger an alarm if disrupted.

He paused about three feet above it, and holding the rope now with one hand, took an aerosol can out of his backpack. He sprayed the hairspray in the air and watched it settle on the thin laser lines that crisscrossed all around the sides of the object. But as far as he could see, there was nothing across the top. A smile twitched at his lips. Their mistake. He could reach in from above.

Sometimes there was a weighted switch. He had read that the vase was approximately twenty-six ounces, so he brought a small bag filled with sand to replace it with. The trick would be to lift the vase and set the sand bag down at the same time, all while hanging from a rope.

He looked around, making sure there were no guards. According to his research, he had about thirty minutes before the guard made his rounds on this floor again.

Tony hooked the rope to his body harness. He was now dangling, but both arms were free. He took the bag of sand and very carefully reached down, keeping his body as still as possible so the rope wouldn't sway. One wrong move and he'd be in the path of the laser beams.

His black gloves were thin and supple. Grasping the vase at the neck with his right hand, he reached down with his left hand, ready to place the sand on the table while he lifted the vase.

But then he saw her. She was standing by the room's entrance, wearing a soft green sweater and tight jeans. Her thick, long, red hair fell in cascades across her shoulders. Big green eyes watched him from under long lashes, and full lips, painted a soft pink, stood out on her fair-skinned, heart-shaped face. She was by far the most beautiful woman he had ever seen.

Hand paused just above the vase, she had caught him in action. He winked at her and gave her his to-die-for smile, which he realized she probably couldn't see under his mask.

"Hey, Babe," he said in his most charming voice.

She frowned, and then there was a sudden screaming of alarms.

"What on *earth?*" He recoiled, careful not to tip the vase. Sandbag in hand, he looked up and around, wondering where he had gone wrong. Then Tony unhooked himself and jumped down, giving his rope a few sharp tugs. It followed him and pooled on the ground around his feet. He pulled his mask off and ran his hand through his unruly hair.

"Gotcha," she said. She leaned against the wall, arms crossed. He smiled at her, which should have more effect now that his mask was off.

"Hey, gorgeous," Tony said.

She refused to be charmed. "You failed."

"That can't possibly be. I'm a *professional!*" He walked over and kissed her on the lips. "Lovely Abigail. *You are my true*

2

and honorable wife, as dear to me as the ruddy drops that visit my sad heart." He saw a smile play at her lips.

A security guard walked out from behind a wall. "Body heat."

"I'll say," Tony said, smiling at his wife and pulling her in for another kiss.

"Not *her.* The alarm. That's what tripped it."

"Can we go home now?" Abigail said, looking at her watch. "It's nearly 11 p.m. Some of us have to work in the morning."

"Some of us are working *now,*" Tony said, feigning hurt.

The guard continued. "You bypassed the entire system until you got to the vase. The museum board members will want to beef that up. But the heat sensor got you."

"I had no idea," Tony said, turning to look at the vase while coiling up his rope. "Where?"

The guard walked over and pointed to the delicate dots surrounding the casing. "Here. And here."

"Hmmm. You learn something new every day." Tony packed his rope in his bag and pulled his gloves off. "Tell them I can come in tomorrow afternoon, and we can go over the shortfalls of the system. I'll give them some ideas to tighten up security."

"Will do," said the guard. Then he grinned. "I have to say. That was pretty neat watching you come in from up there." He turned to Abigail. "Doesn't that ever scare you? Him rappelling from heights like that?"

She looked over at Tony and smiled. "No. He knows what he's doing." She snuggled under Tony's arm and laid her head on his shoulder.

"Tired?" Tony asked quietly, and she nodded. He closed his eyes briefly, still not believing this was his life, that he was so lucky. "Let's go home."

"Let's go see it first," she said.

Tony took her hand. Together they walked down the hall and into the Russo room, which held several paintings of the famous Italian painter Antonio Russo, including his most sought-after, *The Laurel.*

They stopped in front of it.

"There she is," Tony said. Abigail murmured agreement, gazing at the painting. It was a portrait of Tony's great-grandmother, Margaret, whom the painter had nicknamed *Laurel* during their affair in the 1940s. After the painter's wife found it, Margaret had fled back to America, pregnant with his child. They lost touch, and she never received the painting. But then Tony and Abigail found it two months ago.

Abigail held up her hand to examine the ring on her wedding finger, like she always did when she came here. It matched the one in the painting exactly. A light green emerald on a gold band.

"I can't believe I'm wearing it," she said.

"I can't believe you wanted to marry me," Tony said. Tony's grandma had inherited the ring Laurel was wearing in the painting and kept it hidden for years, giving it to Tony to propose to Abigail.

The two of them stood there quietly for a moment. Then Abigail looked up at him and yawned.

"Ready to go home?" he asked. She nodded, and he put his arm around her shoulders, pulling her close to him as they walked out to the car. She had picked him up tonight on her way home from working late.

The snow had quit falling, but the dampness still hung heavily in the air. It brought with it promises of spring, just a few short weeks away. However, it was still cold.

"I love to watch you work," Abigail said when they were in the car.

Tony had his own security company, Black Cat Security. His job was to try to bypass security systems, find the loopholes, and then tighten them up.

"I love to watch you watch me." He reached over and took her hand, keeping his other one on the steering wheel.

They had met in a rather bizarre way when Tony broke in to steal a map from the library where Abigail worked. The map led them both on a treasure hunt to find the lost painting *The Laurel*.

"I have to go in early tomorrow," Abigail said. "We have the French guy coming in at 9 a.m., and the director wants me to have the entire floor cleared and ready."

"For one French guy?"

"Yes." Abigail sighed a long, heavy sigh. This particular project was taxing her. "Everything has to be perfect. Ms. Scott really, *really* wants those maps for our collection."

"And I will do my best to keep them protected."

The library director, Ms. Scott, hired Tony to come in and convince the "French guy," as Abigail called him, that the library was a secure place for his collection. The French guy was a collector of antiquities and wanted to house this particular collection somewhere where they would be both safe and appreciated. He had chosen this university because it was one of the only ones in the United States that was equipped to keep such very rare documents. This collection would bring in millions of dollars to the university and was a very big deal. And Tony was supposed to make sure they were safe.

"I know you will," Abigail said. "Pauline will be there too. She's dying to see you again."

Tony smiled. "Did you ever tell her how we met?"

Abigail laughed. "Not yet. I just told her you came in to check out a map and swept me off my feet. Which is kind of true."

"Kind of," Tony said. "Are you *going* to tell her?"

Abigail turned to look at him. "After you do this job," she said. "It's best Ms. Scott doesn't find out that you were just recently on the other side of the law."

Tony was quiet. Sometimes he wondered if—

"Hey." She squeezed his hand. He turned to look at her. "I'm not ashamed of you. If you want me to tell her now, I will."

"No, it's okay." And it was. He preferred to have a fresh start.

Tony turned down their street. "I never asked you his name."

"Who? The French guy?"

He nodded and parked on the street in front of her house. It was a three-story Victorian home, old, rambling, and perfect for a book-lover and her cat. And now the book-lover's husband.

"Jean-Pierre Mauvais," she said, laughing as she tried using her best French accent. "I haven't met him, but I have a picture." She pulled out her phone and started searching.

"Definitely sounds French." Tony was tired. He stretched his arms up above his head and yawned. He looked forward to getting inside where it was warm and crawling into bed with Abigail.

"Here he is," she said, leaning across to show him. The flowery scent from her hair floated toward him. He wondered if love like this ever dulled.

He took the phone, and what he saw stopped him dead. The name was different, and the hair was not peppered with gray in this picture. He had dyed it a deep black. But there was no mistaking who he was, even if he *was* going under another name. Tony had known him as JP Thomas in different circles. He hadn't looked deeper or done a background check. He preferred not to know his clients too well.

"He seems really nice on the phone, kind of charming," Abigail said. "I love his accent."

Tony stared at the website photo, enlarging it to be sure. Yes, it was him. It was definitely *him*. He swallowed, feeling a lump growing in his throat and cold claws clutching at his stomach.

"Tony?"

He glanced at her, swiped the photo closed, and handed her the phone.

"I've never heard of him," he said, opening the car door and not meeting her gaze. He grabbed his bag out of the back seat and flashed her a smile. "How about going inside? It's cold out here, and I'd love to jump in the shower before bed. Maybe you can join me?"

She looked unsure for a moment but then nodded in agreement. The problem with being this in love was he was too easy to read. It wouldn't do her any good to know what he knew about this man. Not tonight. He'd just have to find a way to make sure that Jean-Pierre Mauvais never got anywhere near Abigail tomorrow—or ever.

Chapter Two

Abigail lay in a tangle of sheets, her head resting on her husband's chest. She could feel his slow, steady breathing, but she wasn't sure if he was asleep yet. She closed her eyes, not quite believing Tony Russo was here in her bed. They had only met nine weeks ago and married after just three. Her close friends—surrogate parents, really—Jimmy and Martha Stout, had tried to get her to wait.

"Honey, it's your heart talking and not your head," Martha told her gently shortly after they announced their engagement. "Give it some time." But Abigail was happy, and she knew Martha could see that. In the end, Martha had helped her plan the small wedding they held at their church and the reception afterward in the church hall. Abigail had worn a lilac sheath dress and carried lilies. Pauline was her matron of honor and wore a darker shade of purple.

She still remembered how Tony looked in his black suit with a crisp, white shirt underneath and his lavender cummerbund. His coworker George had been his best man.

"You don't really know this fellow," Jimmy had said the night before he was to walk her down the aisle, standing in for her father who had died so many years ago.

"But I do," she said, and he let it go. Jimmy was a tough city cop on the outside, but he was a softie where Abigail was concerned. He had plenty of reservations about Tony, but he loved her enough to put them aside. And she believed he truly liked Tony.

She *did* know Tony. When they were together, she could feel what he was feeling, and whenever she looked into his brown eyes, surrounded by those beautiful, thick lashes, she felt like she was looking into his soul. He might have been a charming thief in his past, but with *her,* he wore his heart on his sleeve. Which is why she knew something was wrong tonight. She glanced at the clock. It was half past midnight.

"Tony?" she asked quietly. From his breathing, she was pretty sure he was still awake.

"Hmmmm?" he murmured.

"What's wrong?"

"Nothing. Why?"

She was quiet for a moment. "The reason we work, Tony, is because we're honest with each other. Always."

"And because we're so good in bed together?" She could hear the smile in his voice.

"Well, that too. But don't try to dodge the subject." She traced her fingers through the soft, curly hair on his chest. He smelled good, the sandalwood of his aftershave still lingering from his shower. He had shaved, removing the shadow of a beard he had coming in so it wouldn't be rough on her face. He was thoughtful like that.

He always carried it with him, his scent. It made her think of walking through a forest with him, her hand in his, the leaves underneath their feet making soft shuffling sounds. She started to drift off to sleep.

"You're right," he said, and his voice woke her up. She wondered how long ago she had asked the question. "I know him. I know Jean-Pierre Mauvais, or whatever he calls himself now."

"What? How?"

Tony pulled himself out from under her, carefully putting a pillow beneath her head. Then he turned to lie on his side so they were facing. "This is the hard part about knowing me, Abigail. *My past.*" She could see the uncertainty in his eyes, even in the dark room.

"I *know* your past," she said.

"Not all of it. Not most of it."

For a moment, she was afraid, wondering where this conversation was going, but he must have seen the fear in her eyes. He reached over, entwined his fingers in hers, and pulled her hand close to his heart.

"It's in the past, and it will stay in the past, but he will recognize me tomorrow. And when I knew him, he was a

8

dangerous man. He would do anything to get what he wants. *Anything.*"

"What does he want from the library?"

"Probably exactly what he is asking for. A place to store his maps. He's a legitimate collector, but he also buys and sells on the black market. He deals with some pretty shady people."

Abigail took that in. "Maybe he has changed?"

"Maybe."

The collection was important to the library and to the library director. Abigail herself had found it and wooed Mauvais, promising a display for his maps so the public could see them and researchers and historians could use them. She also promised him they would be safe, as the library had one of the highest quality preservation programs in the world. He would even have his name on a brass plaque in the maps room.

"The maps will bring in a lot of publicity, which will bring in money for the library," said Abigail. "The hope is that researchers from all over the *world,* particularly historians, will come here, to us. That will bring prestige, respect, and more grant money to the university. Plus, it won't hurt my tenure track."

"I know how important it is," Tony said. "But you can't trust him."

Abigail swallowed. "Maybe he has changed," she said again, because she wanted it to be true. And because Tony had.

"Maybe. But Abigail, I don't want you there alone when he comes."

"I won't be. Ms. Scott will be there. And Pauline."

"What I mean is I want to be there too."

"But he will recognize you." She couldn't ask Ms. Scott this late in the game to change security companies, especially since Abigail had first recommended her husband. Tony already had a good reputation, based on the few jobs that Abigail's friend Jimmy had gotten him, so Ms. Scott would wonder why.

"He's smart enough not to say anything. I know him from his illegitimate side of business."

"Oh."

She lay there, thinking. Tony had community service in the morning, restitution for an attempted theft that he was caught in the act of committing. He couldn't skip that. And there was no way she could put off the meeting until later.

"I can't stall the meeting," she said.

Tony turned over on his back, putting his hands under his head. "I don't want you near him."

"It's not really your choice."

They were both quiet for a moment.

"I'm smart," Abigail said. "I can keep myself safe. There will be people around. And you'll be there by 11 a.m."

Tony nodded, and she saw him swallow. He was really struggling with this. She wondered again if she should tell Ms. Scott. But what would she tell her? That her husband was in league with the criminal Jean-Pierre Mauvais at one point, and they should probably not deal with this man? This just meant so much to the university and was such a big deal for her job. Plus, she was excited to see the maps in person. One of them had been hand drawn by Napoleon Bonaparte himself and used during his military campaign.

"How did you know Mauvais?" she asked.

"I got a few pieces for him that he wanted. After the last one, I never worked for him again."

"Why?"

"Because I didn't like what he did with it." Tony turned his head to face her, but he didn't explain more. Instead, he glanced at the clock. "I'll tell you more tomorrow. I promise. Right now, we both need to get to sleep. I'll drive you to the library in the morning, you stay around people at all times, and I'll be there by 11 a.m."

Abigail gave him a small smile. She wanted to know more, but he was right. They needed to get some sleep or she wouldn't be able to concentrate tomorrow. And tomorrow was a big day.

"I'm glad you told me. I know there are things from your past that will come up. It's okay."

Tony rolled over, pressed his forehead against Abigail's, and closed his eyes. She could feel his soft breath on her face, breathing in time to her own.

"I'm always afraid you're going to hate me," he said quietly. "I wasn't a very good person. I never hurt anyone, but I lied a lot. I guess I hurt people that way."

"Tony." Abigail wrapped her arms around him. "I could never hate you. Never." She felt him relax into her.

"What did I do to deserve you?" he whispered.

"You got lucky," she said to lighten the mood. It worked. Tony laughed.

"Do you want to show me how lucky I am?"

She let go and rolled over. "Not again. I have to get up in five hours. Go to sleep." He put his arm around her, spooning up against her back.

"Good night, Abigail. *Good night, sweet prince(cess), And flights of angels sing thee to thy rest!*"

"Isn't that a line from *Hamlet*? Like...when he *dies*? You can do better than that."

Tony chuckled. "I'm sorry. I'm exhausted tonight, so it's all I've got. Try to imagine it differently. Like angels are singing you to sleep. It's a lot of pressure being a Shakespeare-quoting husband."

Abigail laughed and went to sleep with a smile on her face.

Chapter Three

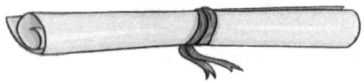

Tony sighed as the community service director gave the work crew their assignment for the morning. There were six men total. Three were in for larceny, himself included. Two were there for skipping on their bail, and one unpleasant fellow was there because he had given the cops a chase when they tried to pull him over for being late on child-support payments.

They loaded into a large van that would take them across the river where they would spend two hours starting work on the embankment. They had to tear apart existing concrete slabs and lay large rocks, by hand, along the river's edge to prevent erosion in the spring. It was hard, dirty work. He kept his eyes to himself. He learned on the first day that Karl, the child-support-payment dodger, hated everybody and was best avoided. The thieves were okay (honor among them, he chuckled to himself), and the two bail jumpers were opposites. Sarge looked like a pro wrestler and talked like a sailor, while Luke was quiet and mouse-like. Tony, being mostly amiable, had been elected captain the first day. It was his duty to hand out tools when they arrived and make sure they were gathered up before they left. Most of the guys liked him, but he kept to himself.

Like them, he was dressed in a bright-orange jumpsuit. It was cold outside, and while he was thankful for its warmth, he hated what it stood for. He hated all of this. The company he was forced to keep every morning, for starters, gave him the willies. When he was thieving, he at least liked most of the people he worked for. And he had never worked *with* them. He worked alone. He preferred it that way. But he had dug his own hole, and now he had to work himself out of it.

"In peace there's nothing so becomes a man as modest stillness and humility," he murmured to himself as they climbed out of the truck.

But he didn't feel at peace today. He felt at war. Ever since he had seen the face of Jean-Pierre Mauvais, he had a restless feeling about him. The majority of the people he had dealt with in his former "job" were okay enough. But not Mauvais. Mauvais had creeped him out from the first time they met.

Then, after that last job he swore he'd never work with him again. And now here he was.

He pulled on his work gloves and handed out the tools. His fellow workers-in-crime nodded, also avoiding eye contact, as they each took the sledgehammers and picks they would use to start demolishing the existing concrete embankment. Except for Karl. He grunted and jerked the tool out of Tony's hand. Their eyes met. Tony kept his eyes hard, masking his emotions. Karl glared, grumbled a few swear words, and moved on.

The men went to work. Tony had to put in two hours, and then he could go rescue Abigail.

──◆────────────◆──

There was a lot of hustle and bustle at the library the next morning. Ms. Scott was running around making sure everything was perfect.

"Pauline!" she shouted from the Women's History section.

Pauline cringed. She was with Abigail at the circulation desk going over a checklist of things to be sure they talked to Mr. Mauvais about.

"Yes, Ms. Scott?"

The director came walking toward them from behind some shelves, the index finger of her right hand held high. She was dressed in her usual attire of mostly black, her long, birdlike legs bound in black tights under her black skirt. Abigail had to give her credit though, because a cream scarf wound around her neck and was pinned with a gold-colored peacock. She must be dressing up for the arriving company.

"Dust!" Ms. Scott said. "This is *dust* on my finger. Do you know where I found it?"

Ms. Scott wasn't typically a mean person. She ran a tight ship, and her nearly thirty years of working at the library made her excellent at her job. But today she was stressed.

"No?" Pauline made it a question.

"In your stacks, Ms. Smith. In your *stacks*." Ms. Scott reached under the desk, opened a cabinet, and pulled out a cotton cloth. "Go dust."

"But I dusted," Pauline said and then stopped talking as Ms. Scott gave her The Stare down her long nose. The Stare is what Pauline and Abigail called it when Ms. Scott was done talking and expected you to do exactly what she had asked. "Yes ma'am."

Pauline went to dust, and Abigail was left with her list of topics for Mr. Mauvais. She was both nervous and curious about meeting him. Tony hadn't told her anything more. This morning, they hit the snooze button, got up late, and rushed out the door to get her here by 7:30 a.m., a half hour earlier than her usual start time.

She glanced at her watch. It was almost 9 a.m.

"He's early!" Ms. Scott announced, nearly running toward Abigail from the front of the library. The director straightened the lapels of her jacket and ran a hand over her tight hair bun. "How do I look?"

Abigail smiled. "You look fine, Ms. Scott."

Ms. Scott smiled and walked quickly back toward the front door. Abigail followed, a knot forming in her stomach. She couldn't tell if it was fear or excitement.

She saw a limousine outside the library. The driver got out, came around, and opened the door. A gentleman stepped out, and Ms. Scott held one of the library's double doors open for him to come inside.

"Mr. Mauvais," said Ms. Scott. "Welcome!"

His eyes traveled around the room, lingered on Abigail, and then landed on Ms. Scott.

"You must be Ms. Scott, the director." He reached out a hand.

Ms. Scott took it, and he lifted her hand to his lips and laid a gentle kiss on it. "You can call me Lulu," she said.

Lulu? Even Abigail and Pauline weren't allowed to call her by her first name. Abigail frowned.

But Mr. Mauvais was moving toward Abigail and holding out his hand. She took it and was surprised by his firm grasp. He had dark, black hair, warm, hazel eyes, and stood about six feet tall. He looked to be in his early forties.

"Bonjour," he said. "And you are?"

"Abigail Russo," she said.

"Oui! The librarian of ancient maps and documents," said Mr. Mauvais. "I had no idea you were this lovely!"

She realized then that he was still holding her hand. He pulled it gently to his lips and gave it a light kiss before letting go. Abigail blushed slightly. "Nice to meet you in person, Mr. Mauvais."

"Call me Jean-Pierre," he said.

Ms. Scott cleared her throat. "We thought we'd meet in the conference room."

"Allons-y!" Jean-Pierre waved his hands, motioning for Abigail to lead the way.

Inside the room, Abigail switched on the overhead lights. She sat down with Ms. Scott to her left and Jean-Pierre on her right. He was a bustle of energy, with his fingers tapping on his knee and his eyes sparkling with interest. Abigail opened up a folder she had prepared earlier and began handing him papers, explaining in detail the library's procedures for map storage and preservation. She told him how it all worked to ensure that his maps would not be destroyed by light, temperature, or handling. Then she went over the details of the display she wanted to have built so others could come in to view the map that Napoleon Bonaparte had drawn and used to conquer his enemies. She had spent countless hours researching and planning and felt her excitement build as she explained this part to him.

He was a very good listener, asking questions and making eye contact. He seemed so pleasant and amiable that she nearly forgot Tony's warnings.

They finished at 10:45, and Ms. Scott went to get a refill on coffee for them.

Jean-Pierre turned his hazel eyes on Abigail. "How did you first get interested in this line of work?" he asked.

"I have always loved old things," she said. "When I was about six years old, my grandpa gave me a weathered old map of the sea. Something he found at a flea market. It wasn't worth anything, but I was fascinated by it. My grandpa made up all sorts of adventurous stories to go with it. I think I was hooked at that point." She didn't usually tell people that. It seemed so long ago. "Anyway, I can't wait to see your maps. I'm so excited that you're giving us this opportunity!" His gaze was penetrating. He was a little too interested in what she was saying. Was he flirting with her?

"I'd love to hear more about your background and your university," he said. "How about over dinner tonight?"

Already? What was it with men? "Um. I'm married." She held up her hand. The emerald caught the light.

"Pardon-moi! I didn't realize that was a wedding ring."

"That's okay. It's...special." Abigail stood, uncomfortable. "Let me show you around the department."

He followed her out to her desk, and Ms. Scott caught up with them. "We're out of coffee," she said nervously.

"Of course, I need to talk about the security before I commit my maps to your library," said Jean-Pierre.

"And here I am."

They turned toward the voice. It was Tony. A rush of relief ran over Abigail. She hadn't realized how tense she was.

Abigail glanced at Jean-Pierre. A shadow crossed over his eyes, very briefly, and then he smiled charmingly.

"I'm Jean-Pierre Mauvais. It's a pleasure to meet you." He held out his hand.

Tony accepted it, and they shook. "Tony Russo."

"Russo?" Jean-Pierre glanced at Abigail. "Same last name?"

"He's my husband," she said.

"Interesting choice," he said to her, so low she was sure Ms. Scott didn't hear. But Tony heard. His eyes flashed.

"Mr. Russo is our specialist in security, very highly trained," said Ms. Scott, coming up alongside them. "He really knows his stuff."

"Oui," said Jean-Pierre evenly. "I hear he's one of the best."

"I was just going to show Mr.—eh, Jean-Pierre—around," Abigail said. It occurred to her that having Tony work on this project might cause them to lose it. If Jean-Pierre knew him and didn't trust him...

"Let's get started," Tony said. He was carrying a cardboard tube, and he opened it, pulling out some papers. "These are the schematics of the library. Before we walk through, I want to show you what's already in place. Then I'll show you what other security we can add to protect your maps."

As he explained the building's perimeter alarms, Abigail ran her eyes over Tony. He was dressed in black slacks and a light-blue, pinstripe shirt with the sleeves rolled up. His short, wavy hair was slightly damp. He must have rushed home and showered after his community service.

"Très bien. That all sounds good," said Jean-Pierre. His eyes traveled up to the skylight, several stories above them. "What about that?"

"Perimeter alarm. There's also an alarm that catches the sound of breaking glass. It's impenetrable."

"I'm impressed. Usually people don't worry about something that high."

"It was compromised once." Tony glanced at Abigail. She bit her lip to hold back a smile.

"Oui. I heard there was a break-in here about two months ago. I admit it almost made me change my mind about storing my maps here. But you've increased security since?"

"Yes. And the thief wasn't able to get anything," Ms. Scott said. "The police practically arrived before his feet hit the floor. Abigail was here working late. She hit the silent alarm, and they rushed in almost immediately."

Jean-Pierre looked at Abigail. "You must have been terrified."

"He wasn't armed."

Jean-Pierre's eyes slid briefly to Tony and then back to Abigail. "I see."

"Let's walk around, shall we?" Tony said, changing the subject.

The tour was uneventful. Abigail's job was done, so she took a back seat and watched as her husband carefully explained how he was going to secure certain areas of the library that seemed vulnerable—the windows on the top floor and the vault room that would hold the maps. Tony also discussed what security measures would be taken to avoid the theft of the maps in plain view as collectors came to view them in the maps room. Nobody else had thought of this. (Except for Tony, Abigail noted proudly.)

"You're probably familiar with the case some years ago when a man named Forbes Smiley used an X-Acto knife to cut valuable maps out of map books in Yale and other prestigious libraries," Tony said.

Jean-Pierre laughed. "Oui! No one suspected him for a long time, since he was a respected dealer."

Tony continued. "He made millions selling those maps on the black market, until one unfortunate day when he dropped his X-Acto knife on the ground with a clatter and was caught."

"Noise does carry in libraries!" Jean-Pierre finished. "You do know your stuff, Mr. Russo."

"Call me Tony, please."

As Abigail watched Tony and Jean-Pierre interact, she knew nobody would suspect they knew each other previously. They were both that good.

At the end of the tour, Jean-Pierre rubbed his chin, thinking. Ms. Scott stood so still in anticipation that Abigail was sure she was holding her breath.

"This all looks très bien!" Jean-Pierre said at last. "I'll have the maps delivered as soon as you can tighten up security."

"I'll have the security ready in a week."

"That fast?"

"I'm good."

"I know."

The two men stared at each other silently, their eyes weighing something that Abigail couldn't read. Was this just an ego contest? She cleared her throat.

Jean-Pierre's eyes cut to hers.

"I'm so glad to be able to work with you," he said. "This project is going to be more interesting than I thought." He nodded to Ms. Scott. "I'll get the maps ready to ship."

Ms. Scott clasped her hands together in front of her. "You won't be disappointed."

"Now I'd like to speak to your security contractor alone, if that's okay."

"Um, yes, fine." Ms. Scott looked unsure.

"I need to be certain of a few things," Jean-Pierre said in a reassuring tone.

"Yes. Please." Ms. Scott motioned to Abigail. Abigail glanced at Tony who gave her a wink. It was okay. She followed Ms. Scott to the conference room.

"Oh, Abigail. I am so excited about this!" Ms. Scott was practically dancing now that she was out of their sight. "This is going to be a great adventure!"

"I'm sure it is," Abigail said. And so far, it seemed to be going very well.

———◇————————◇———

Jean-Pierre waited until the women were out of earshot before he turned to Tony.

"Russo? You changed your name."

"You changed your hair," Tony said.

Jean-Pierre ran a hand through his black waves. "Yes. I did. The ladies don't like the gray. Oui? You know all about the ladies."

Tony didn't say anything. This was Jean-Pierre's way. He tried to get under your skin, get you on the defensive, and then he'd strike.

"What do you want?" Tony asked.

"Want? I merely *want* to have my maps in a safe place. And now that I know who will be building the security system, I'm more than sure it will be adequate. Who better to know how to keep someone *out* than the person who is so good at getting *in*?"

"I will do my best."

Jean-Pierre narrowed his eyes. "Russo. Hmmm. I heard about that city attorney who found the long-lost painting by Antonio Russo. Russo was your...was it your *great-grandfather?*"

"Yes."

"Amazing. After all these years." Jean-Pierre shook his head. "How did he find it again?"

"He was down in an old city sewer system looking for safety issues." That's the story Tony and Abigail had fed to the press.

"Ahhh, yes. That's it. I plan to stop in the art museum for a look at that painting before I leave town." He watched Tony carefully, and Tony did his best to keep his face blank. He wanted this man out of his life *now*, but he also knew how important this project was to Abigail. He was walking a thin line.

Jean-Pierre lowered his voice to a whisper. "Does she know?"

"Does who know what?" Tony asked, casually leaning back against Abigail's circular desk.

"She doesn't. Hmmm."

"She does. She knows what I used to do, if that's what you mean." Better to not let him think he has ammunition to use later. "She knows all about my past."

"Does Ms. Scott?"

"Why don't I ask if Ms. Scott knows about *your* past?" Tony said. "Are all of the maps in your collection even legitimate? Maybe you bought one off Forbes Smiley."

Jean-Pierre scowled. "I'm not an idiot. I'd never bring them out in the open if they were stolen. Looks like we both have a past we'd rather not share. I can work with that."

Tony eyed him levelly. He seemed sincere, but Tony wouldn't trust him if he were the last man on earth. "Good. Me too."

"Mr. Mauvais? Mr. Russo?" Ms. Scott's voice rang out across the library.

"Coming!" Tony said, and decided to end the conversation there. Without waiting for closure, he turned away from Jean-Pierre and headed toward the conference room. "I believe you still have some papers to sign," he said.

"That I do," Jean-Pierre said behind him. "I look forward to working with you, Tony *Russo.*"

Chapter Four

That night at dinner, Abigail was watching her husband across the kitchen table. Tony was in a mood. It was late, and they were both home eating a bowl of soup. Abigail had worked late at the library, and after Tony left the library, he had gone over to the museum to walk people through the upgrades he thought were needed and install them.

"What's wrong?" she finally ventured.

Tony looked up at her. "I don't like this."

"Mauvais? He seems pleasant enough," Abigail said.

"He's not."

She was quiet for a moment, sipping her soup. She should have made a salad to go with it, but she was tired, and they both had another early day tomorrow.

She knew Tony hated his community service work. He never complained, but he kept his orange jumpsuit in the back seat to change in to when he arrived. That way if anybody saw him on his way there, they wouldn't know where he was headed. He was embarrassed, although he never said it.

He worked hard. Yesterday he came home with his knuckles scraped up. Tony was strong, but he wasn't really about getting dirty. When she first met him, he was a sophisticated thief, using his wits more than his muscle. She hadn't asked him much about his past because he was trying to move on. But this she needed to know.

"Last night you said you'd tell me about Mauvais," Abigail said. "About what he did that you didn't like."

Tony kept his eyes on his bowl of soup. "I know I did."

There was a long silence. She thought maybe he was trying to figure out the story in his head, in what order to tell it, but when he didn't answer, she prodded again gently.

"And?"

Tony looked up and met her eyes. His beautiful brown ones were the first thing she had seen of him when he dropped into her library that night, wearing all black, including a mask. Only his eyes showed. Framed by long, dark lashes, those gentle, laughing eyes usually carried a hint of mischief in them. But tonight they looked tired, distant, and even a little sad.

He sighed heavily and put the spoon down on the table. The steam from his bowl rose up and swirled in front of his face, causing a misty screen between the two of them.

"He asked me to get an antique timepiece for him," Tony said. "A pocket watch that belonged to the grandfather of Charles Dickens. It has a moon on the second hand, and a window in it that shows the sun in its various stages throughout the day. A nice enough watch. Probably a bit above average in price for its day, maybe bought for a special occasion, like a birthday. It was said that the grandfather sat little Charles on his lap and let him watch the moon go around." Tony shrugged. "I don't know how true that is. I didn't read up on it. I was just doing a job."

He picked up his spoon and stirred his soup, then laid it down again without taking a sip.

"The owner of the watch was an old man. A very rich old man, who, I was told, acquired the watch through not-quite-legitimate means. He kept it in an enclosed glass case in his bedroom with some rare first-edition books. I believe *Wuthering Heights* was in there. A dreary tale. Anyway, the old man was going out of town on a certain weekend, and I was to go in and get the pocket watch."

Tony glanced across the table at Abigail. She knew he hated to talk about his past. She reached her hand across the table to take his, but he busied himself with his spoon again.

"The night came. I did my homework. His security system was easy enough to get through, the watch was where Mauvais said it would be, and I was in and out in eight minutes. Piece of cake.

"Mauvais was going to sell it on the black market, is what he told me. He had a buyer or two lined up to bid, and it was going to be in the millions. He paid me well. I used the money to get my first car."

"So what went wrong?" Abigail asked.

"He didn't sell it right away. Instead, he used it for blackmail. And he lied to me about where the man got it. It had been a gift from the old man's wife, the love of his life, purchased at an antique auction for their tenth anniversary. She bought it for him the day she found out she was pregnant with their son. She wrote a card to go with it, which was found by the authorities after the theft. It read 'When he sits on your lap, you can show him the moon going around the world.' But when the boy was five, he and his mother were killed in a car crash."

Abigail put her hand to her mouth. She wasn't expecting that. "Oh, Tony."

"So Mauvais took the watch back to the man the day after I stole it and told him to sign over his private collection of maps or he'd never see the watch again. The man was old and sentimental. The next day, in a very public news story, I read about the sale. Mauvais got those maps for pennies. Then, Mauvais turned around and sold the watch on the black market after all."

"What? So the old man never got his pocket watch back?"

"Nope."

"How do you know all of this?"

"Most of it through the news, and the rest when I went back and confronted Mauvais." Tony's face clouded over. "The jerk."

"Oh, Tony. How awful. It's not your fault. Mauvais told you—"

Tony slammed his fist down on the table and stood up. "But it *is* my fault, Abigail! I stole the pocket watch in the first place!"

He had startled her. She had never seen him really angry before.

"Somebody else would have stolen it if you hadn't," she said quietly.

"Doubtful," Tony said. "Nobody else is that good." He rolled his eyes heavenward and murmured "Humility." He looked at her again. When he spoke, his voice was soft, and the anger was gone. "Either way, it's my fault, and Mauvais is cruel. You need to stay away from him."

"So that's why you never worked for him again?"

"Yes. He tried to hire me again. He dangled large sums of money in front of me, but even we thieves have boundaries." He gave a wry smile. "I really screwed up a lot of lives."

"What happened to the old man?"

"He died a year later. Some form of cancer."

"Oh."

They were silent for a while. Abigail toyed with her soup. Tony stood at the table, his hands on the back of his chair, lost in thought. He wasn't looking at her. His eyes were far away.

"Abigail...I can't do this. I can't work with Mauvais."

A bit of anger flared in her from somewhere. When she heard that Jean-Pierre Mauvais was ready to bring his maps into the public eye, she worked for six months trying to figure out how to acquire those maps for *their* library. After she had a solid plan in place, she contacted Mauvais. He had called her two weeks ago, and now they had them.

"Tony, I need this project...I've worked so hard for it, and it will be great for my career. My tenure..."

That was what she really wanted. Not so much the prestige and the accolades, but the *tenure*. The knowledge that her job was safe. She loved her job. A job like this is what she had gotten her degree for, and it was everything she had dreamed it would be. She got to play with some amazing rare documents and maps. Now, acquiring Mauvais' maps for the library might just solidify her chances for tenure.

"This is *important* to me."

"Even if it means working with *him*? After everything I just told you? It's not always about money, Abigail. Where's your integrity?"

"*Integrity?*" She stood, the anger now flaring hotly. "How dare *you* talk to *me* about integrity!"

The words were out before she could stop them. She saw his face fall. She knew their relationship was held in a delicate balance. He was afraid he'd be a disappointment to her, that she'd see his true colors and wake up one day and wonder why she had married him. He had told her as much.

"Tony…"

"No. You're right." He threw up his hands. "You're absolutely right."

He turned and walked into their bedroom, closing the door. She put her head in her hands. What had she done? She had been the one who was so afraid of being hurt in a relationship. And here she was, the one doing the hurting. She could have handled this so much better. Her mind flashed back to the night she had yelled at her husband Nick. The very last conversation they had was in anger. And he had stormed out, closing a door between them. She closed her eyes and pushed the thought down before it could turn to panic. *This wasn't the same.*

She got up, put the unfinished bowls of soup in the sink so the cat wouldn't get on the table to eat them, and turned out the lights. Then she went to their bedroom door and opened it slowly. The room was dark, but she could see from the light in the hall that he was lying on his side in their bed, facing away from the door.

"Tony?" She approached the bed and crawled in beside him without bothering to change in to her nightgown. She spooned up against him and put her arm around him. "I'm so sorry."

He didn't answer, but he took hold of her hand and pulled it closer around him.

"Are we having our first fight?" she asked quietly.

His voice was a whisper. "I never want to fight with you."

"I don't want to fight with you either."

Tony turned over so he was facing her. "Abigail, I love you. I love you so much," he whispered. His eyes were pleading.

"I love you too, Tony. All of you. Please don't ever doubt that."

He nodded and brushed her hair away from her eyes.

"Tony, you have to trust me. I have good instincts, and I'll be okay with Mauvais. I will. I have to do this."

"Then I guess I'll have to help you," he said.

She smiled and moved her head closer to his so their foreheads touched. "Thank you."

Cocoa curled up beside them on the bed, purring into Abigail's hair. Exhaustion took over, and the three of them slept through until morning.

Chapter Five

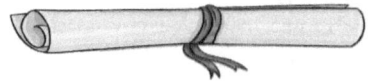

After his community service, Tony spent the rest of Wednesday morning at his desk, going over specs for the library. The vault was solid and would be safe for holding the collection until he finished with some of the other security issues. Ms. Scott had asked for a complete peripheral system on all floors, which would be easy. She also wanted the maps room, which housed the vault, to have cameras at every angle. There would be tables where patrons could view the maps. The goal was to keep the library as just that—a library—where people could view the books, maps and documents for research while maintaining ultimate security so that nothing could be stolen or ruined.

The Napoleon Bonaparte map would be displayed in a glass case near the front of the map research room, where visitors could view it without disturbing the researchers.

The lighting and cameras required an electrician, something Tony wasn't. He had subcontracted with his friend George, who was a handyman in his spare time. George was licensed, and Tony trusted him. He was perfect for hooking up the electronic part of the system.

After a few hours of designing the specs and ordering the parts he would need, he leaned back in his chair and stretched. He still worked out of his apartment. He and Abigail decorated it so it looked more like a business instead of his former living quarters. He could meet with clients here. Plus, it was close to where his grandmother lived, so he had taken up the habit of dropping in for lunch.

His stomach growled at the thought, and he looked at the clock. She would be expecting him. Pulling on his coat and grabbing his keys, he stepped out into the brilliant sunshine. His grandma's house was only a couple of blocks away, but the air was cold, and they were calling for precipitation this afternoon, either snow or rain depending on what the temperature did. He decided to drive.

She was waiting for him, and the house smelled like her homemade Italian tomato sauce. He was pleasantly surprised. He had brought over some lunchmeat and bread earlier in the week so they could have sandwiches, but she must be feeling better if she was cooking.

"How's your day going, honey?" she asked as he pulled his coat off and kissed her on the cheek.

"It's going just fine," he said. "It smells good in here!" He hung his coat up on the coat rack by the front door. The living room of her apartment was small, but neat, and shelves lined the walls. They were filled with books of every genre. She had taken Tony in after his mom died and his dad fled, and she was the reason he loved to read. Raised on Shakespeare, the American classics, and a mixture of Newberry books and recent best-sellers, he was widely read. "You can learn anything from a book," his grandma always said. So far, in his experience, she had been right about that.

"You need something to read?" she asked, noticing he was looking at the books.

"Nope. Just thinking about simpler times."

"Well, come with me, and we can have a nice lunch." He followed her frail, thin frame into the kitchen and sat down at the table.

His grandma was something of a miracle. Two months ago, she had terminal cancer. But Tony had found a cancer strategist who started her on a trial medication that put her into remission. He was so grateful. Before Abigail came along, his grandma was the only family he had. His grandma was living back at home now and regaining strength daily. He checked on her regularly and had come to enjoy his thirty-minute lunches in the middle of the day. This looked to be no exception. The meatball sandwich she made him was warm, and there was cheese dripping out of the sides of the crusty bread, along with her tomato sauce.

"I have cookies for after," she said, gesturing toward a plate of oatmeal raisin.

"Wow," he said.

Grandma looked at him expectantly, and Tony folded his hands on the table and bowed his head. He had started blessing their meals before they ate. It was a ritual his grandma taught him, but he had grown out of it as an adult. He started it up again when he met Abigail. This renewed interest in God warmed him, and he knew his grandma was pleased about it. It felt good, familiar, to talk to the Lord. He regretted the time he had spent away from Him.

"So how are you doing today?" Tony asked after the prayer. He bit into the sandwich. It tasted as good as it looked. He had told her many times she should open a restaurant. She'd make millions.

"I'm doing fine," she said, and she seemed to be. Every day, she looked a little better, a little stronger. "I figure I'll be good as new in another month." She glanced up at the calendar. "My appointment is coming up. Will you still be able to take me?"

Tony nodded, his mouth full of another bite of sandwich. She had to go for regular checkups, and he took her. The doctors didn't want her driving just yet.

While they ate, she told him about the latest gossip in her apartment complex and how her Bible study was going. Marci, one of the women from the church, came by to pick her up for that every Wednesday night. Tony tried to listen, but his mind kept circling back to Mauvais and to his community service work.

"Tony, what's bothering you today?" Grandma asked.

"Nothing. I'm fine." He swallowed the last bite of his sandwich.

"I don't think so," Grandma said. She looked at him across the table, and suddenly he wanted to tell her about his day, like he had done so many times growing up.

He sighed. "What if I'm not good enough for Abigail?"

"Oh, honey, why would you think that?" Grandma asked.

He took a drink of his water to stall for time. "It's just...I went to community service today. It's taking so much time..."

He could only work part time right now in order to fit all of his service hours in. Ordinarily, community service wouldn't interfere with work hours, but his was a little different. He was doing a lot in order to avoid a jail sentence after he had been caught stealing from a jewelry store. He and Abigail had sold his car because they needed the money to start his security company. His savings account had been bled dry from his grandma's medical bills, something he hadn't told Grandma about and didn't plan to.

"I can't even support her. Right now, she's the one with the health benefits and the pension plan."

Grandma pushed the plate of cookies toward him. He took a bite. *Delicious.*

"Milk?" he said, and she nodded. He got up and got it out of the fridge, pouring each of them a glass.

Grandma waited until he sat back down before she spoke. "Your value isn't based on what you can or can't do or how much money you make. It's based on the fact that you are a child of God." She spoke softly and reached her thin, papery hand over and laid it on top of his. "You are amazing, Tony, just because you are *you*. You are created in God's image. That's where your worth lies."

He thought about that. He had forgotten about God for so long, tucked Him away in a closet with his Bible because he thought he didn't need God. But now he was back in church and had started talking to God again. He hadn't realized just how much he had missed Him.

But there was Abigail.

"Maybe *God* loves me," he said, "but how can Abigail? She's so good and sweet and kind and amazing. I'm...well, you know what I am. Or was." Tony had kept much of his thieving from his grandma for so many years, but after he was caught, he confessed to her what his lifestyle had become. Somehow, she had suspected. Yet all the while she had known, she had still loved him.

"That girl is head over heels in love with you."

"I didn't realize how much of my past she still doesn't know. Nor do you." He looked up at her a little sheepishly, afraid of what she'd say. He didn't usually open up to her like this, not since he became an adult. But Grandma only squeezed his hand and gave him a little smile. There was no condemnation in her eyes.

trusting the cat burglar

"Just love her, Tony. That's all you need to do. Love her and make sure she knows how much you love her. Tell her every day."

Tony nodded. That part would be easy. His heart nearly burst every day with how much he loved her. And with how afraid he was of losing her. But he tried not to let that last part show.

He put their dishes in the sink and kissed his grandma. "Thank you," he said. She smiled and walked with him to the front door. As he pulled his coat on, she took his hand again and patted it. "It will all work out, grandson. It always does."

As he drove, he thought about that. Maybe it would work out with Abigail, but Mauvais was another story.

Back at his apartment, he sat in his office chair and thought about last night. Was he so insecure that he couldn't work with Mauvais and help Abigail set up the project she had worked so hard on? Or was he just being careful? After all those years as a thief, his senses were finely tuned to trouble. That was how he avoided it.

He opened up his web browser and typed in Mauvais' name. He saw the usual articles on him. Mauvais at fundraisers, giving thousands to charities. Mauvais donating pieces to museums. Mauvais and his private collections. Nothing suspicious. No criminal record. No lawsuits.

He decided to look deeper. His computer security was updated and his phone line was secured by additional software, so he could pretty much control his part of the Internet safely. Clicking on a specific software program, Tony opened up an application and typed in his memorized, cryptic password. He was now on the dark web.

He browsed some auction sites and saw that a piece he had stolen three years ago was going for six figures in bitcoin. He didn't recognize the seller's code name.

He typed in "DominoXavier" into the search bar. It was Jean-Pierre's code name on the dark web, one Tony had worked hard to figure out. Several older items popped up, mostly maps for auction and a few pieces of ancient pottery. The latest sale date was marked a year and a half ago. He hadn't sold anything since, at least not that Tony could see. He didn't see anything else unusual, so he logged off before somebody got suspicious of his poking around and figured out how to put a trace on him.

He powered down his computers and decided to call it a day.

———◇————————◇———

When Abigail got home, he had a surprise waiting for her. He had baked a chicken with seasoned vegetables and set the table with a bouquet he picked up at the grocery store. Two candles flickered in the middle of the table, providing coziness against the cold rain that had started outside. He found some cloth napkins in the kitchen drawer and put them out.

She let herself in the front door and pulled the hood of her coat down, shaking her hair out and putting her umbrella in the stone holder. She hadn't seen him yet.

"Tony?" she mumbled, her head in the closet as she hung her coat up. "Why is it so dark in here?"

"How do I love thee? Let me count the ways."

She closed the closet door and turned to look at him. Her delighted reaction was exactly what he hoped for. A smile played at her lips. He bowed long and low.

"I love thee to the depth and breadth and height, My soul can reach, when feeling out of sight, For the ends of being and ideal grace."

She smiled broader. "That's not Shakespeare," she said. "That's Elizabeth Barrett Browning."

She crossed the room and put her arms around his neck. Her eyelashes were damp, and there were a few drops of water on her face. The rain must have been blowing at her.

"She probably wrote it for Robert, her husband," Tony said. "It's a great marriage poem."

"She did," Abigail said. She moved closer, and her lips were almost touching his. He had dressed for her—changing into the cobalt-blue button down that she loved on him, leaving a few buttons open down his chest. It seemed to be working.

33

trusting the cat burglar

"They were madly in love," she said breathlessly, "and he affectionately called her 'his little Portuguese' as a nickname. The book that poem is in is called *Sonnets from the Portuguese*. There are forty-four sonnets in the book and "How Do I Love Thee?" is placed at number forty-three, making it the climax."

"Climax?" He raised his eyebrows. "Librarians are *so hot*."

"We are." Abigail grabbed his collar and pulled him to her. The kiss was intense, and if it had gone on any longer, he would have been happy to forget about dinner and go right for dessert, but she pulled away.

"What's this?" Her gaze took in the table. "Did you cook for me?"

"I did, indeed, m'lady," Tony said. He pulled out a chair for her, and she sat. She took a cloth napkin and unfolded it on her lap.

"Mmmmmm. Smells good. I'm starving."

Tony sat across from her and said a blessing over the meal. Then he carved up the chicken. "White or dark?"

"Dark," she said.

"There's still so much I don't know about you." Tony put a chicken leg on her plate and spooned up some vegetables. "Like, I had no idea if you preferred dark or white meat."

"It's weird, isn't it?" Abigail said. "But so fun! It's like dating only you don't have to go home at curfew." She took a bite of the vegetables. "Tony, this is incredible."

"I got the recipe out of a cookbook. I quit work a few hours early. We've been so busy that we haven't done much of this since we got married. We didn't even get a honeymoon."

"We'll go away eventually," said Abigail. "Or we can stay right here. I'm happy as long as I'm with you."

Cocoa meowed and put her front paw on Tony's leg.

"I *told* you that you would spoil the cat by feeding her from the table," she laughed. But Tony tore off a tiny piece of chicken and gave it to Cocoa. Abigail tsked. "This is a bad habit you started, my dear husband."

"I had to let her know I was a friend," Tony said. "I took over her half of the bed. This is how we've made peace."

"So where should we go when we *do* go on a honeymoon?" Abigail asked. "Paris?"

"Oui!" Tony agreed, cutting in to his chicken again. This piece was for him. "Paris sounds perfect. We can walk the River Seine together."

"Whenever you are in Paris at twilight in the early summer, return to the Seine and watch the evening sky close slowly on a last strand of daylight fading quietly, like a sigh." Abigail quoted softly.

Tony put down his fork. "You are so amazing," he said, and he meant it. She was not only beautiful, she was smart. He loved that they shared a passion for reading. "Who's that?"

"Kate Simon. She was a Polish-born American author and poet. Her travel books are amazing."

"Have you ever been to Paris?"

"Me? No. I haven't been many places. But I've read about them all. All the places I want to go."

"Same with me," Tony said. When they were alone together, they talked endlessly, but it still amazed him what he didn't know about her. Like this. "Being with you is like opening a book and reading a new chapter. I'm still learning."

"The story that never ends," she said. "You and me."

Cocoa meowed loudly, as if to say enough of this nonsense, feed me. Tony discreetly handed her another piece of meat.

"I saw that," Abigail said from behind her glass.

"Saw what?" The rain picked up outside, and Tony was glad of the fire they had burning in the fireplace. Cocoa, apparently full now, stretched and went over to lie on the rug in front of it. If only they could stay this way. Safe.

Chapter Six

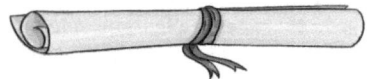

Four men entered the library, none of whom were Jean-Pierre. They were dressed in black suits with black shirts and black ties. They stood just inside the door, two on either side. One pulled out his phone and made a call.

"It's clear. Bring them in," he said.

Ms. Scott and Abigail stepped aside as several more men carefully brought in some wooden boxes and gently set them on the floor.

"These are the maps," said one. "Where should we put them?"

"Uh…" Ms. Scott seemed at a loss for words. She and Abigail had been under the impression the maps would be brought in through the loading-dock area, after Mr. Mauvais arrived.

Then Jean-Pierre stepped inside. "It's okay. Leave them there," he said, motioning to his men with a wave of his hand. They made several more trips and soon there were six wooden boxes on the floor in the lobby of the university library.

"I need to be sure they are safe, no? Where is your security?" Jean-Pierre said.

Abigail looked at her watch. It was 11:05 a.m. Tony was late. "He's on his way."

"They cannot be here without security," said Jean-Pierre. He snapped his fingers, and two of his men reappeared through the doors and stood at attention. "They're armed. They'll protect them."

The elevator doors opened, and there was Tony. Abigail exhaled.

"They were supposed to come in the back," he said.

"I prefer a front entrance," Jean-Pierre replied.

"But I can't keep them secure unless you follow protocol," Tony said levelly. Jean-Pierre was about to say something but seemed to change his mind.

"You are right, of course. My apologies." He gave a brief nod. "Should we go around?"

"Not necessary." Tony, with his usual charm, asked the men in black to bring them into the elevator, which fit two crates and a dolly. "I'll stay with the boxes here," he said to Jean-Pierre. "You travel with the rest."

The Frenchman nodded. Both of these men were so smooth that if she didn't know better, she wouldn't think anything else was going on. She rode up to her floor and then stood at her desk, watching as all of the maps were brought up and moved to the vault.

"Let's open the crates and see what we have," Ms. Scott said, motioning them all into the vault. She was rubbing her hands together, and Abigail could tell she was excited. To see Ms. Scott show emotion was a rare thing. She looked around to see if Pauline was nearby, but she must be working on her own floor. Probably best not to crowd too many people into the vault, anyway.

Abigail's heart was beating quickly from the excitement. Tony took a crowbar and popped the top off one of the crates. Jean-Pierre peered in.

"A great place to start!" he said. "Some of my rarer maps." He carefully lifted a tube out and looked over at Abigail. "You'll love this one."

"Is it Napoleon's map?"

"Non. It's better."

"*Better?*" Abigail couldn't imagine what could be better. In the collection, he had listed some undesignated maps that needed classifying. It must be one of those.

He pulled some white gloves out of his pocket and carefully slid the map out of the tube. He laid it on top of the crate next to them and unrolled it.

Abigail gasped. It was an Italian map that had to be at least six hundred years old. She had heard about a few such maps when she was in graduate school but had never actually seen one in real life. She realized her hand was over her heart. She met eyes with Jean-Pierre, who was beaming.

"This is several centuries old," she said. "It has to be..." She looked back down at it for the telltale signature. "It's a Vesconte!" Pietro Vesconte was a Genoese cartographer who had a profound influence on early mapmaking. "Wow..."

"Oui," he said quietly, almost reverently. "And I need you to classify it for me. I have a very good idea, but you have the knowledge to pinpoint its exact date." He nodded toward the crate it came out of. "I have several more in there that I need some help figuring out."

"Fourteenth century..." Abigail said, still not taking her eyes off it. "Vesconte is a pioneer in Portolan charts... estimating distances, compasses...and is probably one of the first people to sign his works. He was a great influence on Italian mapmaking," she added, for Tony's benefit.

"This is marvelous," said Ms. Scott, smiling. "This is just so *marvelous!* And yes, Abigail is *the* woman for the job. She knows her maps."

"I'm sure she's quite capable," said Jean-Pierre.

Abigail realized she had been holding her breath. As Jean-Pierre rolled the map back up and was putting it in the tube, she looked over at Tony. He was as white as a sheet.

"Tony?"

He swallowed and seemed to regain himself, just as Jean-Pierre met his eyes.

"Something wrong?" the Frenchman asked.

"Nothing. Nothing at all." Tony's smile lit up the room. "You can sleep well knowing it's in this vault. Nothing can get in here."

"I'm counting on that," said Jean-Pierre.

Tony seemed relaxed and all charm, but Abigail knew something was wrong. The look he had in his eyes when she caught him unaware just now was almost horror. What wasn't he saying?

Jean-Pierre replaced the top to the crate and hammered it back down. He followed Tony, Ms. Scott, and Abigail out, and watched as the vault was sealed and the locks set.

"I need to get going," he said, nodding to his men to follow. "Thank you." He shook their hands. Abigail noticed how cool and dry his were. He didn't seem a bit worried about his maps.

Ms. Scott escorted him to the library and went downstairs with him. Abigail was left alone with Tony.

She wondered what had upset him so much. It was true she hadn't known Tony for very long, but it didn't seem that much could rattle him. She turned to him and waited until he met her eyes. When he did, she saw uncertainty.

"What's wrong?" she asked.

"That map is what's wrong. You're right, of course. It's a fourteenth-century Vesconte. It's from a private collection and worth millions."

"You recognize it? How?"

"I stole it."

Tony couldn't believe his luck, or the lack thereof. Of all the things that could go wrong, why on earth did Jean-Pierre have to bring in one of the maps that he had hired Tony to steal for him?

Abigail was looking at him like she didn't understand.

"You *stole* it?"

"Yes." He shouldn't have to explain. She knew what he used to do.

"You mean...you mean..."

"Abigail, let's not discuss this here." He nodded up toward the cameras.

She swallowed. "I have some filing to do. Walk back to the stacks with me?"

Tony knew she was shell-shocked, as was he. She wanted to talk this out. But not here. Not now.

"I need to get home. Or to work. Can we...?"

Abigail glanced at the clock. "Let's do lunch."

"Please, let's talk about this tonight." He needed some time to think.

"No." She looked angry. She picked up the phone at her desk and dialed. "Ms. Scott? I'm going to take an early lunch. Okay. Thank you." She went to the break room and came back wearing her coat. "Let's go."

Tony reluctantly followed her out to their car. As soon as the car door closed, she turned to him.

"What do you mean you *stole* it?"

Her green eyes were flashing. She was definitely angry. He would try charm. "You're beautiful when you're mad."

"*Don't*. Tell me the story."

"That map was not on your checklist."

"No."

"Did you wonder why?"

"He said he brought us a few surprises."

Tony gave a wry smile. "Well, it worked. We're surprised."

Abigail crossed her arms and turned to look out the windshield. She blew some air out from her cheeks in a loud exhale.

Tony sighed too. Here was his past back to haunt him again. "It's what I used to do. You know that," Tony said quietly.

"But I didn't expect...I didn't think..." She turned to look at him again. "Why now? Why does it have to interfere with one of the most exciting things in my career? I mean, this was something I was *so* proud of! Getting *this* map collector to bring his maps here! Did you *see* them? *Napoleon Bonaparte's own map?* Maps from the *fourteenth* century? Hand-drawn maps are so *personal!* And so...priceless. I mean...that one he showed us..."

She was silent, her brow furrowed. "Why on earth would he bring it here and risk someone seeing it?"

"Jean-Pierre has always worked carefully. I'm sure he has covered his tracks."

Abigail pushed her hair behind her ear. He needed to feel her comforting touch. He wanted to reach over and take her hand, but he wasn't sure his touch would be welcome.

"Why would he even show us that map?" she asked.

"He's trying to trap me," Tony said. "Think about it. He shows up and finds me as the head of the security team. Suddenly it occurs to him that he can use this to his advantage."

"Why? How?" She turned to look at him.

"I don't know. He wants something."

Their eyes met. Hers softened. "I'm sorry I'm angry. I'm not angry with *you*. I'm just frustrated." She sighed. "What are we going to do? I need to tell Ms. Scott it's stolen. But I can't."

They both realized the implications of that. Tony would go to jail.

"We're in between a rock and a hard place," Abigail said.

"When we are born we cry that we are come to this great stage of fools."

Abigail raised an eyebrow.

"King Lear."

"Of course."

Tony started the car. "Where do you want to go?"

Abigail looked over at him. "You know, I think I'll stay here. I have a lot to do." She leaned over and gave him a peck on the cheek. "I'll see you tonight."

"Yeah." He knew she was upset, but who could blame her? He supposed he was glad she didn't want to talk more right now. They'd wait until tonight, when they both had time to work it out in their own heads. And hearts.

He watched her enter the building and then decided to go home and eat lunch. He wasn't up to facing his grandma today.

———◇——————————◇———

Tony drove back to the house to fix lunch. There had never been a crisis that affected his appetite. He opened a can of tuna and got some bread out, trying not to trip over Cocoa, who was meowing loudly for a treat.

"I swear you can hear a manual can opener from any room in the house," Tony said. He handed Cocoa a small bite. He found a knife and sliced the sandwich in half, added some chips, and reached into the fridge for a cola.

He sat down at the table and bowed his head in a quick prayer of thanks. He was about to take a bite of his sandwich when he heard a knock at the door. He wasn't expecting anyone.

"Are *you?*" he asked the cat. She blinked at him. He got up and went to the door, looking through the peephole. There stood Jean-Pierre. He was alone. Tony was pretty sure Abigail hadn't given him their address. He must have followed Tony. He cursed at himself for being so careless. Then he opened the door.

"Tony! I wasn't sure you'd be home!"

A lie.

"Hello, *JP*," Tony said evenly.

"Will you invite me in?" he asked when Tony made no move to do so. Tony's mind went to the gun that Abigail kept upstairs in her underwear drawer.

"Sure." He stepped back, and JP walked in, brushing snow off his coat and onto the rug underneath his feet. He stomped his boots.

"Will winter never end? C'est terrible," he said, a wide smile on his face.

Tony ignored the wet mess JP was making with his boots. His eyes narrowed. "Why are you here? I'm on my lunch hour. We can talk at the library tomorrow if you have questions or concerns."

"Oh, I'll be quick," said JP, stepping further inside so Tony could shut the door. He walked through the living room to the kitchen table, tracking snow. He sat in Tony's chair.

"Tuna?" he said, looking at Tony's sandwich. "One of my favorites." But he pushed the plate aside and turned to face Tony. "Would you like to sit?"

"No," Tony said, crossing his arms.

"Ahhhh," JP said. "Then I'll get right to the point."

"I wish you would," Tony said. He was calculating how far away the butcher knives were.

JP slid his eyes in the same direction and then back to Tony. "I'm here to offer you a job."

"What kind of a job?"

"The kind you are best at."

So *that's* what he wants. Tony knew it had to be illegal, or he'd never bring the stolen map out as leverage.

"I don't do that anymore."

JP held up his index finger. "Just this once. It's a piece I've wanted for quite some time now. I remember you let me down once before."

Tony remembered too. It was piece of jewelry owned by a society heiress turned actress who lived on the outskirts of town. A necklace with a large diamond in the center and smaller diamonds around it. It had appeared in some of her films and was especially popular in the 1960s noir films. It was a hot item among collectors on the black market. Everybody wanted it, but it was under very tight security.

"Why me? There are plenty of other thieves out there."

"Because you're the best. You've been inside her house before."

Tony remembered. He had climbed in through the guest bedroom window after turning off the security system. It was a diamond ring he was after that particular night, and it was an easy steal. Practice for the diamond necklace, which he would come back for when the actress was home. She never left without it.

"Only once. I'm sure the security has changed."

"You'll do fine."

"No, I won't." Tony pulled out a chair. He sat across from JP and leaned forward, meeting his eyes across the table. "Because I'm not doing it. I probably couldn't get in there anyway."

JP reclined against the back of his chair and looked at his fingernails. "Well," he said eventually, "then I'll have no choice but to turn you in."

"Turn *me* in?" Tony laughed and leaned back in his chair, folding his arms across his chest. He did his best to look relaxed. After dealing with criminals for so long, he was pretty good at giving off whatever emotions he wanted them to think he was having. "Whatever for? If you claim I stole the map, then it'll come right back to you. We'll both end up in prison."

JP pulled the sandwich plate toward him and took a bite. "Mmmmmm," he said. Tony thought about knocking the man out of his chair. That was *his* sandwich! But he kept his calm, reserved body language. "This is good." JP chewed and swallowed. "And no. *I* won't be going to prison." He glanced around, as if looking for cameras. "If you do some research, you'll discover that particular map was purchased legitimately from a man named Frederich Dietrich. I had no idea it was stolen."

Tony wanted to punch the sweet smile off JP's face. So that was it—JP had rigged up a false identity to make it look like he had legitimately purchased the map.

JP reached into his suit coat pocket and pulled out a flash drive. "You might want to look at this before you say no to me again." He tossed it across the table.

Tony's heart sank. Whatever was on that flash drive must be something that could implicate him in the theft. Or worse. But he kept his eyes neutral, his breathing steady, for JP's benefit. "Whatever you have on me won't stick."

JP pushed his chair out from the table and took the half sandwich in his hand. "This really is a marvelous sandwich," he said, taking another bite. At the door, he turned to face Tony. "It would be in your best interest to take the job. I'll let myself out."

JP closed the door behind him. Tony sat in the chair for a long moment, arms still crossed, thinking. If what JP said was true, he didn't see any way out of this mess without a jail sentence. But he wasn't about to let this jerk ruin his life. He pulled the sandwich plate toward him and ate a potato chip. If JP wanted to play hardball, Tony would strike him out.

He put on his coat and headed out the door to his office to see what was on the flash drive.

Chapter Seven

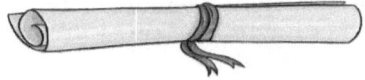

Abigail was chewing her nails, a habit she had picked up this week. She kept thinking about the Vesconte being *stolen* goods. And stolen by Tony, of all people.

Ms. Scott was already writing press releases and having Pauline order banners announcing the maps. A few minutes ago, Ms. Scott had asked Abigail to prepare a workshop where Abigail would talk about the maps, their historic significance, and the library's careful storage of these and other documents. It would be a big premiere event to reveal the maps to the public. Nobody local had much cared about their archival prominence in the industry before, but now that they had Napoleon's map (someone everybody had heard about) instead of just some historic maps of various countries, it was suddenly newsworthy. And Ms. Scott was so excited about the Pietro Vesconte map that she was already planning how to share the news with museums around the world. *Museums,* no doubt! She had twisted her hands together in her excitement as she told Abigail. No other libraries had such treasures that were usually reserved for *museums!*

Abigail frowned at her nails, and their appearance. She'd have to schedule a manicure.

So, what was she supposed to do now? The Vesconte map that Jean-Pierre showed her—and Tony stole—was obviously eclipsing even the Napoleonic map. And there were others, Jean-Pierre had said. How many? She felt a trill of excitement override her nerves as she thought about those maps. To actually hold something that old and rare in your hands... Not many people understood her excitement over old things.

She wondered who owned the Vesconte before. And where he got it. Perhaps he himself was a thief and had taken it from some other awful person. If there was a list of awful people, she could justify having it in her collection. *Her* collection? Was she thinking of it as *hers* now? She'd have to do a search on the Vesconte and see if she could trace it.

She knew the British Library had a few Vescontes in their collection. Now her library had one too! Maybe more, from what Jean-Pierre hinted at...

"Abigail?"

Abigail nearly jumped out of her skin at Pauline's voice.

"I'm sorry! You must have been deep in thought!" Pauline said. "I was coming by to see if you want me to get you some lunch. I'm driving over to Marco's Deli."

"Um..." Abigail's stomach growled but was also feeling a bit queasy from nerves. If she ate right now, she might throw up. "I'm fine. Thanks!"

Pauline left. Abigail took a deep breath and let it out slowly. What if she had never met Tony? Then the map project would be going off smoothly. She wouldn't be worried about Jean-Pierre because she wouldn't know that he was anything other than a charming, good-looking Frenchman. And as for the maps, she would be free to pursue them all, even the stolen ones, with the joy and curiosity that led her to this field of work. Now when she looked at those old maps, she felt sick. Mostly. She had to admit a part of her didn't care *where* they came from. Did that make her a bad person?

She was so excited when she first saw the Vesconte map. Before she saw Tony's reaction to it. Or heard his reason *why*.

She felt some butterflies in her stomach. What else would come up from his past to haunt her? Would there be other things? She had never asked him exactly how much he had stolen. He was thirty-two now...if he started when he was a teen...

The thought of how many lives he had possibly hurt scared her, and she turned her mind away from that. Martha had talked about trust when Abigail told her she was getting married.

And so had her morning devotional.

And really, she couldn't blame him. He had told her what he used to do, and she knew who he was when she married him. He loved her dearly. As much as this job meant to her, Tony meant more. She would do what she could to protect him.

"I thought you were taking an early lunch." Ms. Scott walked up to her desk and dropped off some tubes.

"I changed my mind. I'll go in a little bit." She knew now what she wanted to do.

"These need to be put away," Ms. Scott said, "and there's more in the workroom."

"Okay."

Ms. Scott left her to her work. She'd file the maps away until Pauline got back, and then she'd ask her for a ride. She needed to see Tony now. She wanted to remind him that she loved him and that she was on his side. She'd do whatever she could to be sure he knew that. Feeling newly renewed by her decision, she got to work.

Then her cell phone rang. She looked at the caller ID. It was Nick's mom. She hadn't heard from her in a few years.

"Hello?" she answered tentatively.

"Abigail, it's Sharon." She didn't remember, exactly, when she had stopped calling her mother-in-law mom "Mom" and started calling her "Sharon." It was something that had happened gradually over the years, she suspected, in the once or twice-a-year phone calls she received from her. She couldn't even remember who initiated it.

"Um, hi," Abigail said, wondering why she had called.

"I saw your wedding announcement in the newspaper," Sharon said.

So *that* was it. Abigail closed her eyes. "I'm sorry. I was going to tell you soon. Martha insisted on putting it in, and I didn't want her to, but—"

"I think it's great," Sharon said.

"You do?" Several times, she had thought of calling Nick's parents and telling them the news. It only seemed like the appropriate thing to do. But she couldn't figure out what the right words were.

"Of course! Roger and I are happy for you. In a week and a half, it will be seven years. You're young, Abigail. You need to move on. You have your whole life ahead of you. Have babies. Be happy."

trusting the cat burglar

"Thank you," Abigail said. Just hearing Sharon's voice made her feel like Nick was closer. She should have called them. She needed to tell them that she was finally able to talk about Nick, that just the mention of his name no longer caused a panicky feeling inside of her. They deserved to know that she was finally healing. But maybe they figured it out, now that she had decided to marry again. Another thing she should have told them. It had been over a month since her wedding, and with the anniversary of Nick's death a week from Sunday, she should have let them know. She was sad they had found out in the newspaper, some impersonal source. "I'm so sorry."

"We don't blame you," Sharon reminded her softly, referring to Nick's death.

"I know." It seemed Abigail was forever apologizing to them. But Nick's parents had never tried to put blame on Abigail, even though they knew she and Nick had been fighting when he left that night. Probably because Abigail had punished herself more than enough.

"Well," Sharon said. There didn't seem to be anything more to say. "I guess this is it. You are welcome to call me anytime, honey. You know I love you. But we don't expect you to. You have a new life now."

Tears filled Abigail's eyes. This seemed like a final goodbye, a final letting go of Nick.

"I loved him," she said, upset to hear her voice breaking. "And I loved you too. I still love you."

"We love you too," Sharon said, and Abigail could hear the tears in her former mother-in-in law's voice. Nick, like Abigail, was an only child. There would never be grandkids for Roger and Sharon or a large family coming home for the holidays.

There was a long silence. Nick had Sharon's eyes. Abigail hadn't seen her in-laws in at least five years. It had been too painful for both of them. She wondered what they looked like now.

"Goodbye," Abigail said, her voice a whisper.

"Goodbye, honey."

There was a click on the end of the line. Abigail held the phone to her ear for a moment, her eyes closed and the tears

48

spilling down her cheeks. Then she put her phone in her desk, took a deep breath, and went to look for some tissues.

She had pulled herself together and was filing by the time Pauline came back.

"Can you give me a ride?" Abigail asked. She had a husband who was still very much alive, and she needed to let him know how much she loved him.

Chapter Eight

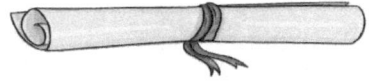

Tony sat in his office chair, waiting for his computer to boot up. He figured it would be best to look at the flash drive here, where he was in control of security. After his computer hummed to life, he plugged in the drive and clicked on the icon to open it. The file was simply titled "Guilty." It looked like a video.

There was a timid knock at the door, and Tony quickly ejected the flash drive just as the lock clicked and the knob turned.

"It's me," Abigail said, peeking around the door, keys in her hand.

Tony stood, crossing the room to her. She closed the door behind her, and he took her in his arms, burying his face in her hair to give him time to compose himself.

They held each other quietly for a moment, and he wondered why she had come. "I'm sorry," he said, because it was all he could think to say. *So* much was going on in his head, so many ways he had hurt her with this map mess. And he was about to hurt her more, even after he had promised not to.

"No, don't be," she said, and she pulled back to look in to his eyes. "I couldn't work. I couldn't eat. I had to see you. Pauline drove me."

She pulled off her boots and walked over to the couch, sitting and pulling him down to face her. "I know about your past, and I'm sorry I reacted the way I did. It'll be okay. We'll make it okay. We just have to figure this out."

Tony's heart was pounding because of all the things he needed to say to her. But piling on the information that JP had stopped by with an incriminating video seemed like too much to tell her right now. He needed to sort it out and give her time to grieve this first before he hit her with another problem.

"Of course, I won't say anything to Ms. Scott. If I didn't know you, I'd have no idea that map was stolen, and when I set this plan into action by inviting Jean-Pierre to our library, I didn't know you at the time. So I've decided to proceed as planned."

Tony swallowed. "Only he probably wouldn't have brought in the Vesconte if he didn't see me as part of the picture now."

"Why?"

"He's using it as leverage. He wants something."

"What?" Her eyes were big, beautiful, and full of trust.

Tony looked down at his hands. "We'll find out soon enough," he said quietly.

She was quiet, and he looked back up at her.

"What's wrong?" she asked.

Tony laughed, a sarcastic sound with no humor. "What isn't? *Let life be short: else shame will be too long.*"

Abigail took his hand in hers. "No shame," she said, and reached over to touch his cheek. "I was remembering my morning devotional, which is why I came over here. It was about trust. Proverbs 3:5. *Trust in the Lord with all your heart and lean not on your own understanding.* So I will trust Him because He loves me and only wants what is best for me. For *us.* We'll be okay."

Tony sighed. "Oh, Abigail, there's so much I need to tell you…"

"There will be time for that, Tony. Right now, we just have to trust in God. He brought us together. He won't let anything tear us apart."

Tony was afraid to ask the next question that popped into his head, but he had to. "You trust God. But do you trust *me?*"

"Love trusts," says Abigail. "And I love you. Remember our wedding?"

Tony did. The scripture they had picked out for the reading was 1 Corinthians 13. Tony quoted: "*Love always protects, always trusts, always hopes, always perseveres…*"

"*Love never fails,*" Abigail finished.

But Tony also remembered the first part of those verses. *Love does not delight in evil but rejoices with the truth.* The truth. He needed to tell her.

Her phone rang. She glanced at it. "I need to take this. It's Ms. Scott."

He half-listened as she told Ms. Scott where to find some documents that the director was looking for. He wouldn't tell her now. Or tonight. Abigail needed a respite from all of this. There would be time later.

She ended the call. "Tony, I'm sorry. I need to go," she said. "Pauline is waiting out front for me. Are we okay?"

He flashed her his charming smile and was pleased to see the worry leave her eyes. They were shining again.

"Yes, we're okay," he said. He reached over and gave her a soft kiss on the lips. "*Hear my soul speak. Of the very instant that I saw you, Did my heart fly to your service.*"

Abigail blushed. He loved that she still did that. He would always try to court her, even when they were old and gray.

"My dearest Tony," she said, giving him a teasing smile. "If thou are at my service, how about you cook us another fantastic dinner tonight? I have to work late."

He laughed. "I am at your service, m'lady!"

She pulled on her boots and a burst of cold came in as she left. He shut the door behind her and leaned against it, closing his eyes. What was he going to do now?

He looked at his watch. A new client would be here in a few minutes, and he was supposed to follow him out to his building to talk about security. He peeked out the window and sure enough, his car was pulling up as Pauline drove off with Abigail. The flash drive would have to wait until later. Tony went into the bathroom and reached under the cabinet, where he kept his toothbrush. There were two there. He grabbed the electric one with the fat, blue handle, popped the bottom off, and inserted the flash drive. He put it back in the holder just as he heard his client knock on the door.

Chapter Nine

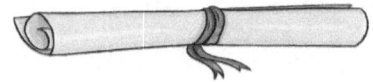

Abigail walked to her desk, feeling much better after her talk with Tony. Pauline had some work to do back in her own section, and now that Abigail was alone, she was looking forward to a quiet afternoon. She had to refile some maps and documents and do some housekeeping chores that would keep her busy, but nothing new or taxing. After the morning she had, she was welcoming it.

Nobody came by her desk to check anything out or ask questions, so she had gotten pretty far into her work when she looked at the clock and noticed an hour had passed. She stretched, rolling the tension out of her shoulders from being bent over the desk for so long. She had just turned back to her work when she heard the elevator door open. She looked up and saw Jean-Pierre coming out of the elevator alone.

"Bonjour!" he said jovially. He gave her a little nod of his head, and when he approached her desk, he leaned over, his hands folded on the cherry wood. "Miss me?"

It was an inappropriate remark, but charming. Suddenly Abigail realized that Jean-Pierre, like Tony, could probably get away with many things because of his good looks and charm. She gave him a small smile.

He pulled back and laid his phone down on the desk. "I wanted to show you these," he said, opening his photos app and tapping on a picture. He slid the phone across the desk to Abigail.

She was planning to be nonchalant and casually glanced down at the photo. She'd show disinterest, or at least not excitement. But what she saw caused her to pick it up. It was Jean-Pierre standing next to an easel with a rare map on it. "Is this an Atillo?"

Jean-Pierre gave her his slow, boyish smile. "Oui!" he said. "It's in my collection." He reached over and swiped the photo, and another appeared.

"An Alexander Tobias?" Abigail exclaimed when he showed her.

"Oui," he said. His voice softened, and quietly he said, "I have been collecting most of my life. My father gave me my first map when I was ten. It was a simple pirate's map, which he bought at auction for a few hundred dollars of your American money. But that began my fascination with maps." He swiped the phone again to a photo of an old book sitting on a wooden table. The large volume was faded, but Abigail suspected it was an original from somewhere in the fifteenth century. He swiped again, and the next photo showed the spine up close.

"*Saints and Peoples,*" she whispered. It was a volume of Prestophenes. Rare.

"Hand copied by Tibetan monks," Jean-Pierre said quietly. Abigail pulled her gaze from the photo to look at the Frenchman standing across from her. Their eyes met.

"This is all in your collection?" she asked.

"My private collection. At home, in Paris," he said. They were both silent for a moment as Abigail pondered what that meant. Maps and documents she had only read about, studied about, but had never actually seen in real life. He had some of them in his *house.*

"Wow," she said softly. "I mean, Atillos haven't been seen in years, they are so rare... And *Saints and Peoples...*" She didn't even know where to begin.

Jean-Pierre broke the spell by pulling his phone across the desk and putting it in his pocket. "Which brings me to my question for you," he said, his voice back to its original timbre, a bit too loud for the library. "We could use you in Paris for a workshop. I was talking with my colleagues at the Bibliothèque à la Paris Internationale and with your expertise, we'd love to have you present at their symposium this summer. In June."

Abigail's mind was spinning. This was far more than she had ever dreamed of! The BPI was one of the most prestigious libraries in the world, containing collections from ancient Greek and Roman times, as well as documents from wars and quests. She had heard some of Christopher Columbus' maps were there! They even had some Sanskrit documents and some on stone.

"June?" she said, her voice shaky.

"Oh my goodness!" exclaimed Ms. Scott, stepping from behind a stack and walking quickly toward the desk, wringing her hands together in her excitement. "Abigail! Do you know what this means? You'd get tenure for sure and possibly more. Maybe even a professorial position, if that's what you wanted!" Her eyes rolled heavenward. "To *present* at the BPI! Can you imagine? And I bet that would bring in some serious grants and donations when people see we have gone international in our expertise!" She looked at Jean-Pierre. "Sir, I can't thank you enough!" She extended her hand to shake his, but Jean-Pierre pulled it to his lips and kissed it lightly.

"You're welcome, Lulu," he said. Abigail saw the blush rise in Ms. Scott's cheeks. Suddenly, Abigail's desk phone rang, startling both women. She picked it up. "Yes, she's here," she said and handed the phone to Ms. Scott. She glanced at Jean-Pierre as Ms. Scott was talking.

"On my way," Ms. Scott said, handing the phone back. "I'm needed in Biblical," she said, flashing Jean-Pierre her smile, which usually caused her crow's feet to wrinkle deeply. Somehow, today she looked younger, and her skin looked smoother. Maybe it was the excitement.

They heard her heels clicking away across the library floor. Abigail finally spoke. "I don't know what to say."

"Say 'yes,'" Jean-Pierre said. "I can make a few phone calls and get you in as a presenter. You have such expertise in this area it would be a shame not to share it."

He was so charming, and she was so excited, that she nearly forgot what Tony had said about him.

"I really don't think..." But she couldn't finish the sentence. She wanted to tell him no thank you, because she shouldn't be flying across the ocean to hang out with someone who dealt in stolen goods. But what if she didn't see him much? What if she just stayed at the BPI and the hotel the whole time? It would be strictly professional. It would be *great* for her career.

Jean-Pierre must have noticed her hesitation. He spoke in a quiet voice. "I know you don't trust me," he said. "Tony has probably told you things. Things that I regret from my past. Some of them may even be true." He slid his hand across the desk and laid it on hers. "But I am a new man now, Abigail. I've changed. For our professional sake, I need you to believe that. This is a great opportunity for you, and it will be great for me if I am the one who sets it up. Bringing such a treasure of intelligence and expertise to Paris! What you've done, what you've written—you have a great body of work already. People are impressed by you. Give them a chance to see you in person."

She gently slid her hand out from under his.

"Bring friends," he said. "I'll invite Ms. Scott to come along, and your friend. Is her name Pauline? They can help you. Bring security if you want. How could anything go wrong that way?"

"I'd want to bring Tony," Abigail said. She watched his eyes carefully but didn't see any hint that this was a problem.

"Very well. Bring your husband too." Then he smiled his big smile, and his boyish excitement returned. "It will be wonderful!" He looked at his watch. "I need to get to a meeting. I'll give you more information later. You have a wonderful afternoon." He reached his hand out, and she gave him hers. Their eyes met as he held it to his lips and kissed it softly and a little lingeringly before letting it go. "You won't regret it," he said. "I'll make sure of that. And I'll make sure you get press coverage and a write up in both the *Journal du Documents Rare* and the *American Rare Maps and Antiquities Journal.*"

He gave her a nod and walked back to the elevator. As the doors closed behind him, Abigail stood there, too stunned to continue her work. What had just happened? That man had literally given her everything she had ever wanted for her career. *Everything.*

And it would coincide nicely with her tenure appointment, which would be considered in July, right after the conference. The timing couldn't be better.

Now all she had to do was convince Tony.

Chapter Ten

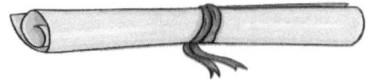

Tony finished up at the client's building later than he expected and checked the traffic on his phone. A crash had closed the road that he took back to his apartment and there was a huge backup. He looked at his watch. He didn't want Abigail to suspect anything, so he had to get dinner made. Plus, he had to work again tonight. With the traffic problems, he didn't have time to go back to his apartment for the flash drive. It would have to wait until later.

He got in his car and fought rush-hour traffic home.

He fixed some broiled cod, flavoring it with lemon and some salt and pepper. He microwaved frozen green beans and put together a salad, all the while pondering what might be on the flash drive. Abigail came home just as he was lighting the candle on their kitchen table.

"Smells good!" she said.

As soon as they sat down, she launched in to her day. "You won't *believe* what I've been offered!" she said, her eyes all lit up. "I," she said, pointing proudly at herself, "I have been invited to the BPI, to give a presentation!"

"What's the BPI?" Tony interrupted.

"The Bibliothèque à la Paris Internationale! It's only one of the most prestigious libraries in the world!" Abigail said. She forked a cucumber and talked as she chewed. "To give a workshop! I mean…most of the top people in the ancient maps and documents world will be there…"

She didn't say how this came about, but he figured it was probably due to one of her publications. He'd ask later. She went about grants and tenure and journal articles. Finally, she stopped, wiped her mouth on a napkin, and put her fork down. "Oh my gosh. I've been rambling on and haven't even asked about *your* day!"

He smiled at her. It was good to see her so happy.

"And how come you're not more excited?" she scolded. "You should be jumping up and down for me!"

"Excited? I'm excited. I'm just not *surprised*, that's all."

"Why not?"

"Because you're *you*!" he said. "Amazing you!"

She smiled.

"Let's clean up, and then I'll tell you about my day," he said.

Later, when they were sitting on the couch with Cocoa curled in between them, she asked again about his day. He didn't want to spoil her mood with news about Jean-Pierre's little visit or the flash drive, so he asked more about hers. "So, tell me more about this trip. Am I invited?"

"Of course!" Then her face did that little twisty thing when she had something to say but wasn't sure how to say it.

"What?" he asked.

"There's just one problem."

Tony raised an eyebrow.

"Jean-Pierre is the one who is setting it up."

Tony inhaled, about to speak, but she held up a hand. "Now wait," she said. "I know how you feel about him—"

"*Feel* about him? Abigail, he—"

But she continued to hold her hand up. "No, he says he has changed. And to prove that, he is letting me bring security, Ms. Scott, and you...I mean, maybe he *has* changed."

"No."

Abigail frowned. "You did."

Tony sighed and ran his hand through his hair.

She was right, of course. She was looking at him with a hint of anger in her eyes, but what he really saw was fear. She was afraid of losing what she had worked so hard for. And it would be all his fault.

"You're right," he said quietly. He had no right to spoil her day. "And I will do what I can to support you. You come first. Always." He moved his hand up to her face and brushed some hair behind her ear.

She gave him that smile that had first melted his heart. She leaned in and kissed him gently on the lips. Then a little harder. Tony kissed her back and then pulled away. It took everything he had to say no to her. He glanced at his watch. "I'm sorry, but this is why I had to get dinner so quickly. I have to work tonight, remember?"

Her face fell. "That's right. The museum." She looked at him, serious. "We could always have Jimmy check Jean-Pierre out if you're worried."

Jimmy Stout was her friend and also the cop who had arrested Tony and assigned him to community service, getting him out of a jail sentence. He and his wife, both in their fifties, had taken Abigail under their wing after Nick died, parenting her since her own parents were long dead and she was on her own. She loved them a lot and trusted them to a fault.

"What if he found out about the Vesconte?" Tony said. "You'd lose a lot. The Paris workshop...it might affect your tenure..."

"Maybe."

Maybe that was the best thing to do. Telling Jimmy would cover them both. If they got the cops involved, would they be off the hook with the stolen map? No, Abigail would surely get the blame for bringing Jean-Pierre in. But how could she have known? Maybe it wouldn't be so bad for her. As for him, it depended on what was on that flash drive. His copy was securely hidden, but certainly Jean-Pierre had more copies.

"Let's talk more about this later. I need to go, or I'll be late."

"I wish you didn't have to leave now," she said.

"Come with me."

"What?"

"Tonight. Come with me. I'll show you how to break and enter." He winked.

She laughed. "Seriously?"

"Sure. I have to go in from the roof again. Let's see what you're made of, woman." He went upstairs to their closet and grabbed his bag. She followed him. "Suit up," he said, pulling on his black spandex cat suit. "It needs to be something light and easy to move in. Your yoga pants would probably work."

"You just like to see me in my yoga pants."

"True enough."

He made sure he had two ropes, an extra safety harness, and of course, his phone with the cool apps.

"Ready?"

"Let's go!" Abigail said. "One thing I have to say is a girl never gets bored with you on a date."

And off they went to break in to the museum.

Chapter Eleven

Abigail stood on the cold, snowy roof, clinging to her husband with both arms wrapped around him. The wind whipped in fierce gusts around them, and even though she had on a black ski jacket that Tony had loaned her, which was supposedly good at some ridiculously low temperature, she was freezing. Or maybe the shivering was from fear. Why on earth had she ever let him talk her in to this?

"Are you scared?" he asked into her ear.

"No," she answered but didn't dare look down. She kept her face against his chest. In truth, she was terrified, but she wasn't about to admit that to her cat burglar husband. There was also a little thrill of adrenaline running through her. She felt wildly alive, and part of her was loving this.

"So, you have to let go of me now," Tony said.

"Um..." She didn't think she could, but he had buckled a harness around her and attached it to the top of the roof before they climbed up.

"You're safe," he reminded her. He told her three times already that it would catch her if she fell.

"I know that." She pulled her face away from his chest with some difficulty and set a determined look in her eyes. "I'm fine."

Tony smiled. She knew she wasn't fooling him.

"Why don't you go first," Tony said. "I'll coach you."

He pried her hands off him and put them on the rope. The black gloves she was wearing kept her hands remarkably warm, considering how thin and supple they were. He had bought her a pair last month. They were expensive, but incredible for the cold winters of Michigan, he said. She wore them for everything and especially loved them for driving. But now they would be put to the test for which they were made.

They had some grip on the palms, so when she grasped the rope, they held and didn't slip. Once she had hold of the rope, Tony opened the skylight. They were five stories up.

"Do you remember what I told you in the car?"

She nodded. Using her upper body strength, she held on to the rope and lowered herself through the opening. Every few inches, she gave a tug to the right, the way he had showed her, and some more rope slid through the catch. Slowly, she lowered herself into the building. The warmth hit her suddenly, as did the quiet, once she was out of the wind. She paused. She thought she could hang there forever, just warming up, but then she looked down at the ground. The circular stairs wound around the five-story opening in the middle of the building, and she could see the Grecian vase directly below her.

"I'm right behind you," Tony said, and he was. He pulled the skylight window closed, leaving only enough room for the two ropes.

The height was making Abigail dizzy. She closed her eyes. "I'm terrified," Abigail admitted.

"No, you're not," Tony said. *"And though she be but little, she is fierce,"* he quoted, dropping down until he was hanging even with her. "Never give in to fear. Feel the adrenaline? Your body is ready for this."

Abigail opened one eye and saw her husband's face. He smiled. She tried to smile back but thought she might throw up.

"Let's go," Tony said and let out some rope. "Just keep your eyes on mine." She did the same, her eyes never leaving his. But then he had to look down to see where they were. "Third floor," he said. He took another rope and swung it over, hooking it on the stair railing. He tugged on it and handed it to Abigail. "Pull yourself over."

She did, hand over hand, until she was at the stair railing. She grasped it, gave a small tug to free some more of the rope she was dangling from, and pulled herself over, landing a bit ungracefully on the third-floor balcony. She had never been so happy to be standing on solid ground.

Tony smiled. "Great job. Stay there. I'm going to need your help in a minute."

trusting the cat burglar

He lowered himself quickly and expertly down two more floors until he was hanging about two feet above the vase.

The guard, who she remembered was named Jasper, stepped in to view. "The sensors around the window tripped the alarm. You nailed that one."

Tony glanced up at Abigail. "That's how I got in last time, remember? So I installed a temperature sensor around the window. As soon as it opens, the sensor reads a change in temperature from the outside air and sets off a silent alarm, which goes directly to the police station so they can come in and catch the thief red-handed. Pretty clever, huh?" He flashed her his smile.

She laughed. "Very nice, cat burglar."

Tony hooked up his harness so both hands were free. Jasper watched his small palm-sized monitor and hollered to the guard at the desk. "Get ready for the second round." He opened a candy bar to munch while he watched. It looked tasty. Abigail realized they hadn't had dessert tonight.

"Abigail," Tony said. "I need for you to walk down the stairs and approach the vase from that stairwell." While he waited for her, he pulled out his can of hairspray and sprayed it into the air. As the liquid crystals fell, they momentarily highlighted the invisible strands of laser lights that zigzagged across the room. He had avoided them the first time by coming in from above but wanted to be sure they worked. As soon as she stepped into the foyer, alarms went off and lights flashed. She covered her ears. Jasper punched in a few buttons and the noise shut off.

"Round two works," Jasper said. "Now for round three." A few other guards had gathered to watch.

"Is *everybody* here?" Tony said. "Who's minding the Crown Jewels?" But Abigail knew he was loving every minute of this.

Small round lights lined the rim of the pedestal on which the vase was centered. They highlighted the object, but the lights had a dual purpose. They stretched slightly beyond the vase, just past the glass area of the pedestal but not so far as to reach the roping around it, which was there to keep the crowd back. She watched Tony gently wave his hand through a beam of light and instantly put her hands over her ears. But this time she only heard beeping as another alarm went off. Jasper shut it off.

"Sha-bang!" the guard said, pumping the fist that was holding his half-eaten candy bar. "That's a really cool trick. Who would have thought of lights being alarmed?"

Tony glanced at Abigail. "That particular safeguard tripped me up once in a jewelry store."

True enough. She rolled her eyes.

"Okay, here's my last trick," Tony said with a wicked grin. He reached his hand toward the vase, right through the heat sensor that got him the first time around. Abigail saw him glance at the guard and then at her to be sure they were watching. She couldn't help but smile. He was somewhat of a showoff. Then, because he was a bit naughty, he touched the forbidden vase ever so lightly with his finger.

Jasper gasped.

Tony looked at the guard, mock innocence on his face. "Problems, my good man?"

"You're not supposed to touch it! And how did you do that? Did you shut off the heat sensor alarm that caught your hand the last time?"

"Not at all," Tony said, motioning for Abigail to walk over to him. "Put your hand through," he said. She reached her hand through the now-disarmed lights toward the vase, crossing the threshold of tiny pinholes that she knew represented the heat-sensing alarm. Immediately, loud bells went off. She jumped back. Jasper hit a few buttons and disarmed it.

"But how——?" he said. She could tell the guard was flustered.

"It's my new suit," Tony said, running his hand over his chest, which caused the rope to swing a little. "This body suit blocks heat and body temperature. Your fancy little alarm couldn't detect me."

Tony grabbed the rope with both hands, unhooked the clip, and lightly jumped to the ground.

"Where did you get it?" Abigail asked.

"Amazon."

Jasper laughed and ate the last of his candy bar. "But that's bad news. What if a bad guy gets one too? He'll get in."

"No way," Tony said. "He—" He glanced at Abigail. "Or *she*, let's be politically correct here—will have to get past all of the other alarms. Impossible to do."

Jasper licked his fingers. "Well done, Mr. Russo. Let's get the specs, and I'll arrange to have you paid."

Abigail decided to walk around while the men talked shop. She wandered into the room with the Monets on the wall. She found the colors to be soothing. Then she went to where their painting was. She had come to think of it as theirs, but the real owner was Tony's grandma. They could have sold it and made millions, but Grandma decided to loan it to the museum so it would remain safe and others could enjoy it.

Abigail looked at the woman in the painting, Tony's grandmother's mother, Margaret. Her long, dark hair fell across her shoulders, and her hands rested lightly on the arms of the chair. Abigail touched the ring on own her finger, which exactly matched the ring in the painting. Margaret had given it to Grandma, who had kept it safe all those years.

She knew if she turned the painting around she would see Antonio Russo's famous signature, along with an inscription of love for Margaret.

"To my darling Laurel,
The light of my life, the mother of my child, the joy of my heart. I do love nothing in the world so much as you."

She was that lucky too. She had found a soulmate in Tony, but they didn't have to be kept apart like Antonio and his love. They had been married for six weeks and hadn't spent a single night apart. They had promised each other they never would. Abigail smiled. Tony would definitely be coming to Paris with her.

"Ready?"

She jumped at the sound of his voice in the quiet of the museum. Tony came up to her and put his arm around her. "Gazing at our painting again?"

"Mmmmhmmm." She turned to him. "I'm so blessed to have you in my life." She kissed him gently on the lips.

When she pulled back, she saw a brief look of uncertainty in his eyes. But it passed so quickly it might have been a shadow.

"Is there more of that back home?" Tony teased, never one to miss a beat.

"Let's go home and find out," Abigail said and started walking toward the front door.

"Wait a minute," Tony said. "Where are you going?"

She turned to see why he wasn't following. "Outside."

"Not that way."

Out the back door, then? But they usually left... Suddenly it dawned on her what he meant. She folded her arms across her chest. "Oh, no," she said. "There is no way I'm going back out the way we came in."

"Of course you are," Tony said easily. "You should never go into some place if you can't get back out."

"I *can* get back out." Abigail pointed toward the front door "And that's the way I'm going!" She turned on her heel and started walking.

"*So come with me,*" Tony's voice rang out in the silence of the museum, "*where dreams are born, and time is never planned.*" She stopped, her back still to him. "*Just think of happy things,*" he said, his voice quieter. She turned to meet his eyes. "*And your heart will fly on wings, forever.*" He had a mischievous twinkle in his eye, yet she saw a love there so deep it made her heart ache. Right then, standing in the museum on a cold snowy night, she realized that she'd follow him anywhere.

She rolled her eyes dramatically but couldn't help the warmth that flooded her body. A feeling of ease. A relaxing of the cares of the day.

"*Peter Pan,*" she said, naming the source of the quote.

"Come fly with me, Wendy," Tony said, holding his hand out to her. "I'll keep you safe. I promise."

Abigail walked over to him and put her hand in his.

"You're crazy, you know that?" she said, giving his hand a squeeze.

"Maybe a little," he said.

"If I die, I'll come back and haunt you."

"I'd be disappointed if you didn't."

When they got back to the room with the vase, Tony bounded up the stairs and unhooked Abigail's rope from the railing. He swung it toward her. She glanced up at the ceiling, five stories above her, where the rope was still attached. "You're going to make me climb up *five* stories on a rope next to you?"

"Climb? I would never work that hard," Tony said. He clipped the rope to her body harness. "Now press this lever like this," he said, pressing it. She felt it lift her up slightly before he released it. "The harder you press it, the faster you will fly."

"Why am I doing this?" she asked.

"Because you love me. And because you might need to know this someday. What if I get the flu and you have to cover for me at work?"

Abigail laughed.

"I've got to see this," Jasper said. The other guards had left to go back to their posts. Jasper folded his arms across his chest and settled in for the action.

Abigail looked up toward the ceiling and then back at Tony.

"You trust me," he said. It was more of a statement than a question.

"Yes," she said, because she did. He took her hand and nodded toward the lever. He pressed his at the same time as she did, and together they rose upward toward the skylight.

"Bye, Jasper!" Tony shouted. "Have a good night!"

"Tally ho, Russos!" Jasper said.

Abigail glanced down and realized they were at a dizzying height again.

"Look at me," Tony said, squeezing her hand. She did. Suddenly, they were at the skylight, and he helped her through onto the roof. She caught her breath as the cold air bit into her face. Tony quickly sealed the window shut and put his arm around her. "Let's go home."

Standing there five stories above the streets, with the wind whipping around them, Abigail looked at the moonlight shining on the face of the man she loved and felt on top of the world.

"Let's," she said. And they did.

Chapter Twelve

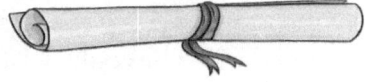

On Friday morning, Tony dropped Abigail off at work and then headed over to the police station. He grabbed his orange jumpsuit out of the trunk and hurriedly pulled it on over his clothes before he went up to the building. The supervisor had the truck in the lot and four of the guys were already there, loading it with tools. Tony grabbed a few shovels and was laying them in the cab when Karl ambled up. Karl leaned against the truck, hands in his pocket, and watched. He was smoking the last of a cigarette.

When Tony brought over another armful of tools, Karl leaned so that he was in the way of the opening Tony needed in the truck. He couldn't get the tools around Karl.

"Excuse me," he said, meeting Karl's eyes.

"Did you pass gas?" Karl said around his cigarette. A few of the other guys snickered.

"Are you going to move?" Tony asked.

"No."

"Come on!" shouted the supervisor. "Let's get to work! Load up that truck!"

Karl still refused to budge. "Maybe you need to move me," he said.

Tony could think of at least a few good ways to do that, but he needed to avoid trouble so his sentence wasn't extended. He moved to the left. He'd go around Karl and put the tools in the other side of the truck. But Karl shuffled left too.

"Come on, Karl," said Marcus, the supervisor. "Move."

Tony eyed Karl. He was huge, towering about a half a head over Tony's nearly six-foot height and weighing nearly twice what Tony did. He doubted he could take him physically, but Karl was dumb as a stump, so he could probably get out of this using his brain.

"Move it!" shouted the supervisor again, and this time the man grabbed Karl by the arm and moved him so Tony didn't have to. Karl's eyes slid over Tony's frame as he was pulled past.

"Next time, jerk-face," he said.

Jerk-face? That was the best he could do? He hoped Karl, who was in here for skipping out on his child-care payments, never saw his kid. The child was better off without his dad or his dad's money, as far as Tony was concerned. If he were the wife, he'd forget about the childcare payments and run far away from this creep.

The guys climbed in the back of the truck, and an armed officer climbed in with them. The ride there was cold and bumpy, and nobody talked. The first hour went well, each man working quietly around the bridge, laying stone. Tony was glad for the thick, warm gloves the city supplied him with. The supervisor blew his whistle, signaling the five-minute break. Tony pulled out his thermos of hot coffee and opened it. Karl lit a cigarette, leaning against the wall next to him.

"Your wifey pack that for you?" Karl asked.

Tony took a long drink, watching Karl. The man was looking for a fight. Why he picked Tony, he wasn't sure, but he was certain that Karl wasn't going to be happy until he got to take his anger out on someone.

Then Luke, the quiet one, pulled out some beef jerky and was about to take a bite when Karl snatched it out of his hand and stuffed half of it in his own mouth.

"Hey, that's my breakfast!" said Luke. Karl leaned in toward Luke, whose mouse-like nose twitched slightly. He dropped his eyes, grumbling. Luke was about ninety pounds and didn't have an ounce of muscle on him.

Tony watched the exchange, quietly sipping on his coffee. Karl finished up the jerky and threw the wrapper on the ground.

"Time's up!" the supervisor shouted and blew the whistle again. Tony screwed the top back on his thermos and saw Karl's movement toward him out of the corner of his eye. As the big, meaty paw reached out to grab the thermos, Tony stepped neatly to the side. Karl's momentum threw him off balance, causing his left foot to slip on some ice. The big man fell, hitting the ground hard.

Tony swore under his breath.

Karl rolled over and got up pretty quickly for a man of his size. He roared some animal noise as he reached for Tony with his left hand. Tony moved out of the way again, but Karl's other fist swung upward into Tony's gut. The punch caught Tony off guard, and he doubled over, clutching at his stomach. He regained his composure enough to block Karl's next punch. Then Karl swung his left hand up. It grazed Tony's chin, just as the supervisor grabbed the big man from behind. The armed officer pulled Karl's hands behind him and cuffed him. "In the truck!" he shouted and pushed Karl forward.

The hit had knocked Tony's teeth together, causing him to bite his lip. He was bleeding and coughing.

The supervisor threw a first aid kit at him. "Clean yourself up and get back to work."

He wiped the back of his hand across his lips and saw it was smeared with blood. "I'm fine," Tony said, setting the kit down and sucking on his lip because that's what manly men did. He didn't think he should show any weakness here. But it hurt like heck, especially because his face was nearly numb with cold.

The second hour went by without incident, with Karl cuffed inside the truck. During the ride back, Luke kept his eyes on the ground, and the other guys were quiet. Tony snuck a few glances at Karl, who was glaring at him for the entire ride.

Karl was taken inside the precinct while the rest of them unloaded the truck. Tony was glad to get out of there.

Back in his own car, he looked at his phone. He had a phone message from a potential new client and a text from Ms. Scott at the library wanting him to give her the final schedule for when the security system would be in place. But today he needed to go back to the museum with his write-up of all the systems, and he needed to shower before any of it.

He decided to go back to the office instead of home. He had a change of clothes there, and he'd have time to look at the flash drive before he did anything else.

As soon as he stepped in the door, his cellphone rang. It was his grandma.

"Tony? Where are you? My appointment is in a half hour."

"Oh geez," Tony said, running his free hand through his hair. "I'll be right over."

How could he have forgotten? He looked at his calendar, and there it was. He didn't have time to shower, but he pulled on some clean clothes and put on fresh deodorant. It would have to do the trick.

It took a while to get Grandma out of the house and into his car. He knew they were going to be late.

"I'm really sorry." It was the third time he had apologized.

"Oh, don't worry about it," Grandma said, waving it away with her hand. "It's just a check-up."

He had to take her to get blood drawn. After that, they had to wait an hour for results before they saw the doctor. He glanced at the clock on the dashboard. He had a client meeting this afternoon.

"Tell me again what on earth happened to your lip and chin," Grandma said, looking over at him. "You said you fell?"

"It was icy at the place we were working," Tony said. It wasn't really a lie. It *was* icy. He hadn't actually fallen, but he wasn't about to tell her some thug had taken a swing at him.

The line at the lab was long, and it was too warm in the room. He found a place to park her wheelchair and took her paperwork up to the desk. The receptionist was cute, and in the old days, before Abigail, he would have flirted a bit. But today, he just wanted to get back to the apartment and look at what was on that flash drive before he had to meet with his client.

He wheeled the wheelchair down the long corridor from the lab to the elevator and then up to the third floor to oncology. It seemed like forever before a nurse called them back and settled them into a room. She took her blood pressure. "The doctor will be in shortly," she said with a smile.

This part always made Tony nervous, the waiting to see if the white blood cell count was up, which would mean the cancer was raging through her body again. But the doctor came in the room with a smile on his face. Tony's grandmother was doing well, he said. No sign of the cancer's return. Tony let out a breath and felt his shoulders sag with relief.

"Of course, it's impossible to really tell without a scan, but her RBCs would be dropping and her WBCs would be up if she were fighting the cancer. We'll scan her again at the three-month mark."

Then he told them they could reduce the in-home care to twice a week, instead of daily, if Tony checked on her every day.

"He doesn't have time for that," Grandma said. She hated to be a burden.

"It's fine," Tony said. He wanted to take care of her, plus there was a co-pay for the in-home care. It was just $25 a day, but that was adding up. With her current seven-days-a-week schedule, that was $175 a week. Neither Grandma nor he and Abigail had the money to keep that up. For a moment, he thought of the necklace in the actress' house and how easy it would be for him to make millions in just a few hours. A quick in and out and a sale on the black market. Mauvais would never know, and he could tell him the actress no longer had it to steal.

"Tony?"

"Hmmm?" He was pulled back to the present.

"The doctor was asking you which days you want the nurse to come to my house. Those are the days you won't have to come over. Weekdays? Weekends?"

"Ummm..." There really was no easier day with his current schedule. "I guess any day is fine." They settled on Mondays and Thursdays, which would space the visits out quite a bit.

"You'll need to keep up your strengthening exercises on your own," the doctor said to her and then looked at Tony. "Make sure she does them."

Grandma laughed. "I'll do my homework, Doc. I'm not a child."

The doctor smiled and said for them to make an appointment to come back in two weeks.

trusting the cat burglar

It took a long time to get her back home and inside her house. By the time he got back to the apartment, it was 2:55 p.m. The new client was due at 3 p.m. He would never be finished and back to the library by 5 p.m. to pick up Abigail. He grabbed his phone and called her.

"Tony!" she said. Her voice sounded lively.

"Hello, beautiful," he said. He could hear glassware tinkling in the background and people laughing. "Where are you?"

"Jean-Pierre took us all out to lunch. Me, Ms. Scott, and Pauline."

"I see," he said, although he didn't at all. A short burst of protective anger shot through him at the thought of JP out with Abigail. And why on earth would she accept? But she wasn't alone with him, so it would probably be okay. His doorbell rang.

"I've got to go. My client is here. Can you take the bus home tonight? I need to work late."

"Sure," she said. "Love you."

"Love you, too," he said, opening the door as he hung up the phone. There was an elderly businessman standing on his entrance stoop wearing a bowler hat and carrying a cane. He sounded younger when he called last week and said that he wanted Tony to run security through his mansion. As he slowly shuffled in, Tony took his coat and offered him a seat. The old man put his flip phone down on the counter and pulled a notepad and pencil out of his briefcase. Tony plastered a smile on his face. This was going to take a while.

Chapter Thirteen

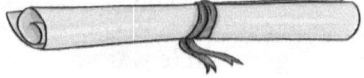

Abigail was enjoying lunch, despite the fact she hadn't originally wanted to go. Even Lulu Scott was giggling. With a glass of wine in her (breaking her own no-drinking-during-work-hours rule), Ms. Scott had loosened up and become quite a bit of fun. Pauline, who usually either picked up fast food or brown-bagged it and always rushed home to make kid-friendly meals, was quite enjoying her sautéed garlic shrimp over some sort of fancy lettuce, with coconut rice on the side. Abigail had ordered a grouper sandwich, which had a delicious slaw dressing on it. Jean-Pierre was footing the bill.

"So, I told the bloke to buzz off, and after that, I never saw him again!" Jean-Pierre finished the story he was telling, and all three women roared with laughter. Abigail had to wipe the tears from her eyes with her cloth napkin because she was laughing so hard.

They had been sitting there for two hours, luxuriating in the food. They started with appetizers: stuffed mushrooms and some sort of artichoke dip on crusty French bread. Jean-Pierre had insisted on ordering a bottle of French wine, but after Abigail and Pauline refused, he and Ms. Scott had settled on just a glass each. Abigail wasn't really a drinker, and besides, it just seemed too strange to drink in the middle of a workday, in front of your boss.

Then the lunches came, and they were just finishing them up.

"This is quite possibly the first real food I've had in months," said Pauline, savoring her last shrimp.

They hadn't discussed work at all. Instead, Jean-Pierre had told them about growing up in the south of France and how he moved to Paris when he went to college. Or *Université*, as they called it there. He told them some stories of how he grew his map collection, mentioning pieces that he hadn't told Abigail about yesterday. She was fascinated and was drawn into his conversation, despite the fact that she kept reminding herself that he had formerly taken advantage of an old man and presently had stolen goods in his possession. But he didn't seem evil or even dangerous. He was just very charming and friendly.

"Let's discuss the workshop in Paris," he said, finally. "I want you all to come."

Ms. Scott giggled again, which made Abigail smile. She had never seen her boss so loose before. "I'm sure we'd love to, but airline tickets are so expensive and the board would never approve the costs."

"Oh, no, Lulu. I'd never expect you to pay. It's my invitation! I plan on covering the costs to get you there! And think of how wonderful and prestigious it would be for your library to have Abigail present at the World Map Symposium!"

Ms. Scott turned an interesting shade of red. Abigail couldn't tell if it was embarrassment or excitement. "Well, if you insist..." she began.

"Is anyone interested in dessert?" the waiter asked, interrupting them. He was a handsome young man with a sharp, pointy nose marring his otherwise perfect face. Probably in his twenties. Very good at his job.

"No thank you," Abigail started, when Jean-Pierre said, "But of course!" in his jovial tone and asked to see the dessert tray.

Dessert was fabulous. Abigail chose a chocolate silk pie. The whipped cream tasted like it was made from scratch, and the chocolate melted in her mouth.

Pauline had a chocolate mousse. "The calories aren't worth it unless it's chocolate," she said. Abigail had to agree.

Ms. Scott ordered an apple torte, and Jean-Pierre had some raspberry trifle.

"The Symposium will give you international exposure," he said. "There will be experts in the field there from all over the world."

Abigail was both thrilled and terrified about presenting in front of such people. She knew she was good at what she did, but *international?* Wow. She could use some of the workshop material she had presented locally in the past. Even what she was working on for next Friday's premiere would work for part of it.

"I'm putting it together, so we can tailor the presentations to your expertise, Abigail," Jean-Pierre said. "Our keynote is Marjorie Vorries—"

Abigail gasped. "The *world-famous* Marjorie Vorries?" That woman was the foremost expert on maps. She was the one who people called in when they wanted something identified or verified. Abigail had read several of her textbooks.

"The very one," Jean-Pierre said.

"Wow," Abigail said.

"Tell me about next week's premiere," Jean-Pierre said. Ms. Scott launched in to how they were going to introduce Jean-Pierre and his wonderful collection. Abigail drifted off, lost in thought about the rich promises of the trip to France and what it would mean to her career and tenure track. All of her career dreams were coming true, in one fell swoop.

Chapter Fourteen

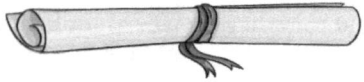

The old man had insisted Tony drive over to his house, which was to be expected. He couldn't properly assess it and give a quote without seeing it. The gentleman lived in a multi-million-dollar mansion on the outskirts of town. He didn't have anything of significant value, just televisions, computers, and all of the trappings that came with living a wealthy lifestyle. He wanted to keep them safe. It would be a straightforward job. Outside lights, perimeter alarm, and a direct police line.

It was past six when he got back to the apartment and sent the man home with a written quote. They shook hands, and he said he'd call Tony back to set up a time to get started.

He made sure his door was locked and then went to get the flash drive. He put it in the computer and took a deep breath. Whatever was on that video was probably about to change his life.

He was surprised to see a slight tremble to his hand when he took hold of the mouse and clicked.

It was a short video of Tony at an auction, walking with Charlotte, another of his clients, on his arm. He remembered the night, two years ago, shortly before he had stolen the pocket watch. Charlotte had asked him to accompany her to a charity event that evening, which was actually cover for a dark auction that took place later that night in the basement of the mansion they were in. He knew what it really was going in and had gone with her hoping to meet some new clientele. It was there he had first met Jean-Pierre.

The Frenchman had been bidding on a piece of jewelry and lost to a higher bidder. Tony was familiar with the piece, a ruby-encrusted brooch filled with other precious stones. He had approached JP.

"That's a shame," he had said, shaking his head.

JP had given him a quizzical look. "Pardon? And you are?"
"I'm a person who can find you a better piece," Tony said.
He remembered how sure he had been of himself. How he
had read up on the beautiful diamond necklace owned by the
actress Vivian Danes and hatched a plan to steal it.

"You have my interest," Jean-Pierre said, and they moved
over to the side of the room where they could talk in low tones
over the auction going on behind them. Tony told him about
the necklace and gave him his price. Jean-Pierre didn't bat an
eye. Soon the two men were shaking hands.

While these auctions weren't usually filmed—all cameras
were forbidden, even security and cell phones—this video
clip showed Tony leaving Charlotte and going on to talk
with yet another client. The video ended with the two men
shaking hands. That in itself was incriminating because Tony
happened to know this particular man had previously been
indicted for selling stolen merchandise. He had served his
time and was back out, ready to wheel and deal again when
this video was made. Then there was the piece that was being
auctioned off in the background—a Chinese vase from the
imperial era that was very old and very much stolen from a
museum in Beijing. It went for an incredible sum that night.
It was obvious in that video what was going on and where
Tony was.

Tony rewound the thirty-second video and swore as he
replayed it. He wondered how much JP had paid for the footage
and how he had found it. The night had ended well, with
Tony giving JP his number, which resulted in the jobs for
the Vesconte maps, the ring, and later the watch. After he
stole the ring, the security had been too tight to get Danes'
necklace, so they had decided to wait. By the time he figured
out how to get in the house while she was home, he was
finished with Jean-Pierre. But that evening, confident and
proud of his successes, he had accompanied Charlotte back
to her place and spent the night with some good wine and a
toss in the sheets.

He pulled the flash drive out, shut down his computer,
and grabbed his coat. He needed to show Abigail, and there
was no time like the present. After she saw it, he'd know for

sure how much she was willing to tolerate about him. Quite possibly, this would be the last straw.

The night was clear and the air cold, so he dug his gloves out of his pocket. He was thankful he had gotten a close parking spot, not parking around back like he sometimes did. As he was unlocking the car door, a figure approached him from the shadows. It was Jean-Pierre.

"Have you looked at the flash drive yet?"

Tony let go of the car door handle and turned. "Maybe."

"Do you have specs for her house?"

Tony didn't, but he was sure he could find them quickly. He hadn't looked because he didn't plan to do the job, but telling JP that right now didn't seem like a good idea. "I'll need a month."

"A month?" Jean-Pierre laughed, a low, rumbling sound so he didn't call attention to them. "Someone of *your* talent? I don't think so. You have a week."

He pulled a newspaper out of his coat pocket. "She will be in town next weekend. Saturday. That's a good time to hit. You know she keeps it with her."

"How do you know she doesn't sleep with it around her neck?"

"That's your problem."

He unfolded the newspaper, and it was open to an article. The headline read, "Society Heiress/Actress to Headline in Local Movie Premiere."

Tony nodded but didn't accept the paper. Jean-Pierre folded it and put it back in his pocket.

"Stay away from Abigail," Tony said.

Jean-Pierre smiled, the white of his teeth showing in the darkness. "She seems quite taken with me and the opportunities I'm offering her. Someone like Abigail shouldn't be wasting her time with someone like you." Jean-Pierre turned to leave. He looked back over his shoulder. "Saturday."

Tony watched him disappear into the darkness on the other side of the street and waited for him to drive off. He stood there for a moment. Then an idea came to him, and he went back inside his apartment.

He no longer had Charlotte's private number. It was in his old cell phone, which he had thrown in the river the night he gave up his life of crime. It had contained the numbers of all of his clients, as well as those of many of the women he had been with.

He guessed she'd be at her new company, working late. Charlotte didn't believe in keeping a nine-to-five schedule, which is how she stayed wealthy. Those she employed either worked hard or moved on. She didn't tolerate anyone who wasn't committed.

He looked up the number and called her main business line.

"Ms. Weber's office." It was probably her assistant. He asked to speak to Charlotte.

"Ms. Weber is out of town," she said. Tony doubted that. Charlotte would never leave a fledgling company in the hands of others to run.

"Tell her Tony Russo is calling."

There was a pause. She was writing it down.

"No. Tell her *now*. I'm guessing she'll take the call."

"Sir, as I said, Ms. Weber is out of—"

"She'd be highly disappointed if she missed my call," Tony cut in, making sure there was authority in his voice.

Another pause. Then, "Please hold."

He heard a few seconds of elevator music and then, "Tony Russo! So good to hear from you!"

"That's quite some gatekeeper you have there, Charlotte."

"Nan is quite the assistant. I thought you had my private number."

"It's at the bottom of the river with the rest of my previous life."

He heard her deep, throaty chuckle. "So, darling, why the pleasure of this call?"

He paused. He was playing with fire, but he could think of no other way. "About six months ago, you invited me to a charity auction, which if I remember correctly, is this Wednesday night."

"Oooooh! Are you back in the game?"

"No. Not really. I just need to chat up a few folks. Figure something out about a current…client…of mine. I'd like to go as your date like we had originally planned."

"Before you went clean and married the redhead."

"Yeah."

Tony heard some shuffling and imagined her going through papers and typing on her keyboard, probably even answering emails while she talked. Charlotte was the master of multi-tasking.

"You don't think there weren't at least a dozen men waiting to take your place when you bailed on me?" He imagined her pout and smiled.

"I'm sure there were. Are. You probably have a date already. But would you dump him for me?"

"You're nothing if not direct," Charlotte said. "Well, there's Oliver. He *was* my date, but he was called out of the country this week. Something about some new-fangled tech piece he invented. I *am* enjoying him."

Oliver was someone Tony had introduced Charlotte to through a work endeavor. The two of them had apparently hit it off.

"You two are still an item?"

"For now. He has quite touched my heart. He's very endearing." Tony heard more clicking on her keyboard, and then it was quiet. "But I'm sure he'd be glad if you'd be my escort. You could keep me out of trouble."

"I'd really appreciate it. Should I pick you up at seven?"

"No. Let's meet there. I'll be coming from work." He heard a click. He guessed she had shut her laptop. "So, what is this about?"

"I'll tell you all about it when I see you."

"I'm intrigued. And what about the redhead?"

"She's still my wife. I love her. This date of ours is business, not pleasure."

"Disappointing," Charlotte cooed. "But very chivalrous. I'll see you Wednesday night." Without waiting for him to say goodbye, she hung up.

There would be a lot of people at this event who were tied in with Tony's past, people he had vowed to stay away from. But they also knew who ran in these circles, and he figured somebody would have some dirt on Mauvais. He needed some, and fast, so he'd have a way to pull himself out of this mess without effecting Abigail's job. He wouldn't tell her about the charity auction. Not until he was sure he had something on Mauvais.

But he would tell her about the flash drive. He locked up the apartment and headed home.

Chapter Fifteen

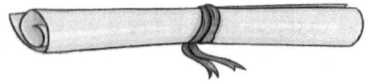

After the huge lunch, Abigail wasn't hungry for dinner. Instead, she decided to do a little research on Jean-Pierre. What if he *had* changed? What if he wasn't the man Tony knew? What if he was no longer blackmailing people and was just a charming thief like Tony used to be?

She typed his name into the search bar. There were pages full of articles and information about him. He even had his own Wikipedia page. She clicked on the most recent link, and it took her to a Paris newspaper, with a photo of him presenting one of those huge poster-sized checks at a big ribbon cutting. She clicked on "English Translation," and the headlines read "Collector and Investor Shares His Wealth with New Children's Hospital Wing." Hmmm. You couldn't say anything bad about that.

She was feeling more hopeful.

She clicked on the next link. "Rare Maps Guru Donates Millions to Museum." She clicked on a few more. Some were in French and had to be translated. One was in a British newspaper, and two were from the United States. In all of them, he was donating or investing either in the arts or in some type of community endeavor, such as funding the rebuilding of a school that had burned down or writing a check to help feed shelter animals over the holidays. Everything she read on him pointed to good works.

She read the Wikipedia article on him. He was an investor and a collector and trader of rare antiquities. He had never been married, had no children, and had apparently inherited his wealth. She clicked on his website, and it brought her to his homepage, which had links to his accomplishments, his bio, and his events page. He spoke regularly on various things related to the collections of rare maps and documents, but she knew all of this from the research she did on him before she invited him to store some of them at her library.

She clicked on his bio, and there was a stunning photo of him. He really was a handsome man. Once again, she didn't learn anything she didn't already know.

She closed her laptop and looked at her watch. It was nearly 7 p.m. She wasn't sure when Tony would be home, so she decided to get in her pajamas and curl up on the couch with a good book. Cocoa seemed impressed with the idea too, and she rubbed against her legs, making it difficult to get dressed.

"What do you think?" she asked the cat. "Can we trust Mr. Mauvais?"

Cocoa didn't have an opinion and followed Abigail downstairs to the living room. The cat jumped up on the couch next to her and curled up by her feet, purring. Abigail opened her copy of *As You Like It*. She was brushing up on her Shakespeare so she could keep up with Tony's quotes.

She was into the second act when Tony came home. "It's still cold out there!" he said. Spring was just around the corner, but in Michigan, the winters could drag on forever.

"Hi, hon," she said, closing her book. She got up and took his coat. "What happened to your chin?"

"Long story," he said. "I hurt it at work today. It's fine."

She asked about his grandma's doctor's appointment, trying to get the niceties out of the way before she launched into her excitement about Paris. He answered her questions, and she pulled him over to the couch to sit down next to her.

"Guess what we talked about at lunch today?" she said.

He raised an eyebrow. He looked tired to her.

"Paris! And you are for sure coming with me because Jean-Pierre is paying!"

He only seemed to be half listening, which was unusual. Tony usually gave her his full attention. Finally, he held up his hand, and she let her voice trail off.

"What's wrong?" she said. Instinctively, she had known something was off as soon as he walked through the door. She thought it must be about his grandma, but that wasn't it.

"Honey, I've got bad news about Jean-Pierre," he said. There were dark circles underneath his eyes that she hadn't noticed before.

She swallowed. She didn't want him to burst her bubble. Not yet. "But I just did some research on him. He seems okay. Maybe he has changed."

He pulled something out of his pocket. It was a flash drive. "I need you to watch this."

He opened her laptop and put the flash drive in. Abigail felt her stomach flutter with nerves. Whatever was on that flash drive wasn't good. Tony looked stressed.

"JP, or Jean-Pierre as you know him, came by the house the other day to ask me to do a job for him."

"*Our* house? He was in our *house?*"

Tony nodded. "He left this as a little incentive." He clicked on the video.

She saw him walking with a woman on his arm whom she recognized as Charlotte. Although she knew that Tony had slept with Charlotte, possibly several times, before Abigail met him, she had a soft spot in her heart. Charlotte had given them the $20,000 they needed to save his grandma's life. And she had helped clear Tony's name in the only theft he had been caught in.

Then the video clip showed Tony leaving Charlotte. The camera followed him over to another man. They shook hands. There was some sort of auction going on in the background. The short video ended at that point. It was maybe thirty seconds long.

"What is this?"

"It's blackmail. This video incriminates me because of where I am and whom I'm with. He can use it to connect me with several crimes."

He pulled the flash drive out and closed the laptop. They sat on the couch together, quiet for a moment.

Everything Abigail had learned about Jean-Pierre slowly dissolved in her mind. The man she was trying to build up didn't deserve the time of day. He was dirty. He was evil. He was out to hurt Tony.

But something else tugged at her.

"My tenure."

"I know."

Tony reached out and took her hand. She still didn't understand. "*Why?* Why would he give you this?"

"He wants me to do a job for him."

"A... job?" She knew it probably wasn't installing security.

Tony leaned his head back against the couch and closed his eyes. "He wanted me to get a necklace for him back when we were working together. He can sell it on the black market for millions. I had promised him I could get it, but I didn't do it right away because I needed to figure out the security system. Meanwhile, I stole the maps for him. Then, after the thing with the pocket watch, I quit on him. He really wants this necklace and has decided that since he found me again, he'd make sure I complete the job. He looks at it as unfinished business, I guess."

Abigail felt a surge of anger toward Tony go through her. It was irrational, she knew. None of this was Tony's fault. Well, it *was* his fault, but it was his past coming back to haunt him, not what he was doing now. So she couldn't really blame him. She thought of what all of this meant for her. Her job. Her tenure. Paris. She stood and paced across the floor. Then she turned to looked at him, sitting on the couch. He was watching her carefully, unsure of her reaction. She knew she should say that it was okay, that they would work it out, but she couldn't help but wonder if any of this would be happening if she hadn't met Tony. Would she just be moving forward in her tenure track, preparing for a workshop at the World Map Symposium in Paris and loving her job? No. She knew she didn't regret marrying Tony, but she needed some place for the anger to go.

"Why haven't you told me any of this sooner?" Her words sounded angrier than she intended.

"Because you've been so happy about your job," he said quietly. "I thought I could figure it out on my own."

"But we're not supposed to keep things from each other!" She paced across the room again and then turned back to him. "How am I supposed to trust you? Here I am, having lunch with Jean-Pierre today, almost convinced he was a changed man. I had no idea! Tony, how could you keep this from me?"

It wasn't really that he had waited a day or two to tell her that made her angry. She understood that he was, in a way, protecting her happiness. But to be honest and say her job was on the line because of this didn't seem right. Did she really care more about her work than honesty?

"He's blackmailing me, which is illegal," said Tony. "There has to be a way around this."

"So, if you don't do the job, he leaks the video?"

"Yes."

Abigail thought about that for a moment. There was somebody who might be able to help them.

"We have to tell Jimmy," she said.

Tony reached his hand over and stroked Cocoa, who had moved closer to him on the couch. "I thought about that," he said quietly. "But that puts him in a tough spot. If we mention the stolen map, he'll have to do something about it. And there will go all the work you put in to securing Jean-Pierre's collection for the library."

"So, let's just tell him about the flash drive," Abigail said. "We can go in with a hypothetical story. Like it's a friend of ours."

Tony gave a rueful smile. "He's smarter than that, Abigail."

"Then *you* fix this. You got us into this mess. You need to fix it." It was unfair, she knew. But after Nick's death, she had turned to her work because it was the only place she found solace. For six years, it had just been her job. No friends. No family. Just her job. It kept her from thinking about...

Her eyes teared up as she remembered her first husband. She still couldn't believe it would be seven years next Saturday. She bit her lip to hold in the tears and turned her back to Tony.

But then she felt his arms around her. "I'm sorry," he said. He pulled her against his chest and rested his head on her shoulder. "I'm so sorry. I will fix this. I promise." She wanted to turn and hug him, but she was too upset. She wasn't quite ready to forgive yet, so she remained silent and stiff. When he let her go and went into the other room, she let the tears fall freely down her cheeks. She walked quickly to the bathroom to get some tissue before he saw that she was crying.

When she came out, he was standing there holding out her coat. "We're going over to Martha and Jimmy's to play cards," he said.

Chapter Sixteen

Jimmy and Martha lived in a cozy little house in a small subdivision on the other side of the university. In the summer, they would be able to walk over, but tonight it was dark and cold. Martha was what Tony thought of as a "housewife." She kept a tidy home filled with the good smells of homemade baked goods and fresh bread. When Tony had called them a little while ago to see if they could come over, Martha said it was perfect timing because she had just put away the leftovers from a roast pork dinner. Would Tony like some? He hadn't had dinner and was starving.

She had a plate ready for him when he walked in the door.

While Tony ate, Jimmy got the cards out. Martha poured them each a glass of water and put on a kettle for tea.

"What's it going to be tonight?" Jimmy said. "Rummy? Euchre?"

Abigail chose Euchre and paired up with Tony. They beat them the first hand. "We don't have a chance against these brainy young'uns," Jimmy said. Martha laughed.

They played cards for about an hour. Tony spent the time watching Jimmy and trying to judge his mood. Jimmy had the night off and was relaxed and happy. He had complained about there not being anything on television these days and was glad the "kids" had decided to come over.

They decided to switch to Rummy. Tony shuffled the cards and cleared his throat. "Jimmy, I have a hypothetical question for you," he said. His eyes met Abigail's, and she gave him an encouraging little smile.

"What is it?" Jimmy was chewing on a straw, a habit probably left over from smoking earlier in his life, Tony figured.

Tony dealt the cards, starting with Jimmy, who was on his left.

"Let's say someone was going to blackmail someone else. Pretend I have a friend who did some illegal things in his past. And let's say someone has proof of some of that and tells my friend he has to do something else illegal or that proof will come out. Can my friend get in trouble for stuff he did in the past?"

Jimmy looked at Tony and raised both eyebrows. "Hypothetically?" he asked.

"Hypothetically," Tony said. Jimmy glanced at Abigail, who dropped her eyes and concentrated on her cards. *It's a good thing none of us play poker,* Tony thought.

"Well, the statute of limitations for…oh, I don't know, let's say *theft*, depends on whether it's a felony or a misdemeanor."

"It's probably not a misdemeanor," said Tony, concentrating on his own hand of cards now.

"I see. Well, *hypothetically*, if it happened longer than five years ago, there may be some leniency. As I said, it depends a lot on the actual crimes."

Jimmy chewed on his straw some more and glanced over at Tony. "On the other hand, blackmail is illegal, so the blackmailer is in trouble too."

"Then it would be best for my friend to come forward?"

"As a cop, I have to say, honesty is always the best policy."

"What if you are out and about and see something that you know is stolen?" Abigail chimed in. "But you don't want to report it because doing so will complicate…well, everything."

Jimmy laid down his hand of cards and looked at Tony and then Abigail. "What is this about?"

"Nothing," Tony and Abigail said at the same time.

Tony laid down a run of three hearts and played his queen on Martha's cards. "I think it's time for snacks," Martha said, scooting her chair out. "Who's hungry?"

"I am," Tony said. Then he looked at Jimmy. "It's your turn."

Jimmy gave Tony an even look. "If there's anything you need…" he said.

"I could use an ace of diamonds," Tony said and flashed Jimmy his most charming smile.

Jimmy scowled at him, but reluctantly let it go. He picked up his hand and laid down three aces. "Hmmmph. Look at that. Looks like I got what you need." He chewed his straw and looked over at Abigail to take her turn. Martha came back with a bowl of chips and nothing more was said about crimes, hypothetical or otherwise.

It was late, and Abigail stood up after the last hand, stretching. "I need to use the lady's room," she said. "And then we should go. I'm tired."

"Sounds good," Tony said. Jimmy collected the cards. Martha reached for a napkin and started wiping up crumbs.

But there was something else on Tony's mind. "So..." he began. Both of them paused and looked at him. "How do I help Abigail get through this coming week? With...the anniversary of Nick's accident coming up."

Martha sat back down at the table. "She'll get through it like she has done every year for the past seven," she said. "It's always difficult, and next Saturday will be the worst day. But this year is different. She has *you*." Martha reached over and put her hand on Tony's.

He nodded. "But what do I say?"

"Just love her."

"Some things can't be fixed with words," Jimmy said. "Like Martha said, just let her know you're there for her. Martha and I are both so grateful she has you to lean on."

"You're a blessing, Tony."

Jimmy frowned slightly. "Just don't screw it up."

"Jimmy!" Martha said, but then they heard the bathroom door open, and Abigail came into the room.

"Ready?" she asked.

Tony got up and got their coats. They gave hugs and soon were in the car headed home.

"Well?" He glanced over at Abigail.

"He's on to us."

"Obviously. We knew he would be. But at least we know our options."

"We don't have any."

He laughed. It wasn't really funny, but he couldn't see any other response. If he turned JP in for blackmail or for being in possession of a stolen map, he himself would go to jail and Abigail would probably not get her tenure. Worse, she might be fired when Ms. Scott found out about Tony's background. Ms. Scott was a smart woman and would put two and two together, which would equal Tony being the one who broke in to her library that night two months ago. She wouldn't be too happy about that.

"We might. I'm still working on it," Tony said.

Abigail sighed and Tony reached over and took her hand. "I'm sorry," he said again, not sure where stood with her.

She looked over at him. A tendril of her red hair fell across her face. "I know," she said. "And I'm sorry for yelling at you earlier. Thank you for trying to fix it."

"I'm still trying," he said. "Don't give up on me yet."

"I will never give up on you."

Her words were sincere; he could hear it in her voice.

"Thank you." He gave her hand a little squeeze.

"I need the car tomorrow," she said, changing the subject. "So, I'll drop you off at community service, and you'll need to take a bus back to your apartment. I have a lot of errands to run, and I'll do some grocery shopping."

"Okay."

He could feel her still looking at him.

"So how *did* you get that cut on your lip and the bruise on your chin?"

Tony had kept enough secrets for one week. He glanced over at her. "Karl decked me."

She stared at him for a moment and then laughed. "What? Why?"

"He hates me."

"*Nobody* hates you," Abigail said. "You and your charming smile."

"He wanted my coffee, and I wasn't going to give it to him."

"Did you?"

"Nope."

93

For some reason that seemed funny, and they both started laughing until they had tears running down their faces. Tony welcomed the relief, because he knew that morning was coming soon enough, and Karl wouldn't be too happy with him.

Chapter Seventeen

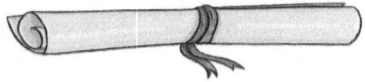

Abigail got up early on Saturday morning to drive Tony to his community service work. She fixed him breakfast and packed him a nice lunch and a warm thermos of coffee. He would be there most of the day.

"You can let me off here," he said when she was about a block away from the police station.

"Don't be silly," she said.

"I'd rather the guys didn't see me being chauffeured by my woman," he said. "Even if she *is* hot. Maybe *especially* because she's hot."

Abigail pulled over to the curb to let him off. "Okay, hon. Have a nice day." Until he got punched, it had never occurred to her how difficult this must be for Tony. Humiliating, yes, but she had never really thought of it as dangerous. But he was surrounded by a variety of criminals, working with them every day on some outdoor project. She vaguely knew that they were helping with a bridge, or at least laying stonework around the base of it. Tony didn't like to talk about it so she didn't ask.

She watched him walk away from the car and turn the corner. She waited a few minutes and then pulled away, deciding to head to the grocery store first. As she stopped at a light, she glanced through some buildings and saw him. He was surrounded by several men in orange jumpsuits, and they were loading up a truck. He looked forlorn there, not like the self-assured, confident man she knew him to be. It made her a little sad to think he'd be outside all day in the cold with people who weren't kind to him. It also scared her a little bit that they might hurt him. She had no idea if Tony could fight. She knew he'd win almost any battle of wits, but she had no idea what would happen if it came down to brute strength. Of course, Tony would probably never let it come to that. He could think himself out of any situation.

The light turned green, and she headed forward, deciding to focus on that positive aspect.

The grocery store wasn't crowded at 8 a.m. on a Saturday morning, so she got her shopping done quickly. She bought him some Oreo cookies, because she knew he loved them, and she thought she'd make him some Alfredo tonight. Something special. She wanted to pamper him.

She had been so wrapped up in her job, the upcoming premiere of the maps, and her grief over Nick that she hadn't properly considered what Tony was going through. Community service must be awful, and now his past was coming back to haunt him. Plus, he was caring for his grandma. Poor guy.

On her way home, she stopped at the post office to buy some stamps and mail a package. She was mailing back a blouse she bought online, which didn't fit. She was standing in line, looking through her phone, when someone came up behind her and said "Abigail!" She knew who it was from his French accent.

She took a deep breath before turning around. "Jean-Pierre!" she said, trying her best to look pleased to see him. "Fancy meeting you here!"

"I'm mailing some trinkets home to my mom," he said. "She likes the...how do you say it? *Brownies?*"

He was carrying a large box wrapped in brown paper. He was impeccably dressed in slacks and a well-ironed shirt underneath his tan wool coat. The hem of the coat came past his calves, and he had a blue knitted scarf hanging loosely around his neck. Abigail felt shabby next to him and was glad she had at least put on some mascara before she left the house.

He saw her looking at the scarf, and he fingered it. "My mother knitted it for me."

"What kind of brownies?" Abigail asked. She was a connoisseur herself.

"The ones that are home-baked at Zipperdoodles, your local bakery here."

"Oh, yes," said Abigail. "I know the Zipperdoodle brownies well. She won't be disappointed." That was at least one part of the conversation Abigail didn't have to fake.

The line moved forward. Abigail pulled her texting gloves off and got her wallet out of her purse. She turned forward and started counting her money. It looked like she had enough on her to pay with cash instead of her bankcard.

"That's quite a ring," Jean-Pierre said softly. She stiffened.

"This one?" She held her hand up. It was a stupid thing to say because the one on her ring finger was the only one she was wearing.

"Oui. Is it the original or a replica?"

"It's not even a diamond," said Abigail, who suddenly felt the need to protect it. "It's just some romantic gesture from Tony. He likes to be different."

"But it's the ring from the painting, is it not?"

Of course, he would know that. He was too smart not to have noticed that the first day.

"Yes. But it's a replica," Abigail lied.

"Let me see," Jean-Pierre said and took her hand. He turned it over so he could see the ring. His hands were warm. "It looks like the real thing. Where did you have it made?"

The clerk became available, and Abigail pulled her hand out of his. "I'm next," she said, and hurried to the counter.

She bought her stamps, mailed her package, and then quickly made her way toward the door. "I'll see you at work!" she said to Jean-Pierre, thankful that he would be at the counter long enough for her to make an escape in her little car.

———◇————————◇———

Abigail thought about the encounter with Jean-Pierre while she put the groceries away. She had never considered that wearing the ring might be dangerous, but now she wasn't so sure. She knew that the stone wasn't that valuable, but with all the publicity the Russo painting had gotten in the last six weeks and the popularity of Russo as an artist, the ring was most likely worth quite a fortune. They should probably have it appraised.

She would talk to Tony about it tonight. To distract herself from thinking about it further, she made a sandwich and sat down with her laptop to work on the talk she was going to give at next Friday's premiere.

She was going to start by telling everyone about the expert system the library had in place for the storage and protection of old maps and documents. That would lead in to the reasons Jean-Pierre Mauvais entrusted them with his collection. She'd also highlight how grateful they were to him for sharing his maps with them, which would boost his ego while letting the audience know how much this meant to the university library.

Her first PowerPoint slide was a photo of a map destroyed by water. The paper was stained, and the ink had run.

Most people are worried about water and moisture damage, Abigail typed. *There is the moisture in the environment, and then there are accidents. That is why we have the maps protected in case our sprinkler system goes off.*

She paused. Paper had a cellulose structure, and she Googled a microscopic image of that. *Even if the paper is in a slightly damp place, such as a basement, its cellulose structure makes it very susceptible to mold and mildew.*

But it can't be too dry, either. She had seen maps and documents come in that were stored in attics and were brittle. *What most people don't know is that paper needs a certain amount of moisture to maintain its structure.* Her next PowerPoint slide had a picture of a desert with a cartoon map fanning itself. Pieces were breaking off. *If it's stored in a place that is too dry, the paper will become brittle and break at the slightest touch.*

The ideal humidity level is between 40% and 50%. The University Library followed the protocol of most museums and maintained a safe environment of fifty percent humidity at all times. And seventy degrees. She worked temperature into her next slide.

She looked up the photos she had taken of their different storage solutions and made them into slides. Then she began the section about light and the degradation and fading it caused.

She had been working on her talk and PowerPoint for several hours when Tony came through the door.

"Hello, beautiful!" he said, pulling his coat off.

She saved her document and went to give him a hug. She took his face in her hands. "You look intact," she said.

"Karl didn't show up today. Rumor has it he is in a time-out for bad behavior." He hung his coat up. "The weather is getting nicer too. Much warmer today. Spring is just around the corner."

That's what they had said the year Nick died. "I've seen some of the worst ice storms ever this time of year," said Abigail. She didn't mean for her voice to sound so shaky. Grief was like that. She'd be doing something mundane, like her PowerPoint, and then something would trigger it.

"Hey," Tony said, coming to her. He embraced her in a warm hug. "I didn't mean to—"

"You didn't," she said, keeping her face buried in the soft sweatshirt he was wearing. She didn't want him to see her eyes. She still wasn't comfortable talking about Nick. She had avoided the topic all together until a few months ago, when she had met Tony and the story had spilled out of her like a dam unstopped. She had finally begun to deal with the guilt and sorrow she had been carrying for so many years.

"Is there anything I can do?" Tony spoke softly into her hair. "Anything at all?"

"No," she said. "It's just a day I have to get through."

"I'll be here to help you get through it," Tony said. "You know that, right?"

She felt the tears sting her eyes and kept her arms around Tony so he couldn't see her face. He held her quietly for a few minutes, and then Cocoa started twining between their legs.

Abigail laughed and pulled back, swiping her sleeve quickly across her eyes. "Somebody's jealous," she said.

Tony smiled and bent down to scratch the cat on her head. She was purring loudly. "Do you want to do anything special next Saturday to remember Nick?" he asked, not meeting her eyes. "We could go put flowers on the grave. Or you could go alone if you don't want me there."

"No," Abigail said quickly. She hadn't been back to the grave since the funeral. She just couldn't face it. Nick's parents had called her several times after his death, inviting her to come with them. On his birthday. On their wedding anniversary.

On the date of his death. She always refused because the pain was too much for her. Eventually, they called her less and less. After a few years, they stopped calling her altogether. That's why she was so surprised to hear from Sharon.

She wanted to change the subject. "I saw Mauvais today," she said. Tony jerked his head up. She knew that would get his attention. "He was at the post office. He was pleasant enough, but he was inquiring about my ring." She turned her hand over and looked at it. "He said it must be worth a fortune."

Tony walked over to the couch and sat down. "It is," he said. "Can you imagine what a collector would pay for it?"

"That's kind of what I thought, too." She sat beside him.

Tony took her hand and looked at the ring. "You need to stop wearing it. I'll get you a real wedding ring. A gold band or something. We can put that in a vault."

"No!" Abigail jerked her hand away. "I love this ring! It's special."

"I know, hon, but I'm not sure it's safe for you to wear it."

"I'm not going to stop," she said. "I'll be fine."

"Abigail..."

"Tony, no. I'm sorry I brought it up. I've been wearing it for nearly two months, and he's the first person to mention its value."

That's because they hadn't made a big deal about it. They had told no one except their close friends about the ring's history because of all the press about the painting. No one else had picked up that it was the ring from the painting. Or at least no one had cared up until this point.

Tony nodded. He was going to let this discussion go for now. She was grateful for that. He got up. "I need to shower," he said. Abigail nodded and petted Cocoa as he went upstairs to the bathroom. She looked at her ring again. She absolutely would *not* stop wearing it just because of Jean-Pierre. The jerk. She would never take it off. It's not like he could cut her finger off while she wasn't looking. She'd keep it safe and everything would be fine.

Chapter Eighteen

Tony sat at the end of the church pew with Abigail to his right, holding his hand. They arrived late and had slipped in next to the Stouts so Tony hadn't had a chance to assess whether or not Jimmy was angry with him. He knew he had aroused suspicion with his questions the other night, but he also knew that Jimmy would let it go because the last thing he wanted to do was lock up Abigail's husband. Then again, Jimmy thought of her as a daughter. If for one moment he ever thought Tony was putting her in danger, he'd probably lock Tony up himself, without hesitation.

The singing was over and the sermon was about trust. "Trust in the Lord with all your heart, and lean not on your own understanding..." the preacher read from the Bible.

Trust. Who could you really trust? Tony knew he trusted Abigail and his grandma. But beyond that? He wasn't sure. He supposed he could trust his friend George. But Tony had lived so long in a world where people played games with trust that he had grown wary of it.

"In all your ways submit to Him, and He will make your paths straight," continued the pastor. That was the other half of the verse, and he was breaking the sermon in to two points.

But could you trust God? Tony wasn't sure. He knew that God would "make his paths straight" and that ultimately God wanted nothing but good for him. He truly believed that. But *meanwhile*, here on earth, God didn't necessarily stop the bad things from happening. He hadn't healed Tony's mom from cancer or kept his dad from drinking himself to death. Tony glanced over at Abigail. And he hadn't kept Abigail's first husband safe from harm. A mere three months after they got married, God had taken him from her.

Tony wasn't sure about trust at all.

His mind drifted during the service, and before he knew it, it was time for the benediction. They stood for one last song, and Tony bowed his head as the pastor blessed the congregation. He needed all the blessings he could get.

Afterward, they went to the reception area for donuts and coffee.

"The weather seems to be warming up," Jimmy said, biting into a powdered-sugar donut, which left a fine trace of white on the moustache he had recently grown. He said it was for warmth, but Tony thought it made him look distinguished. The real reason was because Martha liked it.

"Yes, it does," Tony said, looking around for Abigail. He saw her and Martha over on the other side of the room, talking to friends.

"So," Jimmy said, moving closer. "This hypothetical story you told me the other night..."

Tony shrugged. "Purely hypothetical," he said.

"About a friend." Jimmy's tone was even.

"Yes. About a friend. A guy I happen to like a lot."

The two looked at each other levelly. Tony held Jimmy's gaze and did his best to look innocent.

"Okay," said Jimmy. "But Abigail is my main concern here."

"Yes, sir. I realize that." Tony put his hands in his pockets. He suddenly wasn't hungry for donuts.

"You don't have to call me 'sir,'" Jimmy said. His voice was still gruff, but his eyes showed kindness. "We're practically family."

Abigail came over and linked her arm through Tony's. "I have to get home," she said. "I have yoga class today."

She took a Sunday afternoon yoga class, which she loved, because it wasn't a busy day for yoga and that kept her class small. She always came home relaxed and happy and often took a nap.

Tony was glad to escape.

After lunch, he put his tools and specs in the car and dropped Abigail off at the yoga studio.

"I'm sorry you don't have the car today," he said, glancing at all the junk he had in the back seat for his job. "You'll have to take a bus to my grandma's."

She had no problem with that. Having lived in this city for years, she had taken a bus nearly everywhere before she had met him.

"Give Grandma a kiss for me and make sure she does her exercises," he said.

"See you later, handsome," she said, kissing him before she got out. He lingered a moment, watching her walk into the studio. He wanted to be sure she got in safely. Then he headed to the library to work on installing more of the security system.

George was already there, waiting for him in the parking lot. Tony used the key that Ms. Scott gave him to let them in. They were the only ones in the building today, so it would be easy to get their work done.

"How ya doin', Tony?" George said, as Tony disarmed the security system. "I sure do miss you at Poundstone." The two men had worked together for years at the painting company.

They got caught up on the past few weeks of each other's lives as they unloaded the tools from the car and brought them inside. Laney, George's wife, had apparently taken up ceramics, and George already had a house full of vases, bowls, and other items. "A man can only use so many bowls," he said.

Tony talked about his grandma and how he and Abigail were getting along. He wished he could tell him about JP and ask him for advice. George didn't know about Tony's criminal side, so there was really no way to bring it up. Was he living one big lie? There was so much he had kept from those he cared about. At the time, it hadn't seemed like a big deal. But now, he wasn't so sure.

They had been working for over an hour when somebody rang the bell at the front door.

"I'll get it," Tony said, wondering if Ms. Scott had stopped by to see how things were going. But it was JP.

"I came by to check on progress," he said. Tony reluctantly let him in and introduced him to George.

"George is our electrician," Tony said.

JP politely asked a few questions about what they were doing and then watched quietly for a moment. "Fascinating," he said. "I do appreciate you taking the time to care for my maps."

"No problem," said George, who was on a ladder and had his head stuck through a hole in the ceiling. He was attaching a camera to a light. "And this is a great thing you're doing. It's going to be wonderful for the university, but especially for Abigail and her career, I'll bet."

JP gave Tony a little smirk. "She is very appreciative," he said. "She told me so herself."

Tony was running a wire through the wall and up to George. He ignored JP.

"As a matter of fact," JP said, "I've invited her to Paris. There's a huge symposium in June, and she will be one of the keynote speakers."

"Wow," George said, his voice muffled.

Tony wanted to wipe the smirk off JP's face. Instead, he handed the wire up to George. After a few moments, George descended the ladder. "Got it," he said. "So what type of maps did you bring that are so valuable? I don't know anything about this stuff. Tony told me there's one that was actually Napoleon Bonaparte's?"

"Oui!" said JP. "From my private collection. But the one that Abigail is most excited about is the Vesconte. It's from the fourteenth century."

George whistled. "Wow. Where did you get that?"

JP cut a glance at Tony. "It was acquired through a private sale. I'm not sure where the original owner got it. He wouldn't say."

"Maybe he stole it," George said, laughing innocently as he put a pair of wire cutters in his toolbox.

"Maybe!" JP said brightly. "Wouldn't that be funny? But Abigail would know an illegal item if she saw one. It might fascinate her at first, but I don't think she's really in to that sort of thing."

Something inside Tony erupted at that point, and he launched himself at JP. Grabbing him by the shirt collar,

Tony slammed him up against the wall. JP made an "ooof" sound as the air rushed out of his lungs.

"You creep," Tony said between clenched teeth. He had never hit anybody before, but right now, all he wanted to do was put his fist into JP's face.

"Whoa!" George said.

"You leave her alone," Tony hissed, his face so close to JP's he could smell his minty breath. "Or I'll—"

JP was a man of high class. He wasn't used to getting his hands dirty. Tony could see him fighting his fear. "Cameras," JP said as he glanced up to where George had been working.

"I'm in charge of those cameras," Tony said. "They only record what I want them to see. I could wipe the floor with you, and nobody would know."

"He would," JP gasped, nodding toward George. Tony pushed harder on his windpipe.

"Um..." George's face was white. "I don't see a thing." He turned his back and got busy uncoiling some wires.

"Consider this a warning," Tony said. He dropped his hand, and JP slid down the wall, coughing and rubbing his neck. "Now get off my job site."

JP grabbed his hat off the counter. "Don't forget what you owe me," he said angrily. Still coughing, he left through the main door. Tony went and locked it behind him.

"What on earth...?" George said.

Tony knew he owed George an explanation. They had been friends for so long. George was even best man at his wedding.

"I just... He's after my wife," Tony said. It was true. In a way.

"Oh geez," George said. "Wow. But Abigail would never. I mean. *Would* she?"

Tony gave George a look. "Of course not! But he won't leave her alone. He gives her things and takes her out to lunch to five-star restaurants, and she is all gaga about this trip to Paris!"

"You have nothing to worry about," George said, patting Tony on the back. "That girl is crazy about you. But you let me know if I need to run interference for you. Those men

105

with foreign accents... Laney worked with this Englishman once and said he was the hottest thing since sliced bread."

"Is this supposed to make me feel better?" Because it wasn't. And Tony could hear the blood pounding in his head from his anger. He took a deep breath to calm himself.

George turned red. "I'm sorry, Tony. All I meant was it's fun to listen to those accents, but our women know who really loves them."

The two men got back to work, and the topic wasn't brought up again.

Chapter Nineteen

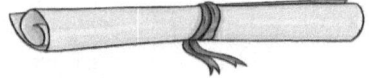

"We need to discuss this," Abigail said when they got in the car to head to work on Monday morning.

"Discuss what?" Tony asked. She felt a flash of irritation. How could he not know? It was the only thing that was on her mind these days: Mauvais and his awful meanness. Wasn't Tony always thinking about it like she was? They hadn't discussed it last night like she planned to. She had stayed and fixed dinner for his grandma and was home in bed when Tony came in from working at the library. He undressed quietly and crawled in next to her. She had slept until 3 a.m., when she awoke suddenly from a dream about Nick's death. She got up to get a drink of water and all the worry about Jean-Pierre came to her mind. She kept trying to figure out how she could turn him in without implicating Tony and still get to go to the Paris symposium.

Tony made a left turn off their street and cranked up the heat in the car.

"*Oh my gosh,*" she said, exasperated.

"I have some ideas," he said.

She turned to look at him. He kept his eyes on the road. "What kind of ideas?"

There was a long pause. One thing she had learned about Tony was that while he didn't lie, he didn't always share things with her. "Tony, I swear, if you—"

"How about we don't start today off with a fight?"

She sighed. There was no reason she should be attacking him. They needed to work together to solve this, because there was a lot at stake for both of them. "I'm sorry. I didn't get much sleep last night. I woke up at 3 a.m. worrying."

"*Worry is the interest paid by those who borrow trouble,*" quoted Tony.

Abigail tried to place the quote. "That's not Shakespeare," she finally said.

"No. I believe it was George Washington. Unless he was quoting Shakespeare."

Sometimes Abigail thought that Tony tossed out quotes to distract her and give her time to calm down. He knew that as an avid reader, she wouldn't be able to resist a quote. She had to admit that while her mind was mulling over the source of the quote, the anger had subsided a little bit.

"And I believe the Bible says something about not borrowing trouble for tomorrow because today has enough of its own," he added.

"Maybe it's *today's* trouble I'm worried about," Abigail said irritably. She looked out the car window. The sun was shining, and the snow had all melted. It was going to be in the forties today. Her snowdrops were up in the front flowerbed, and she could see the crocuses poking their tiny green tips out of the ground when she walked down her front steps this morning. She had plenty to be thankful for. But she was scared.

She hadn't just *worried* at 3 a.m. She had prayed too. But she had enough experience with prayer to know that God didn't always answer it the way she wanted Him too. Her *job* was on the line. A job she dearly loved and was very good at. If she lost this job, and the tenure that came with it, because of a scandal, no other university library would ever think about hiring her. She'd have to find work in the secular world. But she was so comfortable *here*. She loved the university and loved her home, which she had inherited from her aunt. She had Jimmy and Martha close by, and she treasured her dinners with them. She had her yoga studio and Pauline.

"Whatever trouble there is, we'll face it together," Tony said. She looked over at him. She could lose him too.

Loss was something she wasn't good at dealing with. She closed her eyes as she thought of the long, dark months after Nick's death. While the flowers bloomed and the sun shone longer every day, while the rest of the world rejoiced as spring finally arrived and then summer, Abigail had lived in a world of dark despair for what seemed like an eternity. It took a lot of work to climb her way out.

Tony reached over and grasped her hand as if sensing what was going through her mind.

"So, what 'ideas' do you have?" she asked, getting back to her original question, which he had so neatly deflected.

"Ideas you'll have to trust me with. I have a plan, but I'd rather not discuss it yet."

"We don't keep things from each other," Abigail reminded him. "Is it illegal?"

Tony hesitated. "I will keep it legal, I promise."

"Why can't you tell me?"

"I need to work it out in my head before I execute it," he said. "I'll tell you if it works." He pulled up to the library's front door and put the car in park.

"If this relationship is going to work, I need to know now," Abigail said. She wasn't going to let him off the hook. There was too much at stake.

He glanced at the clock on the car's dashboard. "You're going to be late for work."

"Tony..."

He met her eyes. "I need you to trust me. I'm not going to do anything stupid. I just..."

He didn't finish the sentence. He just looked at her with pleading eyes.

"Fine," she said shortly. She opened the door and got out without giving him a kiss goodbye, closing the door a bit too firmly. Then she marched up the steps and into the library without looking back.

"Abigail!" Pauline was in the break room, hanging up her coat. "Good morning! How is your talk coming for Friday's premiere? Ms. Scott is beside herself with excitement. I saw her when I came in a few minutes ago, and she is all aflutter. This is so incredible, what you've brought to our library! And I am sooooo excited about Paris! Do you really think Ms. Scott will let me come with you?"

"Jean-Pierre said he'll pay your way." Abigail forced a smile on her face, but Pauline was sharp.

"What's wrong?" Pauline said. "You look upset."

Abigail hung her coat up and closed the locker. "I had a fight with Tony this morning," she said. "He dropped me off, and I didn't even kiss him goodbye."

"Oh, honey, is this your first fight? It'll be okay. Drew and I fight all the time. Over finances, over parenting. Sometimes over who didn't replace the toilet paper on the roll. It's part of life."

I'll bet you don't fight over stolen maps and clandestine meetings and whether or not you want to continue to work in league with a criminal, Abigail thought wryly. But she said, "I know. It just feels terrible."

She already regretted her abrupt departure from the car, but she was really mad at Tony. He was the one person she could discuss their problem with, and he wouldn't let her in on what plans he had, if any. Now she was left to try to figure something out on her own.

"I've got to get to my section," said Pauline. "Ms. Scott has a bunch of stuff for me to do for Friday's premiere."

"Okay," Abigail said. "Maybe we can get some lunch together later."

Abigail made herself a cup of green tea and took it to her desk. She looked at the tall stacks of books and documents and the rows of drawers where the maps were kept. She loved her circular desk, which sat not quite directly under a skylight a few stories above her that let in sunlight. And, she had to admit, a little bit of a draft in the winter. But it was hers, and she loved it.

She took a sip of her tea. Just two months ago, she had never even heard of Tony Russo. Then one night he had dropped down on a rope from that skylight in front of her. It was late, and he hadn't expected Abigail, or anybody, to be there. He simply wanted to find the map that led to his grandmother's stolen painting. She hadn't been afraid. There was just nothing about Tony that had scared her. His eyes twinkled with merriment, and he smiled. It helped that he was very hot looking in his black spandex outfit that outlined his muscles quite nicely. As well as other parts. She smiled.

"Oh, Tony," she said softly.

What would things be like right now if he wasn't part of her life? She'd still be setting up for the premiere on Friday to introduce the Napoleon Bonaparte map as well as some others. Jean-Pierre, though, would be just a man whom she was working with. A famous collector, yes, but not a threatening person with stolen goods. Would he still have invited her to present at the symposium in Paris? She liked to think so. She had the expertise and was somewhat known in the rare and ancient documents and maps world. Not *well* known, but as the librarian of that area in a university this big, she *was* known.

So if she had never met Tony, this would be a stress-free and exciting endeavor.

But what had her life been like then? She'd still be wearing baggy clothes and her old wedding ring to ward off potentials suitors, and worse, she'd be facing another anniversary of Nick's death with the same emptiness she had for six previous years. She'd be alone. Yes, she had the Stouts, but they had their own lives, and she did feel a peculiar need to protect them since they were older. So she didn't share everything with them.

When Tony dropped into her life that night, everything had changed. A feeling she no longer thought she wanted was reawakened in her. *Love.* And yes, even a little bit of lust. He was *hot*, and their marriage was young enough that she still appreciated it. And he was charming. And he loved her more than the moon.

She knew that.

She loved him too. How she could love somebody so deeply that she had only met months ago was beyond her. But she did. Passionately and enough to die for. As she had thought the other day, she'd follow him anywhere.

But that didn't mean she wasn't still mad at him. Married couples weren't supposed to have secrets. She wondered what her cat burglar was up to and prayed to God that he would stay safe.

Chapter Twenty

Karl was back at work for community service and wasn't looking too happy. The first thing he did was snarl at Tony when he arrived. Then he "dropped" his gloves and told Luke to pick them up. With trembling hands, the small man did as he was told, but to his credit, when Luke handed them to Karl, it was with a rough slam into his chest. Karl only grunted.

"Later," Karl said to Luke.

The day was warmer, but the melting snow and ice made for wet work. Tony's insulated rubber boots kept his feet dry and warm, but it wasn't long before his gloves were damp. He had switched from the heavier work gloves he had used in the colder weather and realized now what a bad mistake that was. His fingers were cold, and it was making it painful to stack the stones up on the bank. They were building up the embankment to keep the river from eroding the shoreline around the bridge.

Tony stood and was considering taking his gloves off when he saw Karl walk by Luke and "accidently" drop a large stone down on him. It landed with perfect precision on the man's hand, and there was a screech of pain.

"Hey!" One of the guards ran over, pulling his billy club out of his utility belt. "Karl!"

"It was an accident," Karl said, holding his hands up innocently. "I slipped. It's icy out here." Karl swore some, for added benefit. "I'm sorry, man."

"It was *not* an accident!" yelled Luke, cradling his injured hand. He had turned an impressive shade of red. "I think it's broken!" Luke was biting his lip and dancing around.

"Let me have a look," said the guard. He was a big fellow that the men called Butch. Luke showed him the hand.

"This isn't a monkey show," Butch said to the men. "The rest of you get back to work."

Tony decided to keep his gloves on and resumed his labor. Soon, an ambulance pulled up, and Luke went and sat inside of it. Eventually they pulled out, with Luke inside, accompanied by one of the guards.

Butch approached Tony a few minutes later. "Luke says you saw what happened," he said quietly. "Was it an accident? Or did Karl drop that rock on purpose?"

Tony hesitated. In his previous line of work, you never snitched on anybody. No matter what. Honor among thieves.

"Look, I know you don't want to get involved in this, but if you know something and you don't tell, that can get you in trouble too." Butch still had his billy club out and was tapping it against his palm. "Would you rather be in trouble with Karl, whom we plan to remove, or with the law?"

With the law, Tony thought, looking over at Karl's massive bulk. Obviously.

"It was hard to tell from here," Tony said.

"Did Karl trip?"

"I'd say no," Tony said.

"Then you'd say he dropped that rock on purpose." Butch put his billy club away and pulled out a notebook and pencil, like he was a detective or something.

"Oh geez," Tony said. "Put that away." They had attracted Karl's attention, and he was looking at the two of them.

"So, I'll put down that you aren't sure, and if there's a lawsuit we can use you as a character witness."

"I don't think—" Tony began. But the other guard blew his whistle, which meant the end of their shift. Tony gratefully grabbed his tools and headed for the truck.

The crew was quiet on the ride back to the police station, and Karl went to the back lot where he kept his car parked, not causing any trouble. Tony kept a wary eye out. He reached his own car without incident, but he knew Karl's type, and the big thug would never let this go.

He drove to his apartment to change and shower. While he was munching on some lunch, he thought he'd see what he could find out on the job JP wanted him to do. He needed something to give to him to get the Frenchman off his tracks for a few days.

He Googled the actress, Vivian Danes. Recent photos showed her wearing the necklace. At a movie premiere last month in Cannes. In a restaurant in LA the previous month. He Googled the necklace, and of course there were several fan pages showing its appearance in each of her movies.

So it was still a thing.

He needed to figure out which security system she was using. She might have changed it up since he was last there. He logged onto the dark web and purchased an app, which he uploaded to his phone.

Since today was Monday, he didn't have to go check on his grandma. The visiting nurse would be there. He looked at his watch and had about an hour before he met with a client.

He grabbed his keys and thought he'd take a quick drive over to Danes' place.

It didn't look like anybody was home, but that was hard to tell through the front gates as he drove down the street with other traffic. He turned off the main road and down a side street, where he parked his car. He got out and casually walked down the sidewalk toward the park that her property backed up to. Tony took a quick turn down a walking trail. He pushed through some bushes, and there he was, at the back of her acreage. The house loomed about 500 yards away, large, brick, and surrounded by trees. That was a mistake.

The property's perimeter was alarmed, and she had dogs, he remembered with a bit of trepidation. Unless they had died in the past few years.

The fence was made of wrought iron bars with brick pillars every ten feet. Very attractive. He took out his phone and used his new app to scan the fence line. It showed a low frequency current, which he calibrated. It matched a security system he was familiar with, the same one she had been using when he broke in before.

He didn't see any dogs.

He looked across the vast yard. She had taken down the bushes that surrounded the house, so it was more open. He'd have to approach the house at night.

He could disarm the property's perimeter alarm from his home computer system, now that he knew which company it was hooked up to, thanks to his nifty calibrating app. Then he'd scale the fence and head along... He looked around the property. Probably along the north side, would be best. He could climb the big oak just off the veranda. That, he knew, led right into her bedroom.

If she was sleeping—and she most likely would be because he'd go in around 2 a.m. He could go in the sliding glass door. Cut the glass, maybe? Or would the cold wake her?

He thought about that and hoped there would be no dogs barking on the lawn to awaken her either. Or eat him.

There would be an alarm on the doorwall, but he could figure that out from home too. Once he got in, he'd have to get in the safe. He was sure she must keep it in a safe at night, and the fan pages agreed. He had done some research on her when he was going to break in before and had come up with several possible combinations. But he was just guessing. He needed another way into the safe.

Wait. *What was he doing?* He was just here to get enough information to satisfy JP. He hadn't really planned to break in. He just got caught up. Old habits...

He had enough information. Satisfied, Tony went back to his car. He needed to get home before his client arrived.

It was late when his client left, and he had to go back to the library to work, after hours. He called Abigail.

"Hey, beautiful."

"Hi." She didn't sound thrilled he had called. But she had answered.

"Are you still mad at me?"

"No. Yes."

"Which is it?"

"Both. We need to talk."

He sighed. She wouldn't like what he was about to say. "I need to get over to the library. George will be waiting for me." He couldn't show up late a second day in a row.

"Of course."

Tony propped the phone between his ear and shoulder as he quickly made a peanut butter and jelly sandwich from the meager findings in his kitchen. "I won't be home until late," he said. "Did you want to come over to the library?"

"It's not like we can talk with George there."

That was true. And he was a little behind on the library security, which he had to have ready before Friday. He would lose Wednesday night as a work night because he'd be with Charlotte.

"I'm doing this for you," he said, which he knew was a cheap way to deflect blame. It was both true and not. Installing the library security system was his *job*, a well-paying gig she had gotten him for his fledgling company. But it was also to prepare for her premiere. There was no way JP would let her display his maps publically without maximum security. They were worth a lot of money, but they were also worth a lot to him personally, as a collector. JP was very fond of his treasures.

"So tell me over the phone," she said.

"Tell you what?" He was stalling for time. He spread some strawberry jam on his sandwich and took a bite.

"Tony!" she said. "You know perfectly well! You have plans, and I need to know what they are!" She was angry.

"Not over the phone," Tony said. "Abigail, I have to go. We will talk. I promise."

"Fine," she said.

He held his sandwich in his teeth while he pulled his coat on. He grabbed his tool bag.

"I love you," he said, chewing.

He heard her sigh. "I love you too," she said. Then she hung up.

Tony closed his door and dashed for his car. He was pushing his luck, but he didn't want to tell her that he was taking Charlotte to an illegal auction to dig up some dirt on JP. She'd never approve, and so far, it was the only idea he had to get himself out of this mess. He had to get something on JP that was just as good as what JP had on him.

He'd have to do something special for Abigail tomorrow.
Or stay away from her until after Wednesday night.
Either way, he was headed for trouble.

Chapter Twenty-One

Abigail blow-dried her hair. She was dressed and ready for work and had yet to see Tony. She tried to wait up for him last night, but he came home late, and she fell asleep before he arrived. She vaguely remembered him climbing into bed, but then he was up early this morning before their alarm went off.

She walked out into the kitchen where he was scrambling some eggs.

He turned to her and motioned to a sack on the kitchen table. "I packed your lunch."

He was trying to make nice for blowing her off yesterday. Then again, Tony was always doing kind things for her, even when he wasn't in the doghouse.

She went up behind him and put her arms around him. "Thank you," she said, giving him a kiss on the cheek.

She handed him some plates, and he put the eggs on them. They ate a hurried breakfast as he told her about the progress at the library.

"Just two more evenings and George and I should have it finished," he said. "I plan for it to be done on time."

"Thursday morning is when Ms. Scott expects it," Abigail reminded him. "Today is Tuesday. You promised it in a week." It made her a little nervous hiring somebody she knew. Or worse yet, was *married* to. If something went wrong, she couldn't actually sue him. Abigail sighed.

"I'll get it done," Tony said. "We're in good shape."

"I know," she said. And she did. She finished her eggs and took her plate to the sink. While she was in the shower, she had decided she wouldn't bring up yesterday or press him to talk about his plans. She didn't want to start the morning off with a stressful conversation. It wasn't good to part ways angry with each other, and she didn't think the conversation would go well. Plus, she had her own ideas.

Tony got the car today because he had to go check on his grandma, so he dropped Abigail off at the library. She kissed him on the cheek.

The library felt like a refuge to her after her long night waiting up for Tony and then skirting around issues this morning at breakfast. Finally, she could relax a little bit. Her job was something she was comfortable with, and the silence of the library wrapped around her like an old friend. Gray light came in through the windows around the room, and filtered down from the skylight. It was dark on cloudy days, so she had her desk lamp and a few incandescents overhead. She had removed the fluorescent lights years ago because she didn't like their harshness.

Surrounding her desk on all sides were stacks where the research books were kept and drawers for her maps. The maps room was off to her left. She was pleased to see the cameras and locked cases that Tony and George had installed last night.

She pulled out a worksheet and took it over to a table nearby. Today she would start categorizing some of Jean-Pierre's maps and figure out where to house them among the others in the library. She'd start with the more mundane maps and leave the rare ones until later. She needed more security set up before she brought those out. That's what Tony would work on tonight.

"Good morning!" Pauline said. Abigail glanced at her watch. She had been working for about two hours. "Ms. Scott put me to work as soon as I walked in the door! I'm finalizing the brochures that we will hand out, and I have a few questions for you."

While they were going over things, the elevator doors opened and Jean-Pierre walked through.

"Bonjour, mademoiselles!" he said, taking his bowler hat off and tipping his head to them.

"Bonjour!" said Pauline. Abigail only gave him a smile.

He ooohed and ahhhed over Pauline's brochure and then walked around and looked at Tony's work on the security.

Finally, he announced that he needed to talk to Abigail about Friday's plans.

"And I need to get back upstairs," Pauline said. "Au revoir!"

As soon as she left, Jean-Pierre sat down beside Abigail. She felt the skin on her neck prickle.

"Can you give me a rundown of what you plan to talk about on Friday, and at what time you want to introduce the Napoleon Map?"

Abigail told him, keeping her tone very polite and businesslike.

"And when should we reveal the Vesconte?" he asked.

"About that," Abigail said, firmly putting her pencil down. She looked around her. Ms. Scott would be in a meeting now. Nobody else was around, but she lowered her voice anyway.

"How *dare* you bring stolen goods into my library!" she hissed.

"Stolen goods?" He feigned innocence. "What has Tony been telling you?"

"This is a huge deal for me...this...this whole thing about having you here and housing your maps," Abigail continued. "*You* are the collector I was so excited to invite here. *Your* maps were the highlight of six months of preparation—of *me* preparing this place for *you*. Not to mention, how good all of this was going to look for my tenure track. Those maps... this project...was something I have always dreamed about."

"Merci—"

"But you have *ruined* it!" Abigail said, slapping the palm of her hand down on the table. In the shower this morning, she had prepared what she wanted to say to him. But her anger was getting in the way, and it wasn't coming out as she had planned. She took a deep breath to calm herself.

"Merci boucoup," Jean-Pierre continued, putting his hand on hers. "I meant no harm. I knew how thrilled you'd be to see the Vesconte, and really, I had no idea it was stolen."

Liar.

Abigail leaned in toward him, as close as she dared. She let his hand remain on hers. Her hair was down and freshly washed, and she knew the scent of her lavender shampoo lingered. She locked her big green eyes on his and noticed how handsome he really was. His hazel eyes looked so charming, so innocent, that she almost believed him. But he was a snake. She moved toward him until she could feel his breath on her face. She saw him swallow. Good, she was making him uncomfortable.

In the research she did on Jean-Pierre, one thing she had learned about him was how much he loved his maps. His collection was like his children to him, and he'd do anything to keep them safe.

Her voice was a whisper when she spoke.

"Here's what I want," she said. "I want to go to this symposium in Paris and present. I deserve to be there. I'm very good at what I do, and you know it. I want this premiere to go off without a hitch on Friday. I will not say a word about the Vesconte being stolen, but you need to remove all of the other illegally obtained goods from this library before Ms. Scott sees them." She was desperately hoping that didn't include the Napoleonic map. "And if you *ever* show that video of Tony to anybody, I will make your Vesconte disappear."

Jean-Pierre's eyes narrowed at the mention of his precious Vesconte. "You wouldn't."

"Try me."

They stared at each other for a moment in a stalemate, and then a smile spread across his face. "You're a feisty one," he said. He laced his fingers through her hand and squeezed. It hurt. "You're playing with fire, Abigail Russo, and you're going to get burned. You don't know who you're messing with."

"Nor do you," Abigail said, sitting back and ignoring the pain in her hand. "Tony's not the only one who can steal something. I have a few tricks of my own up my sleeve. Also, don't mess with my husband. This deal is between you and me. Leave him out of it."

Jean-Pierre leaned in toward her. Taking his free hand, he put it up to her cheek. She tried not to flinch.

"You *are* beautiful," he said softly. "And if you want this to be kept between you and me, that's fine." He traced his finger down the side of her cheek and then to her shoulder, where he fingered her hair. "But you're in over your head.

121

You might be able to flirt with danger with your little thief, but you couldn't handle a man like me."

He let go of her hand and stood.

"Remember what I said," Abigail told him, trying to ignore the pounding of her heart.

"Au revoir," he said. "Until we meet again." He smiled and turned to leave.

That's when they saw Pauline standing just across the room, holding some documents. She cleared her throat and pretended not to notice anything.

Jean-Pierre stepped into the elevator, and as the door closed, Abigail took a deep breath and tried to calm her racing heart. She wondered how much Pauline had seen.

Pauline walked past Abigail and over to the desk, dropping off the documents. She stood there for a moment, her back to Abigail.

Abigail took that chance to regain her composure. She bent over her notebook and tried to look busy. She noticed her hands were trembling.

"Abigail...?"

She looked up. Pauline was standing beside her.

"Pauline, I have a deadline."

Instead of leaving, Pauline sat down across from her at the table.

"This is none of my business, but what did I just see? Was he *hitting* on you? Were you *letting* him?"

Pauline was pale. Her eyes were wide. For a moment, Abigail was about to brush her off. But she had been keeping secrets for too long, and she desperately needed someone to talk to. Pauline was her best friend. Maybe her only friend.

Abigail stood up and grabbed her hand. "Come on!" she said and pulled Pauline down an aisle. The stacks on each side of them reached from floor to ceiling, which gave them some privacy. Abigail stopped in the middle. From here, she had a view of the stairs and elevator, so she could see if anybody entered the floor. She could also see her desk.

"Okay," Abigail said. "I have a lot to tell you, and you have to promise, swear on your mother's grave, that you will not repeat a word of this to anybody. Ever."

122

Pauline's blue eyes got wider. "Uh..."

"*Ever!*" Abigail hissed. "Please. I need someone to talk to."

"Okay," Pauline said. Abigail knew Pauline desperately liked gossip. But she was also a great secret keeper. She loved to listen but rarely spilled.

Abigail took both of Pauline's hands.

"You're scaring me," Pauline said.

"This is one of those conversations where you probably need to be sitting. But there are no chairs."

"Abigail..."

Abigail squeezed her hands. "Remember how I said I met Tony?"

"Yeah. He came in here looking for a map."

"Yes, that part is true."

Abigail was silent. She watched the wheels turn. Suddenly Pauline gasped. "I *knew* it! I told Drew, and he said I was crazy. Tony was the thief, wasn't he? The one who came in here—"

"Looking for a map!" they both said together.

"Oh my gosh." Pauline said. "I do need to sit down." She sank to the floor and leaned against the books. "Does Ms. Scott know?"

Abigail sat down beside her. "Of course not. Nobody does."

"I suspected," said Pauline, "because of how you changed after that. Most people would have PTSD or something but you were...happy. And suddenly this stranger started coming in and dating you. Drew said I was crazy. But it all makes sense."

Abigail proceeded to tell her the story of how the map led to the stolen painting and the mystery they solved, finally finding it. And how they gave the credit to Jonathan Stewart, the city attorney, so no one would connect that they had taken a map out of the library. She told Pauline about Tony needing money for his grandma's cancer treatments and Jimmy catching him in the middle of a theft at a jewelry store.

"He was going to sell the piece for the money," she said. She told her how Jimmy had helped get Tony off and how they hadn't been able to make any of his past crimes stick.

"So how did he get the money for his grandma?" Pauline asked.

"Someone came forward and anonymously donated," Abigail said. *Charlotte.* She didn't mention her to Pauline; she didn't want to incriminate her.

"Wow."

Pauline was quiet, which wasn't like Pauline at all. Abigail could see her thinking. Finally, she looked up at Abigail. "So how does Jean-Pierre fit in to this?"

"The Vesconte is stolen. Apparently, Tony stole it for Jean-Pierre several years ago. Jean-Pierre is using it as collateral for a bigger job he wants Tony to do, which involves stealing a necklace. If Tony doesn't steal this necklace, Jean-Pierre will tell the world that the Vesconte is stolen. He has a whole story that keeps his own name clear but sends Tony to jail. He also has a video of Tony at some illegal auction, which he will release anonymously."

"So, you were playing him just now."

"I was giving him my demands. I want this partnership to work out, so we can go to Paris and the library can still profit from these maps. And I want to keep Tony safe. So I threatened him. Jean-Pierre loves his maps, and I threatened his maps."

"Oh, Abigail," breathed Pauline. "You're playing with fire."

"That's exactly what he said. That's why I'm telling you this. If I disappear, someone needs to know why."

The elevator dinged, and both women jumped up. "Abigail?" called out Ms. Scott. She swore that woman could be loud in a library.

"Coming!" She turned to Pauline. "We can talk more later. You can't tell anyone. Promise!"

"I promise," Pauline said.

Abigail fled to her desk to see what Ms. Scott wanted her to do next.

Chapter Twenty-Two

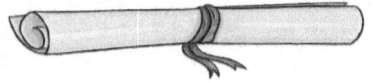

Community service was cold and dirty work, but Tony managed to steer clear of Karl. He went back to his apartment to shower and then dropped by his grandma's. He was disheartened to see how tired she was today, so he helped her get through her physical therapy exercises and fixed them both some lunch. She settled down in her chair afterward, and he put an afghan over her. He remembered when she had crocheted it. It was the winter he was fifteen, and she had twisted her ankle and needed something to do while she healed.

"Are you going to be okay?" Tony asked.

"Of course, dear. I'm just tired."

Reluctantly, he left her and went to get some work done. First, he stopped by the house to get his tuxedo. He didn't want Abigail to see him with it. He found it in the back of their closet, smashed between his suits. It needed ironing.

Back at his apartment, he plugged his iron in and booted up his computers. He took a few phone calls from potential clients, saw that the iron had shut off automatically, and turned it on again. He ran his hand through his hair.

"This is too much," he mumbled after he hung up from a third phone call. He loved the business he was getting from Jimmy's referrals, but he wasn't sure he'd be able to fit it all in.

He ironed his tux and hung it in the closet of what used to be his bedroom. He looked longingly at the bed that was still there. He was exhausted today. But he went back to his desk and decided to do some research on this auction he was attending with Charlotte tomorrow night.

Using special software, he logged on to the dark web and typed in a key code he had memorized from a previous invitation. There it was—a list of items that would be presented at this auction.

trusting the cat burglar

Some very old art—paintings and such. Old vases. Jewelry. The usual. There wasn't a guest list (for obvious reasons) or even a seller's list, but from what was being offered, he had a pretty good idea of who would be there. Collectors had preferences. The man known as Black Jack, for example, would come after the eighteenth-century painting of the woman at the well. He was also pretty certain that Rufus would show up for the rare Chinese vases. He was a collector of ancient oriental items. Charlotte...well, Charlotte always came for the jewelry.

He didn't see anything that should attract the attention of JP except for one map. He didn't expect the Frenchman to be there. He'd be lying low around town and getting ready for his premiere on Friday. But you could never be sure. Satisfied, Tony logged out of the dark web and went to work on finishing the specs for the library work he had to complete tonight with George.

His phone rang. He looked at the time. It was 5 p.m. already. Abigail was expecting him home at 5:30.

"Are you coming home for dinner?"

Not until after tomorrow night, he thought. She'd see right through him. He'd stay out late again; he had to get this project completed anyway. He changed the subject instead of answering her question.

"Grandma needed more help than usual with her PT exercises. I'm worried about her. She looks awfully tired."

There was a silence.

"Abigail, please don't be mad. This is just a really difficult week for me." He clicked on a spec. He needed to get this finished so he could meet George.

"This is a difficult week for me too," she said quietly.

He let go of the mouse and swiveled his chair around so he was no longer looking at the computer. She deserved his full attention. He wanted to run home to her, but he knew how important her job tenure was to her, and this was the only way he knew how to fix it.

"I know it is," he said gently. "And I love you." He wondered what she would be doing tonight if Nick were still alive. Probably not worrying about where her husband was.

126

"I love you too. I don't mean to be angry with you. But we are supposed to share things, and I know you're up to something. I think you're avoiding me."

"What?" But it was true.

"Yes."

Tony looked at his watch again and resigned himself to being late. He leaned back in his chair. "Maybe."

"Well, you don't need to worry about anything. I put Jean-Pierre in his place today. I told him that if that video ever sees the light of day, the Vesconte will disappear."

Tony sat up so fast he almost fell out of his chair.

"You *what?*"

"You heard me." Abigail sounded smug.

"Abigail, you can't threaten Jean-Pierre! Do you have any idea who you're dealing with?"

"Yes, as a matter of fact, I do. Not only have *you* told me about him, but I did quite a bit of research on him myself. He loves his collectables. Like they're his children. He'd do anything to keep them safe."

"That's what I've been saying," Tony said. He couldn't believe it. But he should have figured. She was smart, she was a researcher, and she wasn't going to wait around for a man to fix things for her. "Abigail, listen to me. You need to stay away from him and leave this to me. I know how to handle him. He's a predator. You need to stay safe, and dealing with Jean-Pierre Mauvais is no way to do that."

"Why? Because I'm a *woman?*" She sounded irritated.

"Oh geez, no. Don't play the sexist card. You know that's not me." Tony was getting frustrated with this whole conversation.

"Then let's have a conversation right now about how you plan to fix this."

"Abigail, these next few days and evenings are going to be crazy. Let's set aside some time to talk about this Friday night, after the premiere. Or Saturday."

"It's a bit late then, right?"

Tony sat up. "Look. I have to go. If you want your premiere to happen on Friday, George and I have to get our work done tonight. I've had a bad day, a busy day, and now I'm not even

127

going to have time for dinner before I have to head over there. I need to meet Ms. Scott at 6 p.m. before she locks up tonight because she has a few things she needs to ask me. You know this."

"So, we're going ahead with the premiere?"

Tony thought about that. There didn't seem to be anything he could do about the Vesconte right now. As long as he played ball, JP would behave himself.

Abigail spoke up. "I told Jean-Pierre that I wanted this premiere to go off without any problems. We'll show the Vesconte. His tracks are covered, which mean yours are too. I can live with knowing one of the maps is stolen, because apparently nobody is going to come forward and claim it or Jean-Pierre wouldn't be so sure of himself. If nothing else comes of this, that's it."

"Okay," Tony said. "So, I guess we're going ahead with the premiere."

"I don't see any other way."

Neither did Tony. At least not yet. But if he didn't deliver that necklace, the whole thing could fall apart. JP would have someone come forward and claim the Vesconte after it went public, and he'd release the video. That would bring both Tony and Abigail down. JP would do it, too. Tony had no doubts about that.

"There's still the small matter of the theft he wants me to commit."

"I took care of that. I told him to back off and leave you alone. I'll make sure he does."

Tony rubbed his forehead. He felt a headache coming on. She was getting in too deep. "Don't threaten him. I'll figure something else out. I told you I'm working on it. Promise me you'll leave this to me."

"No," Abigail said. "But I promise you that I still love you."

He smiled. "I guess that's something. That a lot, actually."

"Cocoa misses you."

He thought about Abigail sitting at home on the couch with Cocoa curled up on her lap. She'd have to eat alone tonight. Was he wrecking their marriage? Or was he saving her? He didn't have enough experience to know.

"I miss Cocoa," he said. He wished he was home now with the fire blazing in the fireplace. He had enjoyed his bachelor life, but now he felt alone when he wasn't with Abigail. He had grown to love their home and all of its coziness in the few short weeks they had been married. He was actually feeling homesick. "Look, I really have to go."

"I know." Her voice was softer. "Go. I'll be okay. I miss you."

"I miss you too."

As soon as she hung up, he looked at his watch and jumped up. He didn't want to get Ms. Scott on his bad side too.

Chapter Twenty-Three

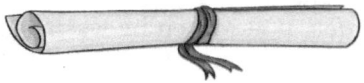

Abigail held the warm phone in her hand, thinking about her conversation with Tony. He was definitely avoiding her. Maybe she should have told him that she told Pauline everything. No, that would freak him out.

Her mind went in circles as she tried to figure out what to do. She wasn't so naive to think that her threat against Mauvais had worked. But maybe it had. At any rate, he now knew she wasn't playing games.

A text came in on her phone, and she jumped. It was Jimmy. He was letting her know that he was out front. He had been doing that since she got married. He didn't want to interrupt anything.

She texted him back, and he knocked on the door.

"Hey there," he said when she opened it. "I'm on duty driving around your neighborhood and thought I'd stop by and say hello."

Abigail invited him in and gave him a hug. "Can I take your coat?"

"No, I'm not going to stay. Is Tony home?"

"No. He's installing the security at the library for the map collection I brought in."

"That's good. I wanted to talk to you alone."

Uh-oh. She invited him to sit, and he did decide take off his boots and walk over to the couch. But he left his coat on and remained standing. She sat, and Cocoa immediately jumped on her lap.

"Are you two in some sort of trouble?" Jimmy never was one to beat around the bush.

Abigail cleared her throat and stroked her cat to buy some time. "Why?" she finally said, although she knew the answer.

Jimmy merely cocked an eyebrow.

"Okay. Well, no." Abigail said. "Not yet anyway."

"Tell me what's going on."

Abigail really didn't want to get Jimmy involved in this. While she would love to ask him for help, she knew he would be obligated to act if he knew a crime was involved.

"Jimmy," she said, trying to sound insulted instead of grateful for his intrusion. "I'm a 30-year-old woman who is married—*twice*—with an advanced college degree and a great job, which I've held on to for all these many years. I'm all grown up. You need to let me live my life." Her voice softened. "I'm *okay*. Really. Let me figure this out on my own."

He frowned. Jimmy always tried to look gruff. "I like Tony, you know I do."

"But...?"

"But I don't trust him."

Abigail sighed and continued to pet the cat. She kept her eyes down on Cocoa so Jimmy couldn't read her thoughts. She was struggling a little bit with that same thing right now herself.

"Then trust *me*," she said, looking back up and meeting his eyes.

He nodded. For a moment, he just stood there and looked at her. He never was a man of many words. Finally, he said, "I need to get back on the road. Call me if you need me."

"You know I will."

She got up and followed him to the door. He pulled his boots on and went outside. "Jimmy?"

He turned. She gave him a peck on the cheek. "Thank you."

As soon as Jimmy pulled away, Abigail got her laptop out. She needed to see if Jean-Pierre was bluffing about the map.

She did a search on the Vesconte. There was a listing of sale, from a Frederich Dietrich to one Jean-Pierre Mauvais. So publically, the map exchanged hands. Then she did a search on Frederich Dietrich. She came up with one living near New York City.

She punched in the number that blocked her caller ID and dialed quickly, before she lost her nerve. Someone with a German accent answered.

131

trusting the cat burglar

"Is this Frederich Dietrich?"

"Yes. Who's calling?"

"I wanted to inquire about the Vesconte map you sold to a Mr. Mauvais. Can I ask where you got it? I'm an avid map collector and am very interested. I might make Mauvais an offer."

There was a low, throaty chuckle on the other end of the line. "Mr. Mauvais told me to expect a call. Only I was expecting a Tony Russo. Is this his wife?"

Abigail was silent.

"I'll take that as a yes," Dietrich said. "I bought the map myself from a reputable dealer. I have all of the paperwork in order if the subject ever comes up."

"I see," Abigail said.

"You have a nice evening, my dear."

He hung up. Abigail sighed. Yes. Jean-Pierre had covered his tracks.

Abigail planned to wait up for Tony because she really needed to talk to him, but she was tired. She figured she'd just lie down until he came home, so she put her nightgown on and climbed in bed. Cocoa curled up beside her, and she closed her eyes to the purring of her cat.

She saw Nick come into the bedroom, which was odd, because they had never lived together in this house. But there he was. He was cold, she could tell, because he was shivering and he still had his coat on.

"Get undressed and come to bed," she said.

"I need to go get you some milk first." He smiled when he spoke, which was wrong, because they had been fighting. "I'll be right back, Abby." That was his name for her. Abby.

"No!" She couldn't let him go. This is how it always ended. He left, slamming the door behind him, and then she never saw him again. "I don't need the milk. You're cold. Come here."

She sat up in bed and patted the mattress, but Nick only smiled more and turned to leave. "No!" she said again, this time louder, but he turned and shouted back, "This is your fault!" and slammed the bedroom door. She tried to jump out of bed, but her feet tangled in the sheets, and then she slipped

132

on ice. She was running and slipping and tripping, trying to reach the door. "No!" she shouted again. "Come back!"

Then she woke up. She sat upright in bed, breathing heavily. It took her a minute to figure out where she was. Cocoa was gone. Tony's side of the bed was empty. The clock on the nightstand said 2:13 a.m.

"Tony?" She took a few slow breaths to calm herself and tried to remember if it was icy outside. She hadn't had a nightmare in months. After her heart rate settled a little and the shaking stopped, she got up to go find her phone and call Tony.

But when she walked out of the bedroom, he was on the couch, covered with a blanket, apparently asleep.

"Tony?"

He stirred and rubbed his eyes. "Hi, beautiful," he said sleepily. "I didn't want to wake you so I crashed here."

Something like a sob escaped her. She realized tears were running down her face.

"Abigail?" Tony sat up. "What's wrong?" He reached for her, and she went to him, gave him her hand, and sat beside him. She felt his strong arm around her.

"What's wrong?" he asked again.

"Bad dream," she said. "I was afraid that you..." She started to cry harder.

He pulled her to him and wrapped both arms around her. "I'm okay," he whispered, rocking her gently.

"I had a nightmare," she said. "About Nick. And then I woke up, and you weren't in bed, and I thought, maybe—"

"Shhhh," he said. "I'm here. I'm 100% okay."

She relaxed into his arms, and the tears slowly stopped. It was her typical dream. Nick was going out for milk, after she had gotten angry with him for forgetting it at the store. But the roads were icy, and it was late. And he never came home. Except this time, Nick was here at this house, instead of back in the apartment that they had shared.

"Tony, don't ever leave me."

She closed her eyes, breathing in his closeness. She knew he wasn't perfect. Who was? He had his past, he had his faults, but there was no doubt how much he loved her. She could feel it in every ounce of her.

"Never," he promised.

After a few moments, she drew back so she could look at Tony. "What time did you come home?"

"After midnight," he said. "You were sleeping so peacefully." He had found some sweatpants somewhere and was wearing those and a T-shirt. "Do you want to talk about the dream?" he asked tentatively.

"I was trying to stop Nick from going out," she said. "And then when I opened my eyes, you weren't here. I just got really scared."

Tony reached over and touched her hair, putting a few strands of it behind her ear. He cupped her cheek with his hand. "I'm here for you," he said. He watched her carefully for a moment, like a father would look at a child, as if to see how okay she really was. "I know this week is hard for you. Saturday will be seven years since you lost him. I want to help, but I don't know how. You need to tell me how."

Abigail nodded and felt her eyes filling up with tears again. "I will. I don't know. Usually I just try to get through this time, this week. The day. But maybe we should do something."

Then she told him about Nick's mom's call. "It was sweet of her to call," she said. "I've ignored them all these years, when they have offered to take me to the cemetery. Did you know I've never been back there? Not since the funeral."

"I didn't realize that," he said. "But maybe that's okay. We all grieve in our own way. I haven't been back to my mother's grave since I became an adult. I used to go with Grandma when I was young, but it was really too painful. So I stopped eventually. I think the last time I went I was eighteen. But it doesn't mean I stop missing her. Or loving her."

Abigail nodded. She took Tony's hand in hers. It was warm. All of the questions she had for him earlier, all of the frustrations she felt, were gone. She just wanted to feel him beside her now.

"Come to bed," she said.

He followed her into the bedroom. Cocoa had curled up in the spot that Abigail had vacated.

134

"She's keeping it warm for me," Abigail said with a little laugh. They lay down, and she scooted closer to Tony so as not to disturb the cat. She spooned her back up against him, and he wrapped his arms around her. She fell into a deep, dreamless sleep.

Chapter Twenty-Four

They overslept. For some reason, the alarm didn't go off. Either Abigail forgot to set it or it was broken, but either way Tony didn't have time for breakfast.

He quickly pulled on his clothes. "I'll take the car. I can't be late to community service." He gave Abigail a quick kiss while she was still changing and headed out the door.

While he drove (a bit over the speed limit), he went over last night's work at the library. He had wanted to finish it up, but George wanted to go home. It was midnight, George had to work the next day, and Laney wouldn't be happy if he kept such late hours every night. They had never worked so late before. They had Wednesday night left, George had said. He didn't understand why they couldn't easily finish it up then.

Because Tony needed to be elsewhere tonight.

He struggled through his community service, narrowly escaping a scrap with Karl, who was in his usual foul mood. The guards were onto the big thug, though, so they pulled Karl away to work on a project on the other side of the road, alone.

That gave Tony time to think about how to handle tonight. He couldn't be in two places at once. There seemed to be only one thing to do, so after his community service, he stopped by to see George. His friend was working at the water and safety building across town, repainting the lab. Tony walked inside and quickly found him. He had to do this before he lost his nerve.

"Hey," Tony said. He had removed his orange work suit and was in jeans. He had on his lighter coat today. The weather was in the forties again.

"Tony!" George said, surprised to see him. He climbed down from his ladder and wiped his hands on a rag. "To what do I owe this privilege?" He was painting with Julio and Marty, two other guys Tony had worked with. They said hello and asked how married life was going. After a little small talk, Tony asked George if he could speak to him alone.

They went out into the hallway and closed the door.

"What's up?" George asked, a little concerned.

This was going to be hard.

"I need to tell you something, and I need you to promise not to tell anybody. Maybe not even Laney." Tony looked around nervously. "Maybe we should have this conversation in the car."

"The car? It's *that* serious?"

But Tony was already heading for the door. He walked across the parking lot, George at his heels, and the two men got in and shut the door.

"Did you cheat on Abigail?" George asked immediately.

"What?" Tony said, taken aback. "No! Geez, George..."

"Laney doesn't *think* you will, but she's giving you six months. I've said never."

"You two are *betting* on me?" Tony had to take that in. "I don't even know how to respond to that. Is that how little you think of me?"

"Not me. Laney," George corrected him.

There was a pause. George raised an eyebrow, but Tony had nearly forgotten what he was there to say. Oh yeah. He was going to tell George about his dishonesty problem. He gave a heavy sigh. How did one go about telling his best friend that he led a double life?

"Do you remember when I used to have all of those extra jobs at night?" Tony asked.

"Yes. You were raking in the dough."

"I was." Tony nodded. "Only I wasn't painting." He kept his voice low, even though the car doors were shut and there was nobody else around.

"What exactly *were* you doing?" George asked cautiously.

"I was...well, I used to have clients, and..."

"Oh my gosh. You were a *male escort!* The ladies have always loved you..."

"George!"

"No? That's not it? Thank God." George sighed heavily and leaned his head back against the headrest.

Nothing seemed too shocking now that he had cleared himself of both cheating and prostitution.

"Why would you think that?" Tony said. "Geez."

George looked over at him. "Because of the way you pulled me out here all sneaky like. We're even talking in hushed tones."

"We're not talking in hushed tones." *Maybe a little bit.*

"Hushed tones only means sex or drugs," George said. "And I know it's not drugs because your eyes are all clear. Laney's nephew was on drugs, and his eyes were half-mast all the time. None of us suspected at the time, but now that we know, when you look back at photos…"

"George, you're an idiot."

"That's what Laney says."

Tony pushed the clock button on the car's dash to look at the time. "Can you please be quiet for a minute so I can talk?"

"I'm sorry. Go ahead."

Now that he was this far in, it didn't seem like it was going to be much of a revelation. He took a deep breath and said, "I was a thief."

"A what?"

"A thief. I stole things. People hired me to get into places and take things. And the night I met Abigail, I was breaking into her library to steal a map. The map that led to the Russo painting. I knew it was there; I just needed to get it. I didn't expect Abigail to be there."

"You *stole* things?" George couldn't seem to get his mind around that.

"Yes."

"Like *Ocean's 11?* Or *Catch Me If You Can?*"

"Well, not quite."

"So Abigail knows?"

"Yes."

"Why are you telling me this *now?*" George said. His brow wrinkled. "After all these years. Man, I thought I knew you. I thought we were best friends."

"We are!"

"No. Best friends don't keep things from each other."

There was a silence in the car. Tony knew he should apologize, but the words "I'm sorry" seemed too shallow. He said them anyway.

George didn't respond. He stared forward, out the windshield. Finally, he turned to look at Tony. "What do you want?"

"I need a favor."

A short laugh came from George, but his eyes didn't light up like they usually did. "A *favor?* You *lie* to me for years, and now you want a favor? What a mess you are."

Tony could no longer meet his friend's eyes. The shame was so strong that he wanted to crawl under the car. How could he ask George for help now? George had every right to hate him. "Yes. You're right. I'm a mess. My life is a mess. And now...now it's affecting Abigail."

George stayed silent. Tony put his hands on the steering wheel and fiddled with it. Anything not to have to look at George right now.

"I need you to finish the job at the library tonight without me," Tony said. "This mess I got myself into, well, I need to fix it. And I don't want Abigail to know. I'm planning to meet someone to get some information that I think can... fix things. Abigail will think I'm at work. She probably won't be able to reach me on my cell, so if she calls you, I need for you to tell her that I'm with you"

"No. No way am I lying to Abigail," George said.

Tony dared to look over. George's eyes were angry. "I need for you to do this, or the premiere won't happen. Please."

George kept his eyes on Tony's, and it was all Tony could do not to look away. "I'll do this for Abigail," George said finally. "I'll finish the work because I know how much this means to her. But I'm not lying to her. Just tell her what you're up to."

"I can't. It involves an element of...danger...and she'll worry."

"Does it involve another woman?"

Tony faced the windshield again and closed his eyes, biding for time. He didn't want to lie to George again. His silence was enough of an answer for George.

"*You're* the idiot," George said. "Don't ever ask me for another thing." He got out and slammed the car door. Tony watched his only friend walk into the building and probably out of his life.

Tony had one more stop to make and then he had to spend the afternoon with his client, the elderly gentleman. But he would need his laptop, so he stopped by his apartment. It only took a little bit of work to find out where JP was staying. It was a fancy hotel in the middle of town. And then a little computer hacking to find the room number.

He had to give him something to think about so he wouldn't get curious and start tailing Tony. He needed to get to this charity event unseen.

Luck was with him and the Frenchman answered when he knocked. "You're in," Tony said. "Good. I figured I'd catch you before you took your after-lunch nap." He didn't wait to be invited in but pushed past JP into the room.

"What a pleasant surprise," JP said, closing the door. The room was tidy, and the maid had already been there because the bed was made. A lunch tray from room service sat at the little table by the window. Tony moved it aside and put his laptop down. "I want to show you this."

He opened up to the specs of the actress' house.

JP nodded, clearly impressed. "So, you've decided to do the job."

Tony told him what he knew about the alarm system and Danes' schedule. "I didn't see the dogs. That's the only problem I can see we'll have."

JP was quiet for a moment, thinking. "I can take care of the dogs," he said.

"How?"

"Leave it to me."

Tony closed his laptop. "Don't kill any animals."

"How touching. You've always been such a softy."

Tony got up to leave. "I'll do it Saturday morning. I plan to go in around 2 a.m. Abigail will be exhausted from the premiere so should be sleeping. She doesn't need to know about any of this."

"I take it she's not on board with your dark side," JP said, laughing. Then his eyes narrowed. "You tell your little wife to stick to her maps. She was threatening me, and you know what happens to people who threaten me."

Tony leaned across the table until he was right in JP's face. "You leave her alone. I'll do this *one* job for you, and then I never want to see you again."

"Oh, but you *will*. You'll see me in Paris. That is, unless Abigail has ditched you by then."

It took all he had in him not to punch JP. Instead, Tony left, closing the door behind him.

Chapter Twenty-Five

The morning was busy. Ms. Scott was in a titter when Abigail arrived ten minutes late. Abigail was hardly ever late, and Ms. Scott said this week was *not* the week to start a bad habit.

Pauline was lingering. "I really need to ask you some questions," her friend said in hushed tones. "Does he still *steal* things? I mean, do you *trust* him?"

"Shhhh!" Abigail said. "Not here. Don't make me regret telling you."

"Does anybody else know?"

"*Nobody* knows." *Except, now, of course you* do. "We need to get our work done. Friday is almost here."

"I know. You're right. You know I'm here if you need to talk."

At lunchtime, Pauline came around and offered to take her out. She was grateful for her friend's concern about her life, but at the same time, she was regretting she had told her. Fortunately, she had an excuse to miss. She had to check on Tony's grandma.

On the bus ride across town, she called Tony. It went to voicemail, which wasn't unusual for this time of day. He had to hustle when he got back from community service. He usually had client work waiting, so he was most likely with a client. She couldn't remember his schedule for today. Probably because they hadn't had time to really talk in a while.

Grandma was looking pretty good and was happy to see Abigail. She got lonely since she couldn't leave the house on her own. Abigail got the stretchy bands and started helping her with her physical therapy. Grandma was getting stronger, she could tell. She loved this woman who had raised her husband. She loved her like she was her own grandma. She wondered about Grandma and Tony's life together. That brought her thoughts back to Tony and their problems. Had he shared any of that with Grandma? Again, she couldn't know because Tony hadn't been talking to her much.

"How long ago did you realize that Tony was working as a thief?" Abigail asked, trying to make her voice sound nonchalant.

"Oh," Grandma said, pausing to give one last pull on her bands before she sat back to rest. "I suspected something when he got his apartment and furnished it and then bought all those fancy computers. A painter's wages can't cover all of that. But he was working a lot at night, doing extra jobs, so I justified it that way, I guess. Tony's pretty clever. I learned early on that if he doesn't want me to find out something, there's no way I'm going to. He also has a strong sense of family and will do anything to protect those he loves. I'm not naive enough to think my cancer treatments were paid for completely by his salary."

Abigail was quiet.

Grandma chuckled. "See? But I don't want to know more. It's over now. Hand me those bands again."

It took over an hour to help Grandma with her exercises and get her settled back in her chair for a nap. Abigail made sure she had everything she needed and then left. She couldn't get Grandma's words out of her mind. *Tony's pretty clever... If he doesn't want me to find out something, there's no way I'm going to.*

He might be pretty clever, but he wasn't more clever than she was. On a whim, she decided to walk to his apartment. She texted Pauline to let Ms. Scott know she'd be late this afternoon. She didn't want to talk to the director herself. Ms. Scott was a nervous wreck this week.

Tony wasn't there when she let herself in. Neither was his laptop. She sat down at his desk and booted his computers up. They were massive, and it took a few minutes. She glanced around, hoping Tony didn't come home right now. She'd have a hard time explaining what she was doing.

She knew all of his passwords. They had agreed that if this marriage was going to work, there would no longer be any secrets. It recognized her fingerprint scan as well, because he had scanned it in for her.

She opened the internet and looked at his browser history. Nothing. Of course not. Tony would always cover his tracks. She wasn't even sure what she was looking for.

She scanned the documents he had recently opened. They were all for legitimate jobs she knew he had.

She got up, went into his bedroom, and pulled out the drawers. There were some clothes, a few T-shirts, and some socks. She found the false bottom in one of the drawers and looked in it. Nothing.

She opened the closet door. He had two pairs of pants hanging in there and his tux. She stopped. It seemed she remembered his tux being at home in the back of their closet. Weird. Maybe he was planning on wearing it to the premiere. But why bring it here unless he was going to come to the premiere straight from work? She'd have to ask him about that.

She decided to watch the flash drive again. She went into the bathroom and reached under the cabinet, pulling out the fancy toothbrush. Unscrewing the bottom, she got the flash drive. She smiled. He had told her all of his secrets.

At least the ones she knew about.

She put the flash drive in and looked at the video. The first thing that came up was Charlotte on his arm. She frowned. She liked Charlotte a lot, but she knew Tony had a past with the beautiful woman. Heck, Charlotte had known Tony much longer than Abigail had. Did *she* know his secrets?

She put the flash drive away and decided to get back to work. She'd return later and check out the laptop, maybe tonight while he was at the library. Right now, she had work to do for the premiere.

The afternoon went by fast, and she kept busy at the library until 6 p.m. She was hoping to run in to Tony and George on their way in, but they weren't there yet. She couldn't remember if they were starting at 6 or 7p.m. Must be 7p.m. As she walked out to catch the bus, she called Tony.

"Hi, beautiful!"

"Hi, hon. What time will you be at the library? I was hoping to see you."

He said he was busy finishing some work at the apartment, and he and George would be starting late tonight. Probably after 7 p.m. "I can't talk now, hon. I've gotta run."

"Tony, this is ridiculous," Abigail said. "We haven't had a proper conversation in days."

"Tomorrow," he said. "I promise. I'll meet you at home for lunch, and we can have a proper discussion then. Right now, I've gotta go. I love you!"

And he hung up. He actually hung up on her.

She frowned at her phone for a moment. Tony Russo had decided to mess with the wrong woman. She caught the bus that was going towards his apartment.

Chapter Twenty-Six

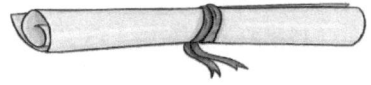

Tony straightened his bowtie and put his phone and his wallet in his pocket. He grabbed his keys and was about to open the door when he heard someone walking up his steps. He peeked through the peephole in his door and saw it was Abigail.

He swore silently, under his breath. Why was *she* here? His car was parked in the back, a habit he had gotten in to in his former life, so she probably wouldn't know if he was home or not. But she had keys. And he had about twenty seconds to get out.

He ran for his bedroom and shut the door behind him. Quickly, he opened the window, climbing out on the fire escape ladder. Shutting the window quietly behind him, he climbed down and ran for his car.

The home where the auction was taking place was enormous. The mansion, built in the style of Greek Revival architecture, had a fountain (which was turned off for winter) it its circular driveway and solid ionic pillars across the front. Tony followed some signs and parked in the designated spaces reserved for tonight. A butler answered the door and welcomed him in. He asked for his name, and Tony told him. He was checked off the list as Charlotte's plus one. Another man asked him for his cell phone. He obediently dropped it in the basket provided. A third gentleman waved a metal-detecting wand up and down him, looking for weapons. Satisfied he was safe, they let him enter. Security was tight.

He walked through the hallway into a large, open ballroom. Crystal chandeliers hung from the vast ceiling, and a band was playing softly up on the stage. The main floor was open for dancing, and long tables lined the walls. They were filled with food and drink.

He saw several people he knew, collectors of many fine antiquities and rare objects. Some were past clients of his, and said hello or gave him a nod as he walked by.

He spotted Charlotte to his right, talking with a couple he didn't recognize. She caught his eye and came over.

"Darling, I saw you come in. Where's your coat?"

"It's a long story," Tony said. "I had to leave in a hurry." Charlotte was dressed in red, her signature color, and had her long, blond hair piled up with a few curls hanging around her face. He had to admit, she was breathtaking.

"You look beautiful, as usual," he said, meeting her eyes. He avoided looking at her cleavage area. Charlotte believed in showing off her assets.

"And you are your usual handsome self," she said, pulling him to her for formalities. Charlotte was big in to ritual, but only in public. He grasped her hands, obediently kissed both of her cheeks, and then gave her his charming smile. He saw that she was wearing a diamond necklace he had lifted for her some time ago.

"It looks good on you," he said.

"Of course, it does."

She took his hand and led him onto the ballroom floor, where dancing had begun. The lights were dim and couples were filling up the floor. She wrapped both arms around his neck, and they started slowly swaying. Her perfume was something she purchased on her trips to Milan, he remembered, and it smelled fantastic. It brought his mind back to other nights they had spent together. He pushed those aside and tried to picture Abigail, as Charlotte put her face up against his and her soft curls tickled his cheek.

"So, tell me what this is about," she whispered into his ear. He could feel her breath on his neck.

"Remember, this is business, not pleasure," he whispered back.

She gave a soft, throaty chuckle. "You know I don't play with married men. You're safe tonight."

Tony decided to get right to the point. "Jean-Pierre Mauvais has a video that incriminates me. You probably know him as JP Thomas. It shows me at the Spangler auction last year, and there is some unsightly bidding going on in the background for the Chinese vase. I'm seen talking with several known collectors of illegal works. And I'm also seen with you."

She pulled back to look him in the eyes. "What?"

"He has both of us on film. As far as I know, he's only after me. But if he releases this video, you'll be recognized. I'm hoping to find some dirt on him tonight so I can blackmail him back."

Charlotte's eyes narrowed, but she put her head back close to Tony's. The music played, and they circled a few times.

"Why does he want to take you down?" she asked finally.

Tony explained about Abigail's job and how she invited JP to store his maps at the library. Then how the Vesconte showed up and the video. "He wants me to do a job for him or he's going to release it to the authorities. He has his tracks covered on the Vesconte."

Their bodies were close, which was a bit of a necessity if they were going to have a discreet conversation. But it was distracting. She was quiet for a moment, and then he felt her stiffen. "He made a mistake," she said, and pulled back to look him in the eyes again.

"What's that?" Tony hoped desperately she had thought of a way out of this.

"He chose to mess with *us*," she said. The slow-dance music stopped, and a faster song started. Charlotte unwrapped her arms from around his neck. "Go," she said. "Get some dirt on him. I'll see what I can do too."

Tony went over to the hors d'oeuvres table. There was some type of pink punch. He accepted a glass from the server and took a sip. Strongly alcoholic and too sweet. He set it down and picked up a plate, adding some Italian pinwheels like the ones his grandma used to make. There was also some type of cheesy mixture on crackers. Those looked good.

Plate filled, he turned to the crowd. Charlotte had a drink in her hand and was chatting with a jewelry designer. The guy had lots of money but was more likely here to sell tonight than to buy. Then Tony saw Marvin Tucker, a thin, nerdy man with a nasally voice who was a collector of rare antiquities, including maps and documents. Tony had picked a few things up for him.

He made his way across the room. Poor Marvin wasn't much of a looker, but he always had a woman or two with him because he was loaded. He was probably here to buy something tonight. Most likely the Atillo. It was a rare and priceless map that someone was willing to let go of. He looked around again to be sure JP wasn't here. He didn't see him.

"Hello, Marvin," Tony said lightly, stuffing one of the Italian pinwheels in his mouth. They really were outstanding. He'd have to ask what spice they used. There was rosemary and oregano, but also something else.

Marvin said hello and excused himself from the two women he was with. He motioned for Tony to follow him off to the side of the room.

"I have my eye on a rare book that's sitting in the study of Charles Vandertoot in Maryland. It's the only one of its kind. I've offered exorbitant sums, but he's not willing to part with it," Marvin said.

"Vander*toot*?" Tony repeated. What an unfortunate name.

Marvin smiled. "I'm willing to pay you well."

Tony put one of the cheese-covered crackers in his mouth to stall for time.

"Well, I'm quite booked at the moment," he said, chewing.

"Word on the streets is that you gave up the life."

Ahhhh. So word was out already.

"There's that, too," Tony said.

"Why? You are so good at it."

"A woman."

"Ahhhh."

The two men were silent for a moment, each thinking.

"But I was wondering if you could help me out with something," Tony said finally. "This woman of mine, she's actually a curator of rare maps and documents. JP Mauvais, or Thomas, is messing with her and threatening me. I need a way to make him stop."

A waiter walked by carrying a tray of champagne-filled flutes. Marvin motioned him over and took one. Tony declined.

"Interesting," Marvin said when they were alone again. He took a sip of his champagne. "I do know that JP wanted a particular book on botany, of early European origin. There are some hand-drawn illustrations, and more importantly, a signature that makes it quite valuable and unique." Marvin nodded slightly toward a blond-haired man who was dancing with his hands much too low on his partner's backside. The dress she was wearing was cut pretty much down to his hands.

"He outbid JP, and it seems soon after that, that young man's reputation was publicly sullied in the rare books world. He lost his professorship at Oxford and has gone underground."

"I see," Tony said, watching the man. "Any proof?"

"I have a text from JP saying that Mr. Oxford there was going down. If it gets out, it'll make JP look pretty bad in the public world. Might even cost him his position on some boards."

Tony smiled. "Perfect."

"I hung on to the text. You never know when you'll need collateral. I'm willing to pass it on if you need it."

Tony nodded to Marvin. "I appreciate it."

"Sure. This one's on me. You've helped me out a lot in the past."

It was true. Tony had introduced him to the blonde he was with and had given him inside information on some of the collections trading hands. Marvin knew where and when to show up for a purchase.

As the song ended, someone pulled the doors to the ballroom shut. A tall, balding man stepped up front with a mic. He tapped it to make sure it was working.

Tony turned to Martin. "Thank you."

Martin pulled his business card out of his pocket. "In case you forget how to get hold of me."

Tony was grateful. Martin's number was at the bottom of the river in his old cell phone.

"And if you want one more job, call me."

Tony smiled. "Will do. Good to see you again, Martin."

Charlotte swept across the room and grasped his arm. She turned so they were both looking at the stage. She had her paddle in her hand so she could bid.

"I'm going for the golden flower piece with the amethyst and diamonds. Have you seen it?

"I saw a picture on the web," Tony said. *Exquisite.*

"Did you get what you needed?"

"I did." It had been easier than he thought.

"I hear that JP is quite the shark," Charlotte whispered while the announcer gave instructions for the auction. "He is almost *obsessed* with his collection. And that man there, Charles Fowler"—she tipped her glass toward a dark-haired man to their left—"said JP was heard bragging that he would one day be the man who held Vivian Danes' necklace in his collection. That man wants it too and says if that snake JP ever gets it, he'll take it from him."

So, JP had a few enemies. Good to know.

Charlotte's grip tightened on Tony's arm. "Speaking of the devil..."

Tony followed her gaze. Entering near the back of the room was JP. The room was crowded, and Tony stepped quickly behind a group of people. "Did he see me?" Tony asked.

"I don't think so," Charlotte said.

"I think it's time for me to go," Tony said. He gave Charlotte a quick peck on the cheek. Unfortunately, the way to the back of the room was blocked, and he couldn't see any other exit.

Charlotte put herself in between Tony and JP. With a group of people blocking their way, Tony was well concealed. He had been in tight spots before and was pretty good at remaining unseen when he wanted to be. JP stood on the other side of the room, his gaze intent on what was happening on the stage.

"I didn't think he was going to be here," Tony said. "He has his hands full with a lot of other stuff right now. And there's not much here for him. He's a pretty exclusive collector. I thought he wouldn't come for just the one Atillo.."

After about an hour of bidding, the Atillo came up. JP watched as Marvin swooped in on it, outbidding everyone else. JP didn't even try to get it.

"Tony, my piece is coming up," Charlotte said. "I need to bid. That will draw attention to me."

Tony glanced over. JP was talking with someone. "I'll go now," Tony said. "Thanks and good luck."

"I don't need luck, honey. I have money."

He smiled as he ducked around her and past the group of people. He stayed close to the wall. His plan was to go around the perimeter of the room and out the door opposite of where JP was standing.

But he saw JP move toward the same door. Their eyes met. He was caught.

JP waited near the door for Tony and then put his hand out. Tony accepted and the two men shook. "Good to see you here, friend," JP said. He kept his voice quiet so as not to disturb the bidding. "I thought this was no longer your crowd."

"And I thought it wasn't yours," Tony said.

"I'm just here to browse. Did you see they have an Atillo?"

"You already have one of those in your collection."

"I know. But it's fun to look. I see you're here on a date. What would the wife think?"

Tony glanced across the room at Charlotte, who was bidding on the necklace.

He changed his game plan. Why hide from JP? He could make him think he was living a double life. Let JP wonder if Tony was trustworthy. "The wife doesn't need to know," he said and gave a wink. "Right?"

JP gave a little smile. "Right. I need to get going. There are other things I need to attend to."

JP left, and Tony lingered at the door. He wanted to see if Charlotte got her piece.

Chapter Twenty-Seven

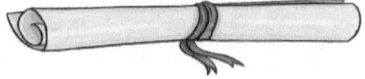

Abigail saw Tony's laptop as soon as she walked into his apartment. It was 7 p.m. and she must have just missed him on his way to the library, so she got lucky. He wasn't home. There it was, just begging to be looked at.

She booted it up, entering all of the correct passwords. His most recently opened folder was titled "Viv". It opened to some specs of a home she wasn't familiar with. She followed the links that were highlighted on it, and it took her to the address of the famous actress, Vivian Danes. These were the specs to her house.

There were more files in the folder. She opened one of the photos. It was a picture of what looked like the rear of Danes' property. She could see the sliding glass door off the in-ground pool, which was covered with a tarp. The timestamp was recent. Yesterday. There were more photos: several of Danes' back yard and a few of her upstairs window and balcony.

She opened his browsing history and clicked on the most recently searched item, "The Crown Jewel of Vivian Danes." The article was about her necklace and the security she had to have at home because it was wanted so badly by collectors and thieves. She had worn it in most of her films, and it had become something of an icon.

What on earth was Tony up to?

Abigail sat there for a moment, putting it together. Tony said he had a plan. Was this it? Was he about to do a job to get some money to pay Jean-Pierre off?

Or was this the job Jean-Pierre wanted him to do? Was he actually going to *do* it? No, Jean-Pierre was an exclusive collector of maps and documents. He wouldn't want a necklace. It didn't make sense.

With a growing sense of dread, Abigail closed the laptop.

trusting the cat burglar

Abigail was done waiting for Tony to find time to explain himself. Deadline or not, she'd go to him. He could finish the security at the library *after* explaining this to her. Tucking the laptop in her bag, she caught a bus to the library instead of home. She'd confront Tony there. *If* he was even there.

The library was locked, so she pressed the button. She wasn't about to call ahead. She wanted to catch Tony by surprise so he wouldn't have time to think his way out of this one.

She'd pull him away from George and open the laptop. With the entire folder there for him to see, he'd have to do some explaining. Maybe it was nothing. But she had a hunch, and Abigail was one to follow her hunches.

George opened the door. "Abigail!" he said. He looked surprised, like a deer caught in headlights.

"Can I come in?" Abigail asked when George didn't make a move to invite her.

"Um, yes." George stepped out of the way to let her pass and then locked the door behind her. He hurried back to the maps room and started tinkering with some wiring. Abigail watched him in silence. When he didn't speak, she asked, "Where's Tony? Is he in the bathroom?"

"Um," George said, concentrating on his wiring. "He's... he had to run out for a bit."

"He what?" Abigail hadn't really expected him to be gone. Tony wasn't a liar. A bit of a charmer, maybe even a con at times, but he had promised never to lie to her. "He told me he'd be here working tonight. That you two had a deadline, and this had to be finished before morning."

"That's right," George said. "But he's not here."

"Where is he?"

George looked pained.

"George? *Where is Tony?*"

George pushed his wires aside and looked over at her. "Abigail, I don't want to get involved in this."

"In what?" Her stomach did a little flip-flop.

There was a silence.

"George?"

George sighed heavily. Around forty years old, George was already greying around the temples and had a slight bulge in his middle. He looked very tired tonight.

"Abigail, Tony's not here. And wherever he is, you won't be able to reach him by phone. He asked me to cover for him if you called. But I told him I wouldn't lie. And besides, you didn't call. You just showed up."

Abigail's stomach sank. For a moment, the room seemed to grow darker.

"Abigail?" George rushed over to her and pulled up a chair. "You look like you're about to faint. Sit down."

Abigail sat. What if Tony was at Danes' house right now, trying to lift that necklace? Where else would he be that he had to lie to her? *Lie* to her! She still couldn't believe it. They had talked so much about trust. He threw out his old cell phone, gave her all of his computer passwords, and kept up an open dialogue just so she'd be able to trust him. But then again, they'd only been married a little over a month. Jimmy had warned her before they got married. *"It's hard for men to change,"* he said. *"Once they get a taste of the adrenaline rush connected with crime, it's hard for them to replace it. For some, it's like a high."*

"Where do you think he is?" Abigail looked up at George. He ran a hand across his forehead, as if a headache was coming on.

"I don't know, and I don't care," he said. He looked at her sympathetically. "Abigail, I'm doing this work for *you*. I'm about finished. This will be in tip-top shape by morning to keep all your maps safe. That's all you should worry about. Go home. Get some sleep. I have a feeling Tony is capable of taking care of himself."

Abigail stood up slowly. She picked up the bag that the laptop was in. "Okay," she said. She felt as if she was in a fog. "Thank you, George."

<hr />

On the ride home, the fear left Abigail and was replaced by anger. Tony had made her all of those promises, and here he was, already lying to her. She wondered what else he had kept from her or *lied* to her about. She had thought she knew him so well, could read him so well. Now, well *now* she had no idea who this man was that she had married.

So, was he on a "job" tonight? She hadn't even thought to look under his bed in the apartment for his bag of tools. He kept one at home, too, but she didn't think he'd be stupid enough to take that one.

She tried his phone, and it went right to voice mail. It was 9 p.m. Wherever he was, he wasn't answering. She wished they had put the apps on their phones so she could find him. For a moment, she had a crazy idea of taking the bus over to Jimmy's and asking him to ping Tony's cell phone.

Instead, she went home. She put on her most comfortable pajamas and made herself a cup of tea, refusing to let herself cry. She had been through tough times before. There was no way she was going to let a man reduce her to tears or worse. She was tougher than that.

Chapter Twenty-Eight

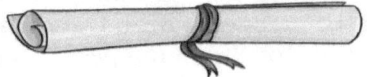

Tony turned the key in the door quietly. It was 1 a.m., and he didn't want to wake Abigail. He had stopped off at the apartment first to change in to his regular clothes and store the tux safely back in his closet. He'd slip quietly into bed and tell her everything tomorrow at lunch, as soon as he figured out what he was going to do with the info he had on JP.

George had texted him earlier. All the text said was "Job done." So that was something else he could check off his list. But George usually put smiley faces or jokes into his texts. Tony would give George a few days to cool off and then find him and talk. He didn't want to lose his friendship.

As he stepped inside, he noticed a light on in the kitchen. Abigail had waited up for him. She was sitting at the kitchen table, dressed in her pajamas, with a cup of tea. His laptop sat unopened on the table beside her. That was weird. She would have had to go back to the apartment to get it.

"Hi, hon," he said cautiously, closing the door.

Abigail looked up at the kitchen clock. "Where have you been?" Her voice was icy.

"At the library. I told you the job was going to take some time to finish up."

"Try again."

A feeling of unease crept over Tony. If there was anything he had learned over the years, it was reading people. And this person was definitely feeling unkindly toward him. Normally he would have turned on the charm, but the look in her eyes tonight stopped him.

"Um, why?"

"Because I was *at* the library. And you weren't there."

Uh-oh.

"Oh," he said. He was still holding the door keys in his hand.

"Is this where you were?" She opened his laptop.

He pulled his shoes off and walked closer to the table. She had opened the specs on Vivian Danes' house. "No," he said. That's what he got for giving people his passwords. It looked like it was time to explain everything now.

But Abigail stood, pushing the chair back so violently that it tipped over. "These are photos of her backyard," she said, clicking on the pictures. "And of her balcony. I matched this up with the specs, and this is her *bedroom*, probably where she keeps her *jewels*." She clicked on the browser, and it opened up to the article Tony had been reading on Danes' necklace.

This was the contents of the folder he had shown JP earlier today. How could he be so stupid as to leave it on his desktop for her to see? He was usually so careful, but his day was so full and stressful that he had gotten careless.

"I—" But she cut him off.

"Were you doing this job tonight? Don't lie to me."

"No, that's not where I was. Abigail, please sit down, and I'll explain."

"I don't want to hear your explanations, Tony Russo!" She snapped the laptop lid closed and turned on him. "Do you have any idea what you have put me through? First of all, this map project I have worked so hard on, you tell me the man I'm working with is a thief. Then, stolen maps turn up *because of you*. We both know Jean-Pierre would never have brought those out if you weren't involved. I take a huge chance by hiring you to do the security for this project, and if Ms. Scott ever finds out what you used to do—or still do—then it's over for me. Because how can she trust the man to do security when just two months ago he *broke in to her library to steal one of her maps?*" Abigail gave herself a knock on the head. "What a fool I was. I put up with all your baggage. I trusted you. I begged *others* to trust you because I thought I could! Our whole relationship is based on trust. You have made such a big deal about that, and now you *lie* to me? Tony, I loved you and this is what you do to me?"

It didn't go past him that she used the word love in the past tense. "Abigail—"

"No. You had a chance to talk and wouldn't take the time. Now you *listen*. All I want is for this premiere to go off without a hitch, for me to get my tenure, and for me to possibly get to present in Paris. Is that asking too much? I've put seven years of my life into this job. *Seven years*. And you're about to blow it for me in one week."

She brushed past him. "I'm going to bed. *You* can sleep on the couch."

Tony still had his coat on, his keys in his hand. "Abigail, let me explain. I wasn't at Danes' house tonight. I was—"

She whirled to face him again. Took a sniff. "You smell like perfume." Her face had a horrified expression on it.

Crap. Charlotte. He should have showered.

"Abigail, please. If you would just listen for a minute—"

"I don't want to hear it."

"I wasn't out sleeping around if that's what you think. I was—"

"No." She cut his words off. She looked away, but not before he saw that her eyes were filled with tears. She scooped up the cat and walked into the bedroom, slamming the door. He heard the lock click.

"Abigail," Tony said. He went over to the bedroom door and tried the handle. He briefly thought of picking it. "Please let me explain."

"Tony! I need some sleep if I'm going to be able to do my job tomorrow. Shut up."

He pressed his forehead up against the bedroom door. He heard her turn on the bedside fan that they sometimes used for white noise if the traffic outside got too loud.

What had he done? She wasn't even talking to him now. Or giving him a chance to explain. Could he blame her? He ran a hand through his hair, a nervous habit he had since he was a teenager. A cold, tight feeling that felt something like fear clenched at his stomach.

He decided to leave her alone and let her cool off. They would talk tomorrow, and she did need her sleep. He walked over to the couch, took his coat off, and laid his keys down on the end table.

The room was cold, and he didn't have a pillow or any comfortable clothes to change in to. He thought of starting a fire, but it seemed like too much work. He sat down on the couch and leaned back. Abigail kept a quilt on the back, and he unfolded it and pulled it over himself. He was surprised to find that he had a few tears running down his cheeks.

Her words rang back over in his mind. *I loved you.* Past tense.

She was right, who could trust him? Ms. Scott would have a fit if she knew how Abigail had met him. That's why they hadn't told anybody. Abigail claimed she wasn't ashamed of him, but how could she not be?

Look how George responded. Tony had lied to all of the people who loved him. His Grandma, George, and now Abigail. Lying to her had been a mistake, but he had honestly thought he was protecting her. If he had told her where he was going tonight, she would have worried. But he had been wrong. And to come home smelling like perfume? That was just stupid. He hadn't even thought about that part because his mind hadn't been on cheating. It had been on not getting caught at a black-market auction.

What if he had lost her? He wiped at his face with the back of his hand. He knew he didn't deserve her. And now he had just proven it.

He closed his eyes and leaned his head back against the couch. His feet were cold. It seemed like forever before morning came. When he heard Abigail's alarm go off, Tony was still sitting there, thinking of all the ways he had failed her.

Chapter Twenty-Nine

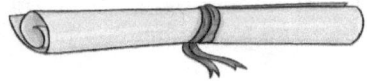

Abigail had gotten up early and quietly dressed. She was sitting on the edge of the bed, thinking, when the alarm went off, startling her. She reached over and silenced it.

She stood and took a deep breath of air for fortitude. Then she put her heels on and opened the door. She glanced at Tony, who was sitting on the couch still dressed in the clothes he had on last night. The ones that smelled like perfume. Or was it on his hair? She quickly turned her eyes away from him. She wouldn't care. Not today. Not now. She had too much to do.

"Abigail!" He rose quickly as soon as he saw her.

"I don't want to talk," she said, and grabbed the keys from the end table. "You can take the bus today."

"Please let me explain. You have a half hour before you need to leave."

She kept walking toward the door. He was following her. There was desperation in his voice, not something she was used to hearing from Tony. It tugged at her heart, and she wanted to turn back to him. But she wouldn't let herself fall for his charm. Not now. She needed to get through this premiere first.

"Leave me alone," she said. "You said we'd talk at lunch. Not now."

"But..."

She grabbed her coat out of the closet, not bothering to put it on, and left, closing the door behind her with a slam. She realized she had forgotten to feed Cocoa.

Tony opened it again. "Abigail! Please. Everything I did was for you."

But she was in the car and shutting the door. She put the key into the ignition. As soon as the motor roared to life, she pulled away, not looking back in her rearview mirror. She

161

fought the tears in her eyes. She would be strong. She would not cry. But then she thought of poor Cocoa and wondered if Tony would think to feed her. That started the cascade of tears.

Her make-up was a mess by the time she reached work. She parked in the lot and pulled her compact out of her purse, trying to clean up her face. It took a while, but her mascara was waterproof, so she only needed to reapply some foundation and blush. She was early, so she sat there for a few minutes, pulling herself together before she went in.

"Hello, hello, hello!" Ms. Scott was in a chipper mood when Abigail walked through the doors. It had been fluctuating between exuberance and stress, depending on the moment. This morning, it was exuberance. At least for now.

"We have so much to do today!" the director said. "And Jean-Pierre is stopping by later, of course!"

Abigail was exhausted. She hadn't slept much at all last night.

"Great," she said, plastering a smile on her face. A fresh new flash of anger seared through her. This was supposed to be *her week*. She should be all joyful and full of expectation. But Tony was ruining it. She knew that was childish, but that was how she felt. She tried to turn her mind away from blaming him for everything, but it just wasn't happening.

And why did he smell like perfume? She had a hard time believing he would cheat on her. Tony just wasn't that type. Well, he was in a way. She had heard stories from George and Laney about his playboy prowess before he met her.

The maps room was sparkling with a mixture of fresh wood and new tech. Cases and shelves lined the sides, and archival lighting with discreet cameras were installed above the tables. Tony had done a great job of making this room both aesthetically pleasing and secure. She had to admit he was good at what he did.

This part of the library, which Abigail had come to think of over the years as *her* part, was closed off today. They were going to be handling the maps, putting the more common ones in drawers and the more valuable ones behind glass. The Napoleon Bonaparte map had its own case right at the entrance of the maps room, where it would be displayed in its

full size behind glass. The rare Vesconte would be displayed
further inside the room, safe for viewing but not handling.
While it was worth more, most of the public probably had
never heard of Vesconte, so they were counting on Napoleon's
name to bring people in.

"Hey, girlfriend!" Pauline said, joining Abigail in the maps
room. She was holding a coffee in her hand.

Abigail looked at the cup. "That has to go, *girlfriend.*"

Pauline laughed. "I'm not stupid enough to drink it while
we work. I wouldn't dream of hurting one of your precious
maps!"

Pauline was in a good mood. She talked about how exciting
all of this was for her, because in reality, most of her job was
a bit boring. She did a lot of filing. There were always items
that needed to be filed or catalogued, and that was Pauline's
job for a large part of the library. She also worked a little bit in
microfilm and would sometimes print off ridiculous articles
she found in old newspapers. Articles about people being
arrested for swearing in front of a lady or something like that.

Her mood began to brush off on Abigail as the two of
them, along with Ms. Scott, started carefully opening up the
lesser maps and putting them in archival-quality drawers for
easy access. They wore gloves and worked slowly and carefully.

After a few hours, the elevator doors opened, and Jean-
Pierre stepped into the room.

"Bonjour!" he said in his usual, cheery manner. "I see you
are working hard, and carefully, with my maps!" He rubbed
his hands together. "This is so exciting! At home, I have to
keep them in tubes and in closets. Here they will be easily
accessible, oui?" He walked over and ran his hands across the
wood that would house the Bonaparte. "Magnifique! Your
Tony does excellent work! I don't even see the wires!"

"But they are there!" said Ms. Scott, worried.

"I believe you," Jean-Pierre said. "When I did my research,
I found out that Mr. Russo is a master of deception. He has
alarmed a few of the most prestigious homes in this city, and
you can't even tell."

Abigail scrutinized him from behind the safety of the
map she was working on. On the outside, Jean-Pierre was

such a pleasant man, happy and carefree. He didn't seem like someone who was a thief. He was handsome, charming, and everyone seemed to like him. In fact, he was a lot like Tony.

"We will put the Napoleon out tomorrow, along with the Vesconte," said Ms. Scott. "I'm saving the best for last. And tomorrow night at 6 p.m., it opens to the public. The world will see your maps, Jean-Pierre!"

"Oui!" he said with a flourish of his hands. "I can't wait!" Then he turned to Abigail. "And for you, madam, I have the Paris symposium schedule." He pulled his phone out of pocket and clicked on something. "You will speak on Tuesday at 9 a.m., and again at 2 p.m., Wednesday will be your day off, and then on Thursday…"—his eyes narrowed, and he did a little drum roll with his fingers on the wall—"you are a closing guest speaker at the wrap-up dinner."

"Oh my gosh!" Ms. Scott's hands flew to her face. "How thrilling!"

"Really?" Abigail said, excitement growing in her. She couldn't believe it. Not only was she presenting several times, but she was a *closing speaker!* She had been to these symposiums before, here in the US, and knew how they worked. To be an opening or closing speaker was the best thing one could hope for. Almost as good as being the keynote speaker.

"Wow," she said. Her phone rang. With a bit of irritation at the interruption, she pulled it out of her pocket. It was Tony.

"Hi," he said. "I'm finished with community service and heading over to the house. Do you want to meet me there for lunch? We can talk."

Jean-Pierre said something to Ms. Scott, and the two were laughing. Abigail cupped her hand over her ear so she could hear Tony better.

"You know what?" Abigail said suddenly. "I have a lot to do here. We can talk tonight."

Tony was silent. In the background, Abigail was watching Jean-Pierre talk to Pauline. She was giggling. He really did have these women wrapped around his little finger. Abigail didn't like him, didn't trust him. But right now, she was angry with Tony and hanging out with Jean-Pierre seemed like the best way to let him know that.

Finally, Tony spoke. "I feel like I'm losing you," he said quietly.

"Abigail!" Ms. Scott said. "Jean-Pierre wants to see where the Vesconte is going to go!"

"I have to go," Abigail said. "We will talk tonight." Without waiting for Tony to answer, she hung up. "You will absolutely love where we are going to put it," Abigail said to Jean-Pierre and went to show him what he came for.

———◇————————◇———

Tony hung up, discouraged by how upset Abigail sounded with him. He was having an awful day.

Community service had been a nightmare. First of all, everything in town was thawing and the riverbank where they were working was a muddy mess. Trying to keep their footing while stacking rocks was nearly impossible. Tony kept slipping, and he fell several times, cutting his hand once on some stone. He couldn't keep his mind off Abigail. The whole time he worked, he had been going over in his head the things he was going to say when he met her at lunch. He had so much to tell her and so much to apologize for. She was right. He never should have lied.

Karl sneered at him several times, bumping in to him once when the big thug went to use the porta-john. He nearly knocked Tony down. Tony ignored him and kept working.

"Hey, idiot," Karl said, after their break. "Did your wifey pack you some coffee? I could use a drink."

Tony had retaliated, something that was so unlike him a week ago. He felt a surge of anger, and before he knew what he was doing, he had grabbed Karl by the collar and pushed him up against the rock wall he had just been stacking. "Listen, thug," Tony said from between clenched teeth. "I'm having a bad day. You may be twice my size, but I'm about ready to take my chances because there's nothing I'd like better than to hit something right now."

A slow grin spread across Karl's face. "And there's nothing I'd like more than to see you try."

A guard walked over. "Karl, that's enough."

165

Tony let go of the big man.

"Hey!" Karl whined. "He started it!"

The guard pointed for Karl to walk over to the other side and continue his job. "Tony, back to work."

Tony was cold and covered with mud by the time his shift ended. Back at the police station, he stripped off his coveralls and packed them in his bag. Then he had called Abigail, only to find out that she didn't want to see him.

He had heard Jean-Pierre in the background. For a moment, he thought about taking the bus over to the library. He could use the excuse that he wanted to show Jean-Pierre all of the things they finished last night. Or had Jean-Pierre stopped by when George was there?

Plus, he was dirty and smelled like sweat. And there was possibly still some of Charlotte's perfume lingering in his hair. He hadn't showered this morning.

He hung up, discouraged by how upset she was with him. He looked at his watch. He didn't have to go to his grandma's today because Thursday was the day the nurse came. But he had a 1 p.m. appointment with his elderly client.

He decided to ride the bus home and shower before he made any more decisions.

Abigail showed Jean-Pierre the Vesconte's case, and he seemed very pleased.

"I'm off to get us some sandwiches," said Pauline. "It's almost lunch time." Abigail gave Pauline her order, and then her friend left.

Ms. Scott was talking to Eileen from insurance. She had brought some folders, and the two women were looking through them.

Abigail turned to Jean-Pierre. "Look. I know I said some harsh things to you the other day," she said. His amazing, hazel eyes watched her expectantly. "I really don't like you, but I admire you, if that makes any sense." She realized she was rambling. "I guess what I'm trying to say is that despite it all, I am very grateful for what you are doing for me for the Paris symposium. I really do appreciate it."

Jean-Pierre nodded, which made his thick, black hair shake. He seemed like he wanted to say something, but he hesitated. "Look," he said, glancing around. "I don't want to upset you, but I think there's something you should know. I debated as to whether or not to tell you."

Abigail waited, a bit uneasy. She glanced over at Ms. Scott, who was still in an animated conversation with Eileen.

"There was an auction last night," Jean-Pierre said. "It wasn't exactly an auction that the public was invited to, if you know what I mean. I don't buy or sell stolen items. I truly meant it when I said I am a changed man. But I still like to look from time to time." He cleared his throat uncomfortably. He looked really upset. "Tony was there last night." He opened up a photo on his phone and handed it to her.

There was Tony, wearing his tux. Charlotte was standing in front of him wearing a dress that showed off her ample cleavage. Tony was leaning in, kissing her on the cheek. With a trembling hand, Abigail swiped to the next photo.

They were in each other's arms, dancing. Tony's face was hidden because it was pressed so close to Charlotte's cheek.

The next photo showed his face. They must have turned around on the dance floor. He was smiling.

The last photo was of Tony standing next to Charlotte with a plate of food in his hand. Charlotte had a wine glass in her one hand and a bidding paddle in the other. They both looked like they were having a good time.

Abigail swallowed hard. So that was why he came home so late last night smelling of perfume.

"He's a playboy," Jean-Pierre said quietly. "He always has been. I'm so sorry."

"Maybe they were just there to buy something," she said. But as soon as she said the words, she realized how naive she sounded. She squared her shoulders. "Can you text these to my phone?"

"Sure," Jean-Pierre said.

"Abigail!" Ms. Scott called across the room. "I have some papers for you to sign for Eileen."

"Are you okay?" Jean-Pierre said. He laid a comforting hand on Abigail's.

She pulled it away. "I'm fine," she said crisply. "Thank you." She turned and went to see what Ms. Scott needed. On her way, she opened her own phone and blocked Tony's number. She didn't need to deal with this now.

Chapter Thirty

Tony was waiting on the couch for her when she arrived. He could tell by the look in her eyes when she saw him that she had already made up her mind about their relationship.

She took her coat off without speaking. It was late, nearly 7:30 p.m. She usually got off at 5 or 6 p.m., and he was beginning to wonder if she was even coming home. He had resisted calling her, thinking what he wanted to tell her should be said in person.

There were roses on the table. He had picked out a pretty vase from under the counter, and taken his time clipping the stems and arranging them. He had thought about fixing dinner but didn't want them to feel rushed talking, worrying about the food getting cold.

"Hi," he said quietly, because it was the only thing that seemed safe to say. He remained seated on the couch, petting Cocoa. The cat yawned, stretched, and languidly rose to go greet her owner. Abigail bent down to give her a good scratch behind the ears before turning her attention to Tony.

"So talk," she said, still standing in the doorway. She looked tired and stressed. He wanted to go put his arms around her but was afraid he'd be pushed away.

"Can you come and sit by me?" he asked.

"No."

Tony took a deep breath. This was going to be tough. He wondered how much damage he had done and how much poison Jean-Pierre had been spouting in her ear.

"Let's start with last night."

"Let's." Abigail crossed her arms.

Tony tried again. He spoke slowly and softly.

"I was at a black-market auction trying to dig up some dirt on Jean-Pierre. I figured if I could get something on him, I could stop him from blackmailing me."

"By blackmailing *him?*"

"Yes."

He dropped his gaze to his hands. It sounded bad when you said it that way. "Anyway, I got some good stuff. I'll share it with him tomorrow so that your premiere can go off with no problems."

"So you were at an auction instead of working at the library, like you said you would be?"

"Yes."

"Why did you lie to me?" Her voice was shaky.

Tony looked at her. She had her arms wrapped around herself like she was cold. Her hair had fallen across her face, nearly obscuring her eyes, but she hadn't brushed it back. She looked like a small, frightened child. He had done this to her.

"I was trying to protect you. I thought if you knew where I was going, you'd try to stop me."

"Or if I knew who you were with?"

Tony was quiet for a moment. How much did she know? Had Jean-Pierre said anything? But he was not going to lie to her again. "Charlotte was with me. She was my way in. She had a ticket, and I went as her plus one. It was probably her perfume you smelled on me. But it was just business. I promise."

Abigail unfolded her arms and pulled her cell phone out of her purse. She tapped a few buttons and walked over to him. "Just *business?*"

There was a photo of him kissing Charlotte on the cheek. They were both smiling and looked like they were having a great time. The dress she was wearing wouldn't help his case.

"That's when I first got there. It was a greeting. That's all."

Abigail flipped to another photo. Charlotte was in his arms, dancing. They were very close. That's when Tony was telling Charlotte the plan, and he didn't want anybody else to hear or read his lips. Abigail showed him the next two photos. If he didn't know better, even he would have trouble believing the steamy pictures were innocent.

"Abigail, I know how it looks."

"It looks like more than business."

"But you have to trust me. I wasn't there to cheat on you, I promise."

"You keep saying that, Tony, but the fact is, you *lied* to me. And whether or not you were there on business, pleasure, or some other sordid scheme, you were *there*, and you were dancing with and kissing another woman who wasn't *me*. Not only didn't you tell me where you were going, but you didn't even consider bringing me along. You went with *her*."

The look in her eyes caused a lump to form in his throat.

"Look, just hear me out," he said. "JP is a terrible person. He was there last night too, and I suspect that's where you got those photos. He is still dirty, Abigail. There are things about him I haven't told you, which I probably should have, but I didn't want to scare you. I have been trying my hardest to figure out a way for this mess not to touch your career."

He took another deep breath. He seemed to be having trouble getting air. "Please sit down." He patted the couch beside him, but she remained standing.

"I told you he came to see me here and gave me the flash drive," Tony reminded her. "You saw it. He is now demanding I break in to Vivian Danes' house and steal her necklace. You've read about it. You know what a collector's item it is. Mauvais is crazy about rare stuff. He wants it, and he wants it bad. I don't want to do the job, and I needed a way to keep him from releasing that video, so I figured I'd get some dirt on him, and that would give me equal leverage."

He looked up at her, but she waited for him to continue.

"In the meantime, I needed to make him think I was working on a plan to steal the necklace, which is why I did some of the legwork."

As Tony spoke, he knew how twisted his story sounded. Hearing it out loud made him wonder what he had been thinking.

He stood. "Abigail, you need to stay away from Jean-Pierre. He's dangerous. I haven't told you half of what he does. He has his place stocked with stolen goods, rare finds, and stuff pried from the fingers of people by blackmail and deceit. Rumor even has it he has tried to have people killed."

"Rumor?" Abigail said. "Now you're making stuff up."

"No, I'm not."

"Maybe you're just jealous."

"Maybe I am. But that isn't clouding my senses."

They were both quiet, in a stalemate. Her hair was still across her eyes. He reached out to touch her, but she stepped back.

"Tony, I can't do this now. I can't have these conversations. I need to focus on the premiere on Friday. I need some time to think, to sleep, and to not have to worry about what you're up to."

"Then let's go to Jean-Pierre right now, together. I can tell him what I have on him and make him promise to leave us alone. It'll work, Abigail."

"No. Leave it alone. Jean-Pierre might be a creep, but right now, he's propelling my career to the top rung of the ladder. And he's not hurting anybody."

"He's trying to hurt *me!*" Tony said, raising his voice. "And he's hurting you. And us—our marriage. Don't let him tear us apart, Abigail. Don't work with him. He's a thief. He's a charming, cunning thief who is full of lies."

"Kind of like you," she said quietly.

Tony closed his eyes as the words hit him. He concentrated on breathing, because he felt like he was losing his balance. "Like I *used* to be."

She didn't respond. He felt Cocoa twine around his legs, and he opened his eyes. Abigail was looking at him with a mixture of pity and sadness.

"I need for you to leave," she said. "I'd like it if you slept in the apartment tonight."

Tony felt tears fill his eyes. "Please, Abigail, no. You can't mean that." He was losing her. Fear rose in him, twisting his insides. He wanted her to reach out to him, to say this was all a bad dream, and that they could go back to the way things were a week ago.

She glanced at the table. "Thank you for the roses. They were a nice touch. Now please get your things and go."

The tears spilled down his cheeks. "Tell me one thing first," he said. "Do you still love me?"

She met his eyes. Those deep emerald pools he had first lost himself in, falling in love the moment he saw her.

"Yes," she said. "I do. Which is why this hurts so much. And why I need for you to go."

He nodded. He held her gaze for another moment, hoping to see some spark in her eyes that would bring her back to him or her hand reach out to take his. But she remained motionless. He wiped his face with his palm and went to pack a bag of clothes.

Tony drove through the dark, silent streets as if in a fog. He had never felt so empty in his life.

His phone rang, startling him, and he grabbed it, thinking it was Abigail changing her mind and wanting him to come back. But it was JP. Angrily, he punched the button to answer the call.

"Stay away from Abigail," Tony said. "And leave my marriage alone."

The Frenchman tsked. "You need to quit playing with other ladies. That was your fault, not mine."

"I swear if I see you again—"

"Let me keep this short," JP said, his tone changing. "Nobody blackmails me. *Nobody*. Last night, I saw you cozying up to Marvin Tucker and a few others who aren't so fond of me. It's true I have some enemies, but no more than you do. You made two mistakes at that auction. One with the woman. The other…"—his voice lowered to a growl—"was thinking you could blackmail me. You have so much more to lose than I do, Tony Russo."

JP hung up. Tony put his phone away and punched the steering wheel. He'd deal with JP tomorrow.

Chapter Thirty-One

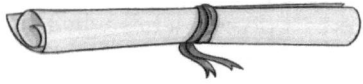

The Friday morning forecast promised to be mild and sunny, as if laughing at Abigail's misery. She saw that the temperatures were going to drop tonight though, with an icy rain mix coming through. She hoped it held off until people got home safely from the premiere.

She had slept due to sheer exhaustion last night after Tony left, so she was refreshed physically, but not mentally. She went to make coffee and saw the roses on the table. The house felt quiet and lonely, but she pushed those thoughts down. She had lived by herself for years. She would be fine.

She just needed to get through today. And tonight.

She didn't have a car because Tony had used it to get to the apartment last night. She sighed because she had forgotten about that, and taking the bus would mean a longer commute.

It was exactly 8 a.m. when she arrived at the library. She quickly put her coat in her locker, along with the outfit she brought to wear tonight, and hurried out to her desk. Ms. Scott was pulling a ladder over to the maps room and directing a young man to hang a banner up across the entrance.

The premiere would take place in the maps room. The desks had not been put in there yet, so they could line up rows of chairs. Abigail would stand at the front by the newly installed AV screen, which was surrounded by vertical glass cases along the walls on either side. The maps were beautifully framed and on display. The Vesconte, which held prominence in a larger case to her right, was covered by a white sheet. Near the entrance, a heavier velvet blanket covered the Napoleon map, which was in a large, vertical glass case as well. The agenda was for Abigail to talk about the library's world-class storage system, showing her PowerPoint presentation on the screen and highlighting some of the maps that were on display.

Then there would be a brief intermission before she came back and uncovered the Vesconte. It was here that she would bring Jean-Pierre up, read his bio, and talk about how much everyone appreciated his contributions. Then, they would unveil the Napoleon map together.

"Our local news station and even some Detroit stations are sending their press people!" Ms. Scott said as soon as she saw Abigail. "This is so exciting!" The young man was having trouble getting the banner to stay. "I'll get you more tacks," Ms. Scott said and scurried off to scrounge through Abigail's desk.

Abigail stayed with the ladder until she returned. Pauline came up on the elevator with her arms full of brochures.

"We need to fold these," she said. Then she took another look at Abigail. "You look terrible this morning. Nerves?"

"Something like that," Abigail said.

She followed Pauline over to her desk, where they started folding the brochures while Ms. Scott and the young man struggled with the huge banner.

"How's Tony?" Pauline asked. She was ever the nosy and intuitive friend.

Abigail didn't want to talk about it, and yet she needed to. "We had a fight. But right now, I want to concentrate on something else. Maybe over lunch?"

"Sure," Pauline said and thankfully didn't press for more details. "We need to check on the hors d'oeuvres order. And there's the recipe for the punch. I have it somewhere in my purse. I bought all of the ingredients last night, but we need to double check that."

"Abigail? Where do you think we should put this photo of Jean-Pierre?" Ms. Scott hollered over to her. She was holding a 20 x 24-inch framed photo of the Frenchman in one hand and an easel in the other.

The morning looked like it was going to be crazy busy.

Because he hadn't slept the night before, Tony managed to fall asleep for a few hours last night, but he was still tired.

He could feel it in his bones as he placed more stones along the riverbank for his community service work. Karl wasn't there today; rumors of a stomach bug or something. For that small gift, he was very grateful.

Without bothering to shower, he went immediately from community service to Jean-Pierre's hotel. He knew the man liked to sleep in and then go for a morning swim, so at this time of day JP would probably be catching up on some work at his desk. He found JP's room, picked the lock, and went in.

JP was sitting at the little table with his laptop open. He looked up, saw Tony, and smiled.

"I was expecting you," he said, "Only I thought you would knock. Some things never change."

"Oxford," was all Tony said.

JP's face fell and his eyes clouded briefly before he regained himself. Tony had apparently scored with that tidbit of information.

"And I have more if you'd like to hear it."

"Listen, you little swindler," JP said, closing his laptop. "Like I told you last night, you have way more to lose than I do. Remember, if I go down, I'm taking you with me."

"So, here's the deal," Tony said, walking over to the table. "I'm not getting the necklace for you. I told you, I don't do that anymore. Find yourself another thief. Secondly, this premiere had better be spectacular for Abigail. I think it's in all of our best interests for it to go over well, wouldn't you agree?"

But JP was seething. "Then you had better not show up tonight," he said. Tony could see his jaw working.

Tony relaxed a little. He was winning this round. "Oh, I'll be there to support my wife. And to keep an eye on you."

He turned to leave but stopped with his hand on the door. "One more thing," Tony said, turning back around. "After this premiere, I want you to go back to Paris or whatever scum hole you crawled out of and leave Abigail alone. If she comes to Paris, it will be with me, and you'll keep your distance."

Before Jean-Pierre could answer, he left, closing the door behind him.

Pauline drove them to a little restaurant not far from the library. They had great burgers, and Abigail loved their beef barley soup, which was on special today. She ordered a cup to go with her burger, and the warm soup was just the balm she needed to relax her frazzled nerves.

"So, tell me about this fight," Pauline said.

"I think he was with another woman," Abigail said.

"Oh, honey." Pauline was all sympathy. "I'm so sorry."

"I'm not sure they did anything, but I know he was with her."

"What do you mean?"

Abigail sighed, wondering how much to tell Pauline. "He went to a black-market auction last night," Abigail whispered across the table. "And apparently Jean-Pierre was there looking at an old map. He showed me photos. Tony was dancing with her."

Abigail wanted Pauline to react with anger, to say bad things about Tony and how right Abigail had been to kick him out last night. But instead, her friend was thoughtful.

"Maybe he was undercover."

"What?"

"Well, you told me all about Jean-Pierre and his nasty threats. Maybe Tony is trying to figure out a way to stop Jean-Pierre by playing his own game."

Pauline was sharp. Abigail never gave her enough credit. "Well, that's what he claimed."

Pauline raised an eyebrow. "So maybe he's telling the truth?"

"But that doesn't change the fact that he lied to me!" she said. "And this woman he was with, he has slept with her before."

"How do you know?"

"He told me. It was before we met. But still."

Abigail pulled her phone out and showed Pauline the photos.

"Whoa," Pauline said. "She's hot."

"That's not helping."

Pauline reached her hand across the table and took Abigail's. "Honey, I don't know what to say about these photos. But I see the way he looks at you. That man is crazy in love with you. I'm not excusing him, but whatever he did, I don't think it's because he is ready to move on. And remember what I thought when I saw you with JP? Things aren't always as they seem."

Abigail squeezed Pauline's hand and then pulled hers away. She went back to her soup, stirring it to cool it off some more. "But I can't trust him, Pauline."

"But you can trust God."

The words were so simple, so true, that Abigail had to repeat them over to herself in her head. *I can trust God.*

"No matter what our circumstances are, no matter how crazy our life is, God is still in charge. Remember I told you that Drew cheated on me? I had a young child then. Those were the darkest days of my life. But at the same time, they weren't, because God revealed Himself to me in such a powerful way. You have a lot going on, Abigail, with the evil Jean-Pierre, your tenure track, and now Tony lying to you. But remember Who has you in the palm of His hand. Ultimately, you can trust *Him.*"

"But God doesn't stop bad things from happening."

Pauline sat back and laughed. "No! He doesn't. He didn't stop Drew from cheating on me. It would have been nice if He had knocked him upside the head and said 'Hey, idiot. Don't put your wife through this.' But He didn't. And while I never wish to go through that again, it made me stronger."

Abigail toyed with her soup some more. "How did you decide to trust Drew again? I mean...with Tony's background. And he's so good at turning on the charm and making a person unable to think clearly..."

"I didn't decide to trust Drew. It's just something that happened over time. A *lot* of time. He was repentant and worked very hard to rebuild the relationship. Now I trust him completely. I don't lie awake at night wondering if he really is working late or if he's with a woman. I know his heart. It's good. He's a changed man."

Abigail sighed. She had believed Tony was a changed man at one time. If she was honest, a part of her still did.

"All I'm saying is that it's okay to give him another chance," said Pauline. "You don't want to be a doormat, but I don't see you ever doing that anyway. People can change, Abigail. But it takes time. Just because he told one lie doesn't mean he's turned back to a life of crime and is committing adultery."

Maybe Pauline was right. Maybe she needed to give Tony another chance. But not until after the premiere. She couldn't handle all of this in one day. "I didn't ever have to worry about this stuff with Nick." Abigail's eyes filled with tears. She sniffed. "Nick was so solid. So different."

Pauline's own eyes filled now. "I know," she said. "I loved Nick. We all did. And I know what tomorrow is."

"It'll be seven years," Abigail said. She told Pauline about Sharon's call. "I feel so terrible. I should have told her. I just keep messing everything up."

"Love doesn't come cheap, Abigail. There's always a price. Usually, it's worth it."

The server returned and asked if they wanted anything else. They had to get back to the library, so Pauline asked for the bill. "I'll get this," she said, pulling out her wallet.

Next door to the restaurant was a flower shop. "Did you want to stop in and buy something for Nick's grave?" Pauline asked. "I can go with you to the cemetery tomorrow if you want."

Pauline knew that Abigail had never been back. But maybe it was time. Maybe she needed to say a final goodbye to Nick and remember all of the good times they had instead of that one terrible, final night together.

"Okay," Abigail agreed. And they went inside to pick out a grave bouquet.

Chapter Thirty-Two

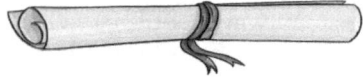

Tony sat at his desk, freshly showered, eating peanut butter out of the jar with a spoon. He looked at his schedule. He had to stop by his grandma's apartment, and then he had some work to do at a client's house, which he was afraid would run later than he wanted. Somewhere in between all of that, he wanted to stop and see George.

He had called his Grandma earlier to tell her not to make lunch today. He didn't have the time. She told him she'd be fine without him, but he really felt he should at least stop in to check on her.

He pulled his phone out and thought about calling Abigail. But instinct told him to give her more time to cool down. He thought about calling Charlotte and begging her to talk to Abigail to straighten things out, but that seemed pathetic. Maybe he wasn't above pathetic. Either way, Abigail was right. He had lied to her.

Tony got up and packed his tool bag. He grabbed his lighter jacket and set off to begin his afternoon.

Grandma looked well. It seemed she had bad days and good days, which he supposed was to be expected. He got her exercise bands out and started helping her with her physical therapy.

"I have to work late tonight, so remember that Jimmy and Martha are going to pick you up and bring you to Abigail's premiere," Tony said.

"I remember," Grandma said. "How late will you be? You won't miss it, will you?"

"Of course not. I'm coming there straight from a client's house though."

"Remember to iron your suit."

Tony smiled at her remark. He had been dressing himself for how many years? But that reminded him that he'd have to swing by the house to pick it up.

His next stop was George. He had no idea where his friend was working today, so he stopped into Poundstone Professional Painters, his old workplace, to ask at the desk.

"He'll be happy to see you," Ginny, their secretary said, as she handed him a sticky note with the address on it.

Probably not, Tony thought as he thanked her and headed over.

George was at a large home on the north side of town. He had his back turned to the door when Tony let himself in, and the Beach Boys was blaring from George's boombox.

Tony knocked hard on the open door. "Hey!" he called out, so as not to scare George.

Julio appeared and turned the music off. He gave Tony a friendly nod. "Someone's here to see you, George."

"Laney?" His friend turned, and his smile faded as soon as he saw Tony. "Oh, it's you."

"Yeah, it's me." Tony stood there with his hands in his pockets. "Can we talk outside for a minute?"

"I have nothing to say to you," George said, turning back to the wall he was painting.

"But I have stuff I need to say to you." Tony glanced meaningfully at Julio, who got the hint.

"I need to go out to the truck, George," he said. "I'll be back in a minute."

As Julio left, Tony walked over to George. "You have every right to hate me," he said.

"Yes, I do."

Tony prayed silently that his words would be heard.

"I came to apologize."

"You already did that. I accept. But it doesn't change how I feel."

"George, please. At least look at me."

George turned to face Tony. His eyes were blazing. "I thought you were my friend. We've had such great times together, but all the while, you were living a double life! It's not like you lied to me once. You *lived* a lie. I don't even know

181

who you are anymore, Tony. Now leave. I have work to do."
He dipped his roller in the pan and started working the paint
onto the wall.

Tony stood there for a minute, trying to think of something
to say that would salvage their friendship. Nothing came. He
had messed up. He thought back to all the times he had told
George he was working late painting a client's house. Or he
needed to take a long lunch to help his grandma, when really
he was at home scoping out some future gig. It's not like he
did it a lot. The money was so good he didn't have to. But
he did it enough.

He nodded, although he knew George couldn't see him.
Head lowered, he slowly turned and walked out of the house,
closing the door quietly behind him.

Back in the car, he took his phone out to call Abigail
again. Then he put it back in his pocket.

He sighed. It seemed he did a lot of sighing these days. He
started the car and headed over to the house to get his suit.

He decided that he would go in late to the premiere so
that he wasn't there for the mingling part at the beginning. It
would be uncomfortable if Abigail felt obligated to talk to him.
They'd have to smile and pretend that everything was okay.
But he was proud of her and wanted to see her presentation.
He'd definitely get there in time for that.

Chapter Thirty-Three

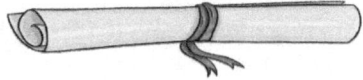

Abigail was nervous. She was watching from her desk, and the room was quickly filling up with people. All of the library board members were here, as were many of the regents, a few deans, and of course, people from the general public. The university president himself was here, smiling and asking Ms. Scott to show him around the room. He nodded politely as she pointed out various details about each map, but he probably had no idea what she was talking about.

"Come and mingle," Pauline said to Abigail. "I know that's not your thing, Ms. Introvert, but it's expected." She held up the glass of punch in her hand. "It turned out really tasty!"

Abigail walked over to the maps room and entered. Jean-Pierre came to greet her, introducing her to some friends of his. All map collectors. She nodded and smiled politely and escaped as soon as she could. Thankfully, Ms. Scott grabbed her elbow and directed her up front.

There was a little stage at the front of the room that somebody had brought over from another building. There was a podium on it, and two chairs. One was for Ms. Scott, and the other was where Abigail would sit while Jean-Pierre gave his short talk.

Abigail already had her laptop plugged in and ready to go. Ms. Scott asked her to take a seat to the left of the podium.

People started taking their seats. The first two rows were reserved for University staff, board members, and donors. She saw Jimmy and Martha come in, with Tony's grandma hanging onto Jimmy's arm. They found a seat near the middle of the room. They smiled and waved at her, and she smiled back at them.

She looked around but didn't see Tony anywhere.

Pauline's husband came in. He looked handsome in his brown suit and navy tie. Pauline said they hired a babysitter to watch the kids tonight, so it was kind of like a date.

Jean-Pierre directed his guests up to the front, where they had four seats reserved in the first row. He unbuttoned his suit coat, sat down, and nodded encouragingly to Abigail. She gave him a brief nod back. They were in this together.

It was time to begin. Ms. Scott stood at the podium. She welcomed the board members and the president and thanked them for their support. Then she turned the microphone over to Abigail.

Abigail had chosen to wear a black pencil skirt with a soft green sweater. She had the front part of her hair pulled back on top and pinned with her favorite hairpin, which was given to her by her grandmother. It was the one she had been wearing the night she met Tony.

She cleared her throat. "Good evening, and welcome to our exciting premiere! Some of the maps you will see tonight are very rare, and we are so thrilled to have them here at our library."

Tony quietly came into the room and slipped into a seat near the back. He was wearing his charcoal pinstripe suit and a tie. He looked amazing. He caught her looking at him and gave her a small smile.

She felt her stomach twist. He had come after all. He was so late she thought he wouldn't show up. She wasn't even sure she wanted him there. But there he was, smiling at her, a look of pride on his face.

Ms. Scott cleared her throat, and Abigail realized she had paused for too long.

"But first, before we unveil some of these maps, I want to tell you about our world-class storage system that we have here in this library for maps, rare books, and other documents." She clicked on her first slide.

Abigail got wrapped up in her talk. She lived and breathed this work every day, so it came out smoothly as she explained in layman's terms what they did here and why collectors like Jean-Pierre were satisfied leaving their maps in this collection. She glanced briefly in Tony's direction as she mentioned the security system that had been recently installed by Black Cat Security. He was sitting there, listening intently to every word she said.

She wondered why he decided on the pinstripe suit and if he had gotten the tux dry-cleaned or if it was smelling up his entire apartment with perfume. Then she wondered where that thought came from and pushed her mind back to her work.

The presentation was lengthy. She thought it was a bit *too* long, but Ms. Scott insisted that they cover everything for the benefit of those donating large sums of money. "Let's impress them, and maybe they will donate more," Ms. Scott had said.

When Abigail wrapped up, they had been there about forty-five minutes.

"Okay," she said. "Let's take a brief intermission." She gave them an encouraging smile. "Then we get to take a look at the marvelous maps behind these sheets!"

People got up and wandered back toward the punch table. Jimmy and Martha came to meet her as she walked down from her little stage.

"This is marvelous!" Martha said. "I had no idea your library was such a fortress! And isn't this interesting, Jimmy, about how they take care of these rare maps?"

"Yes," Jimmy agreed, but Abigail could tell he was bored to death. Her eyes cut over to Tony, who had gotten up and was talking with his grandma.

"Thanks, Martha," Abigail said.

"You're doing a marvelous job." Martha hooked her arm around Jimmy's. "Let's go refill our punch. And I want to try one of those almond cookies."

"Okay," Jimmy said with more enthusiasm. He was more interested in the food than in the maps.

Abigail's eyes kept going to Tony. She didn't notice when Jean-Pierre came up to her.

"Is he going to cause trouble?" he asked, nodding toward Tony.

Tony had gone to get his grandma some hors d'oeuvres and punch.

"No."

"What's he doing here, anyway?"

She met Jean-Pierre's eyes. "He's my husband."

Jean-Pierre grunted and was pulled away by someone who wanted to talk to him.

Tony noticed Abigail was alone and made his way across the room toward her. Her stomach tied itself in knots, and she suddenly had trouble swallowing.

He stopped in front of her. His hands were in his pockets, and he was carrying himself in that relaxed manner he had.

"You're doing a great job," he said. "I can tell all of these guys are impressed." He glanced over to where the board members were gathered.

"Thanks," Abigail said. She felt her hands trembling and clasped them together.

"You okay?" Tony asked.

"No." She wasn't. She wasn't okay at all. She was giving a presentation that her entire career could be balancing on. All of the board members were here and most likely members from the tenure committee. She wasn't allowed to know who they were. She had two thieves in the room, both known for stealing maps and both wanting to kill the other. And all she could think about was Tony and where their relationship was headed.

"I need for you to go."

She saw the shock register in his eyes. "Go?" he said.

"Yes."

"I know you're mad at me, but I'm here to support you. Can't I at least do that? I know how hard you've worked for this."

"It's just that you're making me nervous. I can't concentrate. Please go."

She felt her face getting warm. She couldn't possibly cry now. "Please," she pleaded.

She saw the hurt in Tony's eyes, and she glanced over at the hors d'oeuvres table. She couldn't look at him anymore.

"Okay," he said quietly. "Whatever you need."

"Abigail!" A woman approached her and took her by the arm. "I want you to meet my husband. He has been collecting maps since he was a child."

Abigail shook his hand and listened politely as he told her about his expensive hobby. Then Ms. Scott said it was time for people to take their seats again. When Abigail turned to look, Tony was gone.

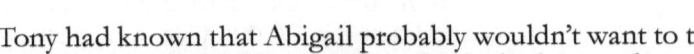

Tony had known that Abigail probably wouldn't want to talk to him much during the premiere, but he had never dreamed she would kick him out.

He had slipped out of the room quietly to make sure his grandma didn't see him leave. He didn't want her worrying or Jimmy following and asking questions.

He pushed the main door open and stepped outside into the dark night. The air was cooler, and the rain had turned to an icy mix. He hoped it held off freezing on the roads until their loved ones were home safe.

He thought about leaving her the car and looking for a cab, but it was expensive taking a cab all the way back to his apartment, which is where he thought he should go. Plus, she had mentioned earlier in the week that they might all go out to dinner afterward. She wouldn't want him there. She could find a ride to the restaurant if they went, but just in case, he would call her around the time he thought the premiere ended and offer to come and pick her up.

He was foolish to have thought they would be going home together.

He walked carefully on the sidewalk to avoid slipping and fished for the car keys in his pocket. He went around the corner of the building to the parking lot and was surprised as a rough hand grabbed his shoulder and spun him around. Before he had time to figure out who it was, a fist landed in his stomach, knocking the air out of him. He doubled over in pain, gasping for breath. He tried to look up to see who had hit him, but another fist came at his face, catching him in the jaw. He fell backward, seeing stars.

He still had his keys in his pocket. If he could get to them, he could use one as a weapon. He started to reach for them when a face leaned over him and came in to view.

187

"No, you don't," Karl said and hit him with a Taser.

Tony's body went completely stiff. He lost all control of his muscles, but his brain was still working and what he *wanted* to do was scream for help. But he couldn't. The pain, which was the most intense pain he had ever felt, seemed never-ending. Somewhere in the back of his mind, which was fighting for survival, he remembered reading about the power behind a Taser and knew that 20,000 volts were passing through him. But it was the amperage which would kill him. Luckily, the amperage with Tasers was low enough that he probably wouldn't die.

Hopefully.

When Karl pulled the Taser away, the pain stopped and Tony's limbs went limp. He felt like a wet noodle. He tried to move, but his body wouldn't cooperate. He felt Karl digging in his pocket for his keys, and then the big man hefted Tony up and over his shoulder. He carried him to Tony's car, unlocked it, and tossed Tony in the back seat. Tony felt his arms starting to work again, but before they could get their full strength, Karl rolled Tony over. He grabbed his hands and feet and tied them with a thick cord. He found Tony's phone in his other pocket and turned it off. Then he shut the door and climbed in the front seat.

Tony lay there listening as Karl started the car and drove off. He was lying face down on the back seat, so he couldn't tell where they were going. After a while, they stopped.

"You came out of the library early, jerk-face," he said, turning around. "You wasn't supposed to be out for another hour. Now we gotta wait."

Tony had most of the use of his body back. He rocked until he got momentum and rolled himself over on his back so he could see Karl.

Karl grinned at him, which looked more like the snarl of a rabid dog. "I'd like to have messed up that pretty face of yours some more, but the boss needs you in working shape."

Tony tasted blood in his mouth from a cut on his lip. "The boss? Who hired you?"

Karl laughed. "Wouldn't you like to know."

He was wearing a thick, brown jacket that was stained, and he smelled like beer. He reached into his pocket and pulled out a Bluetooth earpiece.

"This is for you," Karl said. "John-Pierre wants you to wear it when you break in to that house."

He said the Frenchman's name with a hard "J". So that was who was behind this. Tony should have known. He hadn't even been watching when he walked out alone into the dark because his mind was on Abigail.

"I'm not breaking into that house," Tony said.

"Yes, you are," Karl said. "The boss will see to it that you do." Karl dug in his pocket again. He brought out a damp, dirty paper towel. Something was wrapped in it.

"You're supposed to give this to the dogs, if you see any. Jean-Pierre says to tell you to relax, it won't kill them. It'll just make them sleepy."

Tony looked at it with disgust. "What is it?"

"It's a slice of T-bone with a pill wrapped inside. There are two here, because that's how many dogs there are." Karl gave the paper towel a sniff. "I was tempted to take a bite, but it ain't cooked."

Tony used his core muscles to lift into a sitting position. He couldn't tell where they were. It looked like a deserted area in a park because the car was parked in an empty lot with trees along both sides. No one else was around. Tony tried to figure out if he could open the door and make a run for it. But Karl put the meat down on the passenger seat so that his hand was free to use the Taser that was on his lap. Tony didn't want to encounter that a second time. And he hadn't yet been able to work the rope off his legs. If he could get to his tool bag...but it was in the trunk.

"What makes JP think I'll do what he says?"

"Because he can listen to you on this here device. And if you don't do what he says..."

"Then what?"

Karl was slow. He had been kidnapped by an idiot. But maybe he could use that to his advantage.

"Well, he'll have your girl by then. That cute little wifey of yours."

"What?" Panic brought a fresh surge of adrenaline through Tony. He had to get out of here! He threw himself forward and head-butted Karl. The force knocked the big man backward and in to the steering wheel, but he quickly recovered. Tony was rewarded with another hit of the Taser.

Abigail adjusted the mic on the podium and cleared her throat.

"This is the exciting half!" she said, and the audience laughed. She looked around the room. The chairs were filled. There were people here who could make a difference in her future and people from the general public who just loved old things and libraries and wanted to hear about what she did. And, of course, her family and friends were here to support her.

This was her moment.

She looked over at the Vesconte on the wall to her left, covered by the white sheet. No one outside of the library had seen it yet.

"This map that I'm about to reveal is made by a very well-known fourteenth-century cartographer," Abigail said. "Some of you may have even heard of him." More laughter. She glanced again at the covered Vesconte. Would any of them realize it was stolen? She doubted it. As a matter of fact, she was betting her career that they didn't. Jean-Pierre was very clever. He covered his tracks.

But what was she doing here? She thought about the comment Tony had made about integrity. Was she throwing hers away for her career?

She looked toward the door. The Napoleon was up there, covered in velvet. "And then we'll see the big thing you have all come for. A map drawn by Napoleon's own hand." There was a murmur of excitement. She was doing a great job working the crowd.

"But before I show the Vesconte to you, I want to tell you about the man who made this possible."

She looked at Jean-Pierre, who gave her an encouraging nod. She tried to smile at him, but her stomach twisted again and she felt ill. He wasn't the man who should be giving her encouraging looks. She looked toward the back of the room and saw the empty chair where Tony had been. That's the man who should be here.

And she had sent him away.

She thought of the past few weeks of their new marriage and how he doted on her. How he was working so hard to turn his life around and make himself a better man. "I want to be worthy of you," were the words he used. She had tried to convince him that he already was, that she loved him tremendously, but he was so afraid that she'd see him in a different light someday and leave him. She had promised him she never would. And yet here she was. What had she done?

Was her job more important than her marriage?

Ms. Scott cleared her throat. Abigail looked down at her notes, at the biography she was about to read on Jean-Pierre. The room was very quiet. The door was open, and she could hear the rain beating on the skylight above her desk, just outside of the maps room. It had turned to ice and sounded like tiny pellets hitting the glass.

The roads were probably icy.

She felt a familiar wave of panic coming over here, and her breathing speeded up.

The rainy mix seemed to respond to her fear and picked up, coming down harder on the glass. It reminded her of the night she had sent Nick away. Just like she had sent Tony away.

"Abigail?"

Ms. Scott's voice came from somewhere to her right. She looked up at the crowd, and some of them were growing restless. She was having trouble breathing. She had sent Tony away, angrily, into an ice storm.

She saw Jean-Pierre stand up, buttoning his jacket. He started to approach the podium. Shaking, she stepped down off the stage and fled.

She didn't stop for her coat but pushed through the doors out into the night. She thought about looking for her car, but figured Tony had it. She tried to flag down a cab, but the driver didn't stop. He already had a fare.

"Abigail!" She heard Jean-Pierre's voice shouting and was vaguely aware he was coming out of the library door after her. She ran further down the street. She had to find a cab.

"Abigail!" Jean-Pierre shouted again. In a blind panic, she turned to him.

"I have to find Tony," she said.

"Come with me." He grabbed her hand and pulled her quickly across the street, both of them slipping on the ice. They were in the deserted parking lot of a breakfast café. There was a trash bin near them and beyond that, some bushes. She saw a car parked by them. She realized that neither of them had a coat on, and her sweater was getting soaked with icy rain. She glanced back toward the library and thought she saw Jimmy standing in the doorway.

"Wait!" she said, pulling on Jean-Pierre's hand. But he tugged her toward the trash bin and pulled her behind it into the darkness. He wrapped one arm around her and pushed a cloth to her face with his other hand.

"You're making this too easy," he said, and everything went black.

—◇————————◇—

Abigail woke slowly, feeling a bit dizzy. She didn't know where she was, and lay very still, trying to assess her situation. She was lying on her side on what felt like a cold, cement floor. Her wrists were tied, and so were her ankles. Thick cords also wrapped around her legs just above the knees.

She blinked a few times, and the room started to come into focus.

"Well, look who's up," said a familiar voice.

She craned her neck and saw Jean-Pierre sitting in a chair watching her. There was a metal desk beside him, and on it was a laptop. He had a cell phone in his hand.

She struggled to a sitting position, which wasn't too easy considering how she was bound. The room swayed crazily for a moment and then settled as the dizziness receded.

She was in what appeared to be a large warehouse. It was a big, open space, probably about five stories tall, with the only windows being way up toward the ceiling. The rest was metal and concrete. It looked deserted because it was pretty much empty except for a twenty-foot-tall stack of old cardboard boxes in a corner. The light near Jean-Pierre only let her see so far into the old building.

"Where are we?" she asked.

"You're safe," Jean-Pierre said and got up to pull a chair over to her. He picked her up and set her on it. "Comfy?"

"Why are you doing this?" Her sweater was wet from the rain and ice, and she had goosebumps. The building was cold, and she started to shiver.

Jean-Pierre grabbed a fleece blanket from his chair and draped it around her. "I keep this in my car. There's no reason for you to freeze. I apologize that it's so cold in here, but I hadn't planned on being here for a few more hours. When you bolted out of the library early, I had to improvise."

The blanket felt good around her shoulders. Her skirt was long enough to cover her thighs, but her legs were cold in the nylons she was wearing, and her feet were practically numb.

"I have a space heater on, but it'll take a few minutes to warm the area up." He made a few more adjustments to the blanket, tucking it in tighter around her. "That's better. Oui? Are you comfortable?"

She shook her head. "Untie me."

"I'm sorry for the ropes. I need to keep you here, and I don't want a fight on my hands."

Abigail's teeth started to chatter. She looked around. They seemed to be alone. Her head was still a bit fuzzy.

"What are we doing here? What happened?"

"I just need your husband to do a favor for me, and then you'll be free to go. I needed a little insurance. Tony can be... difficult."

At the mention of Tony's name, Abigail started trying to kick the ropes off her feet. They were on tight, as were the ones around her wrist. Her blanket started to slide off.

"Calm down," Jean-Pierre said. "Tony will be okay as long as he does what he's told." He tucked the blanket back around her and went to sit down. He typed a few things into his laptop.

"He'll find me," she said.

"No, he won't. There's no way to trace you here. Your phone is somewhere back in the parking lot across from the library."

"Jean-Pierre, this is ridiculous. We weren't going to say anything about the map. This whole thing was supposed to go off okay. Is it because I ran?"

He chuckled. "No. That actually helped facilitate my plan. I was trying to figure out how to get you away from Tony and your friends after the event. But you helped me with that little panic attack of yours. What on earth happened, anyway?"

If he wasn't holding her hostage because of the map, what was he doing?

"Why do you need Tony? What job are you talking about?" *The heist?*

"You'll find out soon enough."

The space heater was finally starting to warm the place up. Abigail's teeth had quit chattering, and she could feel her toes a little bit.

Jean-Pierre's phone rang, and he answered it. Abigail couldn't hear the voice on the other end. "Fantastic!" Jean-Pierre said.

"Hello!" Abigail screamed. "Help me!"

Jean-Pierre scowled at her. "Okay," he said into the phone. "Call me back when he can talk."

He hung up. "Abigail, where we are, nobody can hear you scream." He fished in his pocket and pulled out a rag. He tore it, came over to her, and forced it in her mouth. She tried to bite him but couldn't. He tied it around her head, gagging her. "Still, we can't take any chances."

She wondered who he had been talking to. Call back when *who* was awake? Did they have Tony? And why?

"To answer your question from earlier," Jean-Pierre said, as if reading her mind, "I have your husband. He's with my associate right now. That's what the call was about." He waved his phone. "I need him to steal something for me, and you are my insurance that he doesn't try anything smart."

Jean-Pierre turned the laptop around so she could see the screen. "I'm going to watch him from here. It'll be like a television show. So nice of you to join me for the viewing." He gave her one of his charming smiles.

The phone rang again. "Ahhh, looks like this is him."

Chapter Thirty-Four

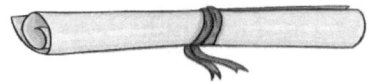

While Tony lay in the back seat, cursing the invention of electricity, Karl made a phone call. Then he took out a knife.

"Are you going to kill me?" Tony asked weakly. His muscles were starting to work again.

"I'm going to cut you loose," Karl said. "And then here is what you're going to do." He tossed the Bluetooth earbud, a box, and a small electronic device into the back seat. "That there is a tiny camera. Clip it onto this." He tossed back a baseball cap. "Clip the box onto your belt. And you'll wear the earbud. John-Pierre will be able to hear everything you say and see everything you do. That's his assurance that you don't deviate from the plan."

"What exactly is the plan?"

"You steal the necklace and bring it to him. Then he lets your girl go."

Tony glanced at the clock. The premiere was probably ending now. "He'll never catch her. She's too smart to go anywhere alone with him."

"Apparently, she's not as smart as you think." Karl punched some numbers into the phone and spoke to someone. "He can talk now." He nodded at the voice on the line and put the phone on speaker.

"Tony!" said the voice of Jean-Pierre through the speaker. "So good to be working with you again!"

Tony struggled back into a sitting position. "JP, I swear, if—"

"Now, now. No swearing. Not in front of the lady."

A chill went through Tony. He had her.

"I don't believe you. I need to hear her."

There was a brief pause, and then he heard "Tony!" It was Abigail's voice.

Tony tried to come forward again toward Karl, but the thug held up the Taser in warning. "If you hurt her," Tony growled at the phone, "I will kill you with my bare hands."

"She's fine," Jean-Pierre said. "All tucked in with a warm blankie. But how fine she stays depends on you. Did Karl explain how the tech works?"

"I'm not doing anything until I know Abigail is okay," Tony said. "I want to talk to her. I'm not doing a thing for you until I hear that she isn't hurt."

There was a pause and then silence as Jean-Pierre possibly muted the phone for a moment. Tony could feel his heart pounding in his chest. At least that was working. He was still shaky from the Taser.

"Tony?" It was Abigail's voice back on the phone. Tony closed his eyes briefly and took a calming breath. He had to be strong for her.

"Hey, beautiful," he said. "Are you all right?"

"Yes," she said. Her voice sounded strong. "He gave me a chair and put a warm blanket around me. But I'm tied up so I can't leave. It's cold in this warehouse—"

The call was muted again. More silence. Finally, Jean-Pierre's voice came back on. "I had to gag her again. She's a talker, that one. But you have my word she'll be fine as long as you hold up your end of the bargain."

"I never made a bargain."

"You did, a few years ago. You promised me that necklace. And now you're going to get it for me."

Tony didn't know if he could. He hadn't studied the security that much.

"I'll need my computers to shut Danes' security off remotely," he said. "It's a complicated system, and there's no way I can do it from inside."

Jean-Pierre laughed. "And there's no way I'm letting you near your computers. You'd send a message off to the entire police force or the FBI or who knows who through some encrypted means."

"No. I would never take a chance now that you have Abigail. And besides, you'll be able to see what I'm doing. You have a camera on me, right?"

"I'm not taking the chance. You'll have to go in blind. What harm can it do? She's an old lady."

"It can do a lot of harm when I trip a silent alarm," Tony said.

"Then I guess Mrs. Russo will pay the price."

Tony glanced at the clock on the car dashboard again. "It's only 11 p.m. I can't go in until after midnight. I need to be sure she's asleep."

Jean-Pierre cursed in French. "This whole plan was thrown off when you all left the library early!" More cursing. "Do what you can. And Tony? If you go to the police or contact anyone in any way, I'll shoot her. I'm tired of messing around with you."

Shoot her?

"JP, please. I really need my computers." Tony was desperate. "Otherwise, this whole thing is not going to work. You said yourself that I'm good at what I do. So let me do it. I will not only bring you the necklace, I'll pull out whatever else I can. I'm sure she has a whole drawerful of diamonds. You can easily sell those at auction. You know you can."

There was a pause. "Very well. But Karl will be with you. And because we can't hurt you, Abigail will be the one to pay. If you do anything suspicious with your computer, I'll start by cutting off her ring finger. She won't need it anymore because I'm taking that ring before we're through with this."

Tony remembered the rumors that Jean-Pierre had people killed. "Don't hurt her. I'll do what you say."

"Good. Let's get started."

Karl pointed to the tech he had thrown in the back seat. "Put those on."

"I can't." He nodded toward his tied-up hands.

Karl grunted and reached into the back seat. He sawed through the ropes that had Tony bound. "Mr. John-Pierre is still on the phone, so don't try anything stupid."

Once Tony's hands and feet were free, he hooked up the Bluetooth, box, and camera and put them on.

"I've got visuals," said JP. There was some clicking in Tony's ear. "And sound. Tony? Can you hear me?"

"I can hear you," Tony said.

"Get up front," Karl said, and Tony climbed over the seat. "I'm gonna drive you to your apartment and then to Ms. Danes' house. Tell me how to get there."

The drive was uneventful. Tony was hoping there would be a swarm of police at the apartment looking for Abigail, but they didn't see anybody as they walked up the steps. Karl used Tony's keys to open the door.

"Only the laptop," said Jean-Pierre. "Grab it and get back in the car."

"I can't do what I need to do from that," Tony said, booting his computers up. The familiar whirl of fans would have been comforting if he wasn't wearing the camera. He wondered if he could get something past JP. The man was smart but might not realize if Tony sent a secured email while also browsing the security site.

Then he thought of Abigail and her finger. He knew Jean-Pierre enough to know he wasn't bluffing. He couldn't chance it.

He quickly brought up the security company and hacked in to it. They hadn't updated it by much since Thursday, so it was easy.

"Walk me through it," JP said.

"Here's Danes' house," Tony said, typing quickly. "Her perimeter is on and the fence is electrified." He typed some more. "But not anymore." He watched as the power went off. Then he plugged in a false code so it would loop and look like it was still up. It should take a few hours before somebody discovered what he had done.

"The house is alarmed as well. Perimeter and sensors." His fingers flew over the keys. "And...done." Again, he plugged in a false code. That would work for a while too before anybody got suspicious.

"Can you take down her phone?" asked JP.

"We don't have all day. This code will only hold for so long," Tony said. "If she wakes up to make a call, we have more trouble than the phone lines being up. I believe she has a gun."

He remembered that tidbit from the first time he scoped out her house.

199

Guns. Dogs. His wife's life on the line. Tony took another calming breath and shut down his computers.

"I need to change," Tony said. "I can't climb in this suit." Karl followed him in as he grabbed his clothes.

"I'll change in the car," he said to Karl. "Let's go."

Abigail watched with Jean-Pierre as Tony did what he was told. She recognized the big man as someone Tony had worked with on community service. How had Jean-Pierre recruited him?

"Remind Karl that he will drop you off at the park behind her house," Jean-Pierre said into Tony's ear. "And then he'll come here for his pay. When you're finished, my driver will be waiting there to pick you up."

She listened as Tony relayed the information.

She struggled again against the ropes. There was no way she was going to be able to loosen them. Jean-Pierre looked at her.

"Is this the first time you've seen your hubby work?" Jean-Pierre said. "He's good. Very good. Watch."

The drive seemed to take forever, while in reality it was probably only twenty minutes. Karl dropped him off.

"I need to get my tools out of the trunk," Tony said, and Karl popped it open for him. He grabbed his bag. The icy rain pelted his face, but his jacket was keeping him warm and dry.

"Don't forget your doggie treats," Karl said. Tony took the soggy paper towel and grimaced. Reluctantly, he put the raw meat in his bag. Everything would need a good dry-cleaning after this.

Karl pulled away, and Tony slipped onto the path that led up to the fence behind Danes' house. It was dark, but he was able to follow it quickly because he remembered it from the other day.

"I can't see anything," JP said.

"And I can't have you yammering in my ear, or you'll distract me," said Tony. "You need to shut up so I can concentrate."

Suddenly, he was in front of the fence. He looked around the yard and didn't see any dogs. Tentatively, he touched the fence with the back of his hand and was relieved to find he didn't receive a jolt. He had had enough of electricity today. Before he could overthink it, he tossed his rope up, hooked it on the fence, and was over in seconds.

He landed lightly on the frozen ground and gave a tug on his rope. It dropped, and he coiled it up. Then he slipped into the bushes close to him. The thick concealment of the shrubbery was why he had chosen to go in this way.

"I need to hear Abigail's voice again," Tony whispered as he carefully made his way across the slippery grass, looking for dogs.

"Tony," she said into his ear after a brief pause. "Don't do this. Please."

"I know what I'm doing. I'll be okay, and I'll come to get you really soon. Don't worry."

"Tony, I—"

"That's enough," Jean-Pierre said. "Get to work."

Tony was almost at the tree by Danes' bedroom window. He had to go across an open part of the lawn to get there. The back floodlights were still on because if they had gone dark it would have alerted a neighbor or passing cop, but he had turned the cameras off. And since he was in the back, nobody should be able to see him from the road. He looked again for the dogs. Nothing. He sprinted across the lawn to the tree. Hooking his rope over a limb, he pulled himself up. He climbed onto a strong branch, where he had a good view of the window. All of the lights were off. His watch said 12:05 a.m. She was in her seventies. Maybe she was in bed at midnight on a Friday night.

He threw his rope, and it caught on the railing of her upstairs balcony. Hand over hand he pulled himself across it and climbed over onto the balcony, quiet as a mouse.

"Is she awake?" whispered JP in his ear.

"Shhhhh!" First Karl and his bad French, and now the whispering villain. Tony was surrounded by idiots.

The sliding glass door stood in front of him, shimmering in the icy rain. He took the glass cutter out of his bag and looked for a good place to cut. He was almost there.

The dogs could be inside. He pulled the meat out of his bag.

Carefully, he knelt down and cut a small hole near the bottom so he could reach in and remove the board in the track. It was an extra security measure to keep the door from opening. As he lifted out the piece of glass, he heard a low growl, and a dog lunged at the door with a bark. He threw the meat through and pressed himself up against the brick on the side of the house, where he couldn't be seen or hopefully smelled. He thought he heard a voice but couldn't be sure over the sound of the pelting rain.

He wondered how long it took for the pills to take effect and make the dogs sleep. His heart was racing, keeping him warm, and as he waited, he started to pray.

Abigail jumped when the dog lunged at Tony. Jean-Pierre watched, looking worried, but Tony soon had it under control. She thought he must be standing against the side of the house because the camera was showing them a view of the yard.

"How fast does this stuff work?" Tony whispered.

"Give it five minutes," Jean-Pierre said.

Karl came ambling into the warehouse. He was a huge man, nearly twice as broad as Tony. He wore baggy blue jeans and a stained, brown jacket that was spotted with dampness.

"Good job, Karl," Jean-Pierre said, and muted the connection. They could still hear Tony, but he couldn't hear them.

Karl's eyes ran up and down Abigail as he walked over to Jean-Pierre. He leaned against the desk. He was staring at her like she was prey.

"I've come for my money," he said.

Jean-Pierre pulled a bag out from under his coat. "Here you go. And if you keep quiet about this, there will be more jobs in your future that pay equally well. You were an asset tonight."

Karl pulled the money out and counted it. It looked to Abigail like about twenty thousand dollars. Satisfied, he grunted and put it back, pulling the string tight on the bag.

He walked over to Abigail. "Maybe I can have a little something extra?" he said and touched her on the cheek with his finger. She flinched.

"Leave the woman alone," said Jean-Pierre firmly. "We're not animals." He turned back to the screen. "At least I'm not," he muttered.

Karl took his finger away but kept staring at Abigail. "Nice legs," he said, showing his teeth.

"I said to *leave her alone.*" There was an iciness to Jean-Pierre's voice that Abigail hadn't heard before. They both looked over at him, and he was pointing a gun at Karl. "Now go sit down over there." He waved the gun toward a chair. "I still need you around. There's another ten grand in it for you if this ends well."

Reluctantly, Karl retreated to his chair in the corner.

"He's in," Jean-Pierre said. Abigail turned her attention back to the screen.

Chapter Thirty-Five

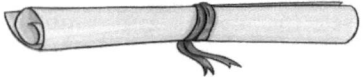

Tony gave it ten minutes. He wanted the dogs asleep, and he wanted Danes asleep. *Please, everybody be asleep*, he prayed. Then he reached through and removed the board. When nothing happened, he moved across to cut another hole near the handle. He carefully put his hand through and unlocked the door. He slid it open enough to squeeze inside and then quickly shut it again. The dogs were there on the floor, sleeping soundly. About ten feet in front of him, up against the wall to his left, was a large queen-size bed. Danes was in it, and from her breathing, she appeared to be asleep too. He had always made it a point to be sure places were empty before breaking in, so this was a new experience for him.

He looked around and saw a walk-in closet across the room, on the other side of the bed. The room was otherwise clear, except for a make-up table to his right. It had a small, metal box sitting on it, with intricate detailing on the lid. It looked like real gold. Definitely a collector's piece. It must be worth a fortune. He turned on his penlight and carefully lifted the lid. It contained make-up pencils, cotton swabs, and a folded, hand-embroidered handkerchief. No necklace. He closed the lid.

"Take the box," said JP.

Tony ignored him.

Silently, he crept to the walk-in closet. It was a big, square room, and there was no door. He shined his penlight around. Her clothes hung neatly above rows and rows of shoes. At the back was a mirror and several drawers built into the wall. That's where the jewelry would be.

He walked back and pulled out a drawer. Diamond earrings of various sizes glittered up at him. He pulled out a second drawer. Different colored jewels shone in his light, some set in gold with silver inlay, some in 24-karat gold or sterling silver. A third drawer showed a pearl necklace with matching earrings. There were millions of dollars here.

"Take it all," JP said.

There was a hatbox on the shelf above the drawers. On instinct, he reached up and removed it. Behind it, built into the wall was a small safe. He had hit the jackpot.

"Ahhhh," JP breathed into Tony's ear. Tony wished he would shut up.

He really needed his old phone for this. There were apps for breaking into safes. But he would have to do this the old-fashioned way. He pulled a stethoscope out of his bag and put it up to the door of the safe. He listened for the telltale clicking as he turned the knob. He had it open in under a minute.

There it was. The coveted necklace. Danes had it displayed on a mannequin neck covered in velvet. It glistened in Tony's light, begging to be touched. The large diamond was surrounded by tiny diamonds and was exquisitely set in gold. He couldn't believe he was seeing it in person, this icon that had graced so many movies. He reached for it, and that's when he heard a click. He felt the cold butt of a revolver against the back of his head.

"Don't move."

Tony slowly raised his hands above his head.

"Turn around." He did. He didn't have his ski mask on, only the baseball cap that had the camera on it. He hadn't been able to get the tech to work with it.

"It's Danes," JP said in his ear.

"I realize that," Tony said.

"What?" said Danes.

"Nothing," said Tony, his hands still in the air. She was in her nightgown, her short hair messed up from sleep. With no makeup on and barefoot, she looked frail, and nothing like the formidable woman who had won several Oscar nominations and an Oscar for her roles in dramas. In fact, she reminded Tony of his grandma.

"I'm not going to hurt you," he said.

"Not while I'm the one with the gun," she said. "Now come out here while I call the police."

He should have cut the phone lines.

"This isn't what it looks like," he said. "I'm not really a thief. I'm..." What was he? She was motioning him slowly out of the closet.

"You're dressed in black. You have a bag. You drugged my dogs. And you cracked open the safe to get to my necklace. I'm pretty sure you're a thief."

He had to think fast. Abigail's life was on the line. "What do I do?" he said into his mic.

"Get yourself out of this mess," said Jean-Pierre. His voice was cold, calculating. "Or I start with Abigail's finger."

"My wife's life is in danger," Tony blurted out. "You have to let me take that necklace." He kept his hands above his head. "Please. I'm not here on my own—I'm being forced to do this."

But Danes was dialing, the gun still trained on him. Tony had one last trick up his sleeve. It might get him killed, but it was all he had left.

God, forgive me, he prayed silently.

While she was busy pushing in 911, he slipped his hand into his pocket and threw some powder in front of him. He closed his eyes as it flashed, and he ducked. The gun fired wildly, and a bullet sunk into the wall behind him. He knocked Danes backward onto the bed, grabbed a quilt, and wrapped it around her. While she struggled to free herself, he picked up the gun. He took the time to grab the necklace and then ran for the sliding glass door, swinging his rope up to the tree. He swung off the balcony and dropped onto the grass, slipping as he ran. When he reached the fence line, he hauled himself over with his rope and landed with a thump, rolling on the frozen dirt. It nearly knocked the wind out of him.

"My driver is waiting for you where Karl let you off," said JP. "Hurry. You've made a mess of this."

Tony ran down the path. There was a black sedan waiting near the entrance to the path. The passenger door opened, and he vaulted inside.

He leaned back, catching his breath. He could hear police sirens in the distance. The driver put the car in gear and pulled out.

"Did you get the necklace?" Jean-Pierre said.

"Yes."

"Good job."

Why didn't Jean-Pierre mention the gun? Was it possible he didn't see Tony pick it up?

It was in his bag. If he could get it inside where JP was holding Abigail... But Tony didn't know how to use a gun. His wife, on the other hand, was professionally trained by Jimmy. He took her to the firing range regularly to practice using the handgun he had bought her when she lived alone.

"Abigail?" Tony said into the mic.

"She's fine," Jean-Pierre said.

"I want to talk to her."

But there was silence on the other end. Tony sat back. While the driver took him closer to his wife, he tried to formulate a plan.

The roadside buildings grew sparser up ahead, with fewer homes and more space between them. He realized where they were. They were about to head out of the south side of town under the river. The tunnel wasn't very long, but it was deep enough to disrupt cell service. He'd briefly lose his connection with JP.

He glanced at the driver, who was a man of medium build with a very French nose. He kept glancing down at his phone. He was using the GPS to get where they were going. Tony looked ahead at the tunnel again. He had about forty seconds to figure something out.

As soon as they went under the tunnel, Tony spoke. "JP?" he said into the mic. Nothing. He muted it just in case, pulled the gun out of his bag, and pointed it at the driver.

"Stop the car."

The driver glanced at Tony. "Mr. Mauvais?"

"I said stop the car!" Tony shouted, waving the gun for emphasis. "He can't hear you. We lost service."

Tony knew enough about guns to realize the safety was still off. Vivian Danes had been pretty serious about shooting him.

The driver slammed on the brakes. There were no other cars in the tunnel, and Tony hoped it would stay that way.

This was a pretty quiet town, and it had to be somewhere between 1 and 2 a.m.

He had to work fast, before JP got worried.

"Give me your phone and your gun," Tony said.

The driver, having no desire to be a hero, handed both over without a problem. "Now drive out, and when we are back in contact with JP, you're going to tell him I got squirrely when we went through the tunnel and you locked me in the trunk. Okay?"

Tony moved the gun closer to the man's head. He started driving.

"Slowly," Tony said. "And no funny stuff, or I'll blow your head off."

He had no idea if he could actually shoot somebody, and he hoped he didn't have to find out. Maybe in the knee. Certainly not in the head.

Tony used his other hand to take the camera cap off his head and stuff it under a blanket. All JP would see is darkness when they emerged from the tunnel.

They drove out of the other side of the tunnel, but Tony kept the mute on his mic. "Stop the car," he said. The driver obeyed. "Now give me the keys and get out." Tony motioned him back toward the trunk. He popped it open. "Get in. I'm going to call JP, and you're going to say what I told you."

He didn't have to look for JP's number because JP was calling *them*. Tony opened the call.

"Johnson! What the—?"

Tony put the phone near Johnson's mouth. The man was curled on his side in the trunk.

"It's okay, boss," Johnson said. "We lost you for a few minutes when we went through the tunnel. Your man got restless, so I had to lock him in the trunk."

"Well geez, Johnson. Get a move on."

"Yes, sir."

Tony hung up while his luck still held. He waved the gun at Johnson. "If you make a sound, I'll come back here and blow your knee cap off." He closed the trunk and climbed in the driver's side of the car. Then he turned his mic on.

"Get me out of here!" he yelled into the mic, knowing he was probably shattering Jean-Pierre's eardrums. He hoped the shock of sound would keep him from wondering why there had been a lag between phone service and the Bluetooth coms coming back up.

"Tony, turn your camera back on!" shouted JP.

"It *is* on!" Tony yelled again for emphasis and looked down at Johnson's phone. He smiled. The GPS was still active and leading him right to where they were holding Abigail. He put the car in gear and drove as fast as he dared. He didn't want to attract the attention of the police. His mind was spinning. He had a phone now. He could text Jimmy. Or call 911. But no. If they came in with sirens, JP would kill Abigail. Or use her as a human shield to escape. He would have to do this himself.

"I can't see anything!" JP said. Tony could hear him breathing heavily. He was getting himself worked up.

"That's because I'm in the *trunk*, JP," Tony said, quieting his voice.

"Oh."

Tony kept quiet. It was another ten miles to his destination. He hoped JP didn't ask to speak to Johnson again.

— ◇————————◇ —

Abigail had slowly been scooting her chair toward Jean-Pierre. She had no idea what she was going to do when she reached him. She was tied and gagged. She had never felt so helpless in her life.

She could hear the icy rain pelting against the roof. Tony was in a car now, on his way here, stuffed in a trunk. She wondered if he was cold.

She was close enough to see the time on Jean-Pierre's laptop. It was 1:34 a.m. That meant it was Saturday. Nick's face flashed in her mind. He had died on this date. Pauline had said she would go with her later to put flowers on his grave.

Where did she leave the flowers? They must still be at the library because she hadn't gone back home before the premiere started. She was supposed to be home now, sleeping after her successful premiere and launch of the maps.

She scooted another inch.

"That's far enough, Abigail," Jean-Pierre said. He had calmed down after his brief loss of a connection with Tony and the driver. There for a moment, she had been truly afraid. An angry Jean-Pierre was a scary sight. He had banged his chair around and shouted into the mic. Then, he had turned and glared at her, threatening her with the gun if Tony didn't resurface. But now he was back to his calm, self-assured self. Of course. His plan was working out.

She glanced over at Karl. He was munching on a bag of chips. She realized she was thirsty.

"So, Tony," Jean-Pierre said. "Since you've got a ways to ride in that trunk, we have time to talk."

"I have nothing to say," Tony said. Abigail could hear his voice clearly. She was bummed they had lost the visual connection because it somehow made her feel closer to him. The screen was dark because he was in the trunk. She wondered if he was scared. Tony didn't seem to get scared, not even when he was caught breaking into that jewelry store to get the money to save his grandma. She had burst in, trying to save him. Even with all those guns pointed at him, he had remained calm.

She had only seen him scared once. That was the other day, when she told him to go sleep in the apartment. Suddenly, her eyes filled with tears.

No. She wouldn't let Jean-Pierre see her cry. *My drops of tears I'll turn to sparks of fire.* The quote popped into her mind. She thought it was from *Henry VIII,* but she couldn't be sure. Tony was the one with the better memory for quotes. *Tony.*

"I have plenty to say," Jean-Pierre said. "And Abigail is here, so she can listen. She won't be able to chime in with her thoughts, though, because she's gagged."

"You'd better not hurt her." Tony's voice was like steel.

"She's fine." Jean-Pierre leaned back in his chair. "That was a pretty impressive escape, Tony. Of course, now that the police are involved, I'm sure they're searching your house and your apartment as we speak."

Abigail thought of Cocoa. What if they broke in to her house and the cat got out? It was so cold outside.

"Abby. Can I call you Abby?" She shook her head no. The only one who called her that was Nick. And sometimes Jimmy got away with it.

Jean-Pierre grinned. "Abby. Did you know that your husband is a very talented man? Do you remember that story about the Grecian urn that was stolen from the Detroit Institute of Arts? That's a local story. Surely you heard about that."

Abigail hadn't. She didn't pay much attention to such things.

"That was your Tony. At least, that's what rumor says. How does it feel to know that he stole something right out of your own backyard?"

Detroit was hardly her backyard.

"He's quite respected in his field. If you want it, call Tony, they say," said Jean-Pierre. "That's why I needed *him* to get me this necklace. Nobody else would do."

"Jean-Pierre, shut up." Tony said.

"What else?" Jean-Pierre continued. "There was the time he broke in to this woman's house to take her jewelry. Those items, he sold himself. I saw it up on the black-market website. What did you buy with that money, Tony?"

Tony was quiet. Abigail could only imagine what he was thinking.

"Tony?" Jean-Pierre inquired.

"Why don't we talk about what *you've* done?" Tony shot back.

"No. Your job is to listen. What else should I tell Abby? Oh, I know!" He turned so he could see Abigail. "Maps. For some reason he has—or had—a keen interest in those. I never understood why until I found out about the Russo painting. He was on a search for a map that led to that, oui?" Jean-Pierre chuckled. "He was great at lifting those. Museums. Libraries. Private collections. Marvin Tucker could give you an earful of all Tony brought to him."

He looked at Abigail. "That's not the only thing he got for Marvin. He also picked up a blonde for him. I saw her the other night at the auction, hanging on Marvin's arm. I hear you introduced them, Tony. You're quite the Romeo, aren't you?"

Abigail scooted her chair again.

Jean-Pierre shot her a sharp look. "You do that again, madam, and I'll be forced to get nasty."

She wanted to distract him somehow. She knew what this must be doing to Tony. He would not only be worried sick about her, but now his dirty laundry was being hung out for her to see. She nodded toward a water bottle.

"You thirsty?"

She nodded.

"Too bad. Now, where were we? Ah, yes. Romeo." JP's grin turned wicked. He plugged his phone in to the computer and brought up the photo of Charlotte and Tony dancing. Blown up to the full size of the screen, Abigail could see how close they were. She closed her eyes.

"Tony has a thing for blondes," said Jean-Pierre.

"I like blondes," said Karl. They both looked at him. He had orange powder around his lips from the chips.

Jean-Pierre turned back to Abigail. "Let's take Charlotte, for instance. He has worked quite a bit for her. Both *in* and *out* of her bedroom, I believe."

"Jean-Pierre," Tony cut in. "Abigail knows I love *her* and only her. Abigail, don't listen to him. He's trying to tear us apart."

"I don't need help with that, Tony. You're doing a great job of that yourself. What were you doing that night, anyway? I hear Charlotte asked you back to her place, and when told her you had to get home, she pulled you upstairs to one of the bedrooms."

"Don't believe a word he says, Abigail."

Abigail swallowed. This was getting to be too much.

"He was all over her the other night," JP said. "Before he met you, they had a thing, you know. It's hard to get a woman like that off your mind."

"It wasn't a thing," Tony said.

"And there were other women. When you hear Tony's name in the dark circles, you hear great thief, excellent lover. Not that I would know," Jean-Pierre said. "That's what the ladies say. But he leaves a string of broken hearts, you know. It won't be long before he gets tired of you too."

Tony was silent on his end.

"He's only coming for you now out of guilt. He's a softie. Look how he was with Vivian's Dobermans." Jean-Pierre opened the bottle of water and took a swig. "He says he never hurts people, but he did. Did he tell you about the old man he stole a pocket watch from?"

"That's old news," Tony said. "She's heard that story. And your twisted part of it."

"What about the jewels you took from the widow? I believe her wedding ring was among them. He thinks because he doesn't shoot anybody, Abby, and goes in unarmed, that he isn't hurting anybody. But there are deeper hurts than losing material possessions, aren't there? He has hurt plenty of people. And now he has hurt you."

Jean-Pierre looked back at the photo of Tony and Charlotte. Abigail's eyes were on it too. Did Tony cheat on her that night?

But now he was risking his life to save her. What if he got killed in the process? She closed her eyes again and began to pray.

Chapter Thirty-Six

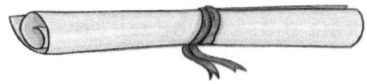

All Tony could do was listen as his sordid past was being spilled out for Abigail to hear. If she didn't hate him already, she certainly would now.

The icy road was practically empty this time of night with only a few solitary cars passing by. Anyone who was sane wouldn't be out driving in this weather. He had left the "bad part" of town behind, and came across a patch of houses, small, cookie-cutter types that were built during the war. There were some odd buildings here and there, and run-down businesses with boarded up windows. He passed an old factory that had been closed for decades. He glanced at the GPS. He was almost there. He would need some time to think once he reached the address.

He needed to give JP a reason not to worry about where they were. *Don't text and drive,* he thought as he punched a message in to Johnson's phone and sent it to JP.

There's an accident up ahead with some police barricades. I can talk my way through. Don't text or call until I'm clear.

Hopefully, JP would believe that.

There was a pause in JP's rambling, probably so he could read the text. Then he continued. "And what else has Tony done, Abby? Don't you wonder?"

Tony gripped the steering wheel hard, wanting to crush something. Abby had been Nick's special name for her, and no one, not even Tony, used it. He remembered with a start that today was the anniversary of Nick's death.

"How did Karl get involved in this?" he asked, trying to change the subject.

"Keep your voice low until the car starts moving again," JP said. "As for Karl, I've been following you around. I saw you two didn't have the best relationship, and I talked to him. He was more than happy to help me. He's getting great monetary compensation for his troubles. You personally know how well I pay."

The GPS indicated for Tony to turn right down a smaller road. He saw a huge warehouse standing tall and dark against the night. It looked deserted.

He had arrived.

He stopped the car behind some bushes far away from the building so he wouldn't be seen. He stuffed the phone and the gun in his bag and got out. The night air was freezing, and the ground was nearly a solid sheet of ice. The icy mix still fell from the sky and coated the branches of nearby trees and bushes. It was also doing a great job of coating his car. A small part of his brain was worried about Johnson freezing to death, but right now, he had to focus on Abigail.

"Are you moving yet?" JP asked Tony.

"Not yet. What's up?" Tony said as he pulled his gloves on. "I can hear people talking. It's freezing back here. Can you text Johnson to let me out?"

JP didn't answer. Hopefully, he was still afraid to contact Johnson. Instead, he began talking more about Tony's exploits. Half of them were made up. Tony muted his mic while JP droned on.

Tony looked at the huge building. He had no idea where they were inside of the place. He also didn't know how many people JP had with him. Were they guarding the doors?

The building was about five stories tall, with several small windows around the top floor. The rest was windowless. He looked for a way up to the roof. He had learned to come in from above when you could. People watched the doors and windows, but rarely did they look overhead.

He walked around to the back of the building and saw a metal ladder leading up. It must be a way for workers to reach the air conditioning units and fans up on the roof. He put a hand on one of the rungs. It was covered in ice. His gloves would only offer so much protection. He looked up again, and the icy wind beat sleet down on his face. It was going to be a long, dark climb.

"I hear your driver talking to somebody. Can't you tell me what's going on?" he said, to keep JP busy. He put his hand on the ladder and began to climb.

"Just stay quiet," the Frenchman said.

He'd love to. Tony muted his mic again so JP couldn't hear him breathing hard and wonder what he was up to. It was to the sound of JP droning on about his sins that he made his way to the top. He slipped at about twenty feet up and almost fell. He had to hang there for a moment before he had the nerve to continue. When he reached the window, he scraped off some ice with his lock pick and looked in. Luck was with him. Or God. There was a light illuminating a small portion of the dark warehouse, and he could see JP sitting at a desk. Abigail was in a chair near him, bound and gagged. From here, he couldn't see Karl. Or anyone else.

He finished climbing on to the roof, out of breath. He turned his penlight on and walked around the roof, but he couldn't see a way in. He would have to go in through the window.

He clipped his rope to the top rung of the ladder and lowered himself back down over the side of the roof. Hanging there, he took his glass cutter and carefully cut through the icy glass until he had a space that his hand could reach through. He unlatched the window and opened it. He saw a platform inside. He could land on that, and the darkness of the warehouse should keep him hidden.

Praying once again, he crawled through.

Abigail tried to tune JP out, but then she heard the ice pelting down on them. *Why were the heavens so angry with her?* Was this date to be the one where she lost another husband?

Why are you doing this to me? she asked God. Over the past hour, her prayers had gone from a desperate cry for help, to fear that He wasn't listening, to anger that He would leave her here.

She opened her eyes, and that's when she saw a figure climbing through the window up near the ceiling. JP's back was turned to that side of the building, and having run out of the Evil Escapades of Tony, he was now blathering on about some map or other in his collection. She had quit listening. The figure landed quietly and expertly on a platform. It was Tony!

He saw her and put a finger to his lips to silence her.

Karl was over in his corner working on a second bag of chips. JP sighed and stood. "Tony?" he said into the mic. "Are they moving yet?" When there wasn't an answer, he started to swear in French. "We've lost this connection again!"

Abigail needed to distract him. She started rocking her chair wildly.

"What's wrong with you now?" Jean-Pierre said. He was getting antsy.

She squirmed and tried to speak through the gag. Jean-Pierre came over and pulled it out of her mouth.

"I'm thirsty," she said. "And I have to pee."

Jean-Pierre shrugged. "You'll have to hold it. There's no restroom. We weren't supposed to be here this long."

"You've had me here for *hours*," Abigail said. "I really have to go. I can use a bucket."

Jean-Pierre wrinkled his nose in disgust but glanced around the room for one.

"I can watch her," Karl said. "Make sure she doesn't escape." About that time, there was a loud crash, and boxes came tumbling down from the far side of the room. They landed on Karl.

"There's somebody else in here!" JP said. He grabbed his gun and ran to check it out.

That was enough time for Tony to swing unseen across and down to Abigail. He landed in front of her, flipped open a knife, and quickly cut her loose. She had never been so happy to see anyone.

"Go!" he said, unbuckling his harness to give to her. "Remember how you did it at the museum? Get up to that window while I distract them."

"He has a gun!" she whispered.

Tony thrust a gun at her, as well as a cell phone. "So do you. Call Jimmy for backup. The address is on the phone's GPS. Now go!"

Abigail hesitated for a moment, but this seemed like the only plan. JP was behind a crate, and Karl was struggling under the boxes. "Don't worry about me. I can hide," Tony said.

Abigail quickly put on the harness and ran toward the platform. His rope was hanging down, and she hooked it to herself.

"Hey!" Jean-Pierre shouted, and she turned to see him running toward her.

"JP!" Tony shouted. The man turned. Tony was dangling a necklace from his hand. Below him was a drain. If he dropped it, it was lost. "I have it. I have Danes' necklace."

JP froze, and Abigail used the moment to ascend upwards. The quick ascent took her stomach, but she was on the top of the platform almost instantly. She unhooked the clip and peeked her head out the window to look for the ladder. She reached through and hooked the rope on the top rung. She could see the dizzying drop, even in the darkness. Then she kicked off her heels and climbed out, slipping once on the rung. The pain of the ice on her feet was excruciating. Holding on with one hand, she dialed Jimmy's number.

"We need help!" she said. She briefly told him the story and gave him the address.

She heard a gunshot. The sound scared her, and she dropped the phone. As it fell to the ground below, she looked in the window. Tony was in trouble.

Chapter Thirty-Seven

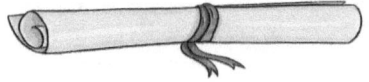

Tony had his hands raised. One was out to the side over the drain, and one was over his head. JP wanted Tony to give him the necklace, but Tony was hanging on to it. JP had fired into the air in an attempt to scare him. It worked. He was plenty scared, but he was still holding that necklace above the drain.

Karl appeared beside JP, having managed to climb his way out from underneath the boxes. He looked a little bruised.

"Karl, grab him," JP said.

Karl walked toward Tony and threw a gut punch his way. But Tony was expecting it and dodged. The force of the punch propelled Karl forward, and he stumbled.

"Fool me once..." Tony said.

JP swore. "Grab him, you idiot."

Tony pushed the necklace down into his pocket and jumped up on JP's desk. With his foot, he kicked the chair toward JP, knocking him off balance. He took advantage of that to leap on JP's back, bringing them both to the floor. The gun went off again, causing Tony's ears to ring. He was on top of JP and about to pin him down when Karl grabbed his shoulders and tore him off the Frenchman.

With a huge roar, Karl flung Tony through the air. He hit the boxes hard, and a few fell on him. Tony rolled out from underneath them and was back on his feet, coming back at Karl.

Karl braced himself. But instead of plowing into the huge man, Tony reached into the bag on his back and wrapped his hand around the glass cutter. As he approached Karl, he pulled it out and sliced it across his face. Karl howled in pain.

"Enough!" JP yelled. Tony turned and saw the gun pointed right at him. He raised his hands into the air.

A gunshot rang through the air. They all looked up toward the sound. Abigail was standing on the platform pointing a gun at them.

"Don't move," she said.

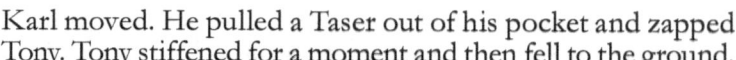

Karl moved. He pulled a Taser out of his pocket and zapped Tony. Tony stiffened for a moment and then fell to the ground.

JP turned his gun up at her. She flattened out on the floor of the platform and looked wildly about. Across the room, behind JP, she saw a pipe. It looked like a gasoline line that led to some of the machines. She had practiced her sharpshooting skills many times with Jimmy, so she took careful aim and shot a hole in it. Gas started pouring out.

"Drop the gun, or the next one is going through you!" she shouted down to Jean-Pierre, praying she didn't have to shoot him. If he shot at her now, the bullet wouldn't go through the floor of the metal platform. But she was trapped up here.

Instead, he swung the gun around toward Tony, who was still lying on the floor. "Abigail, put the gun down, or I'll kill him!"

With quick precision, Abigail fired. The bullet shot a hole clean through JP's wrist. He dropped the gun in a howl of pain.

Karl fled.

Abigail had to get to Tony before JP recovered. His wrist was shattered, but the shock would dull the pain enough for him to act. She hooked the rope onto the platform and looked five stories down. She remembered Tony's words from the museum. "You trust me."

"Yes," she whispered. She looked down at the man she loved and jumped.

Landing lightly beside Tony and JP, she dug into Tony's bag and found some flash powder. The gasoline was pooling below the hole in the line. She threw the powder at the gasoline and then threw herself on the ground over Tony. The huge explosion rocked the building, and for a moment, all sound disappeared as her eardrums reacted. She saw JP screaming and running, his suit coat on fire. He quickly rolled on the floor, smothering it. But she could see bone shards sticking out of his wrist, and the man was deranged from the pain of both. He disappeared through a pair of doors.

The fire was spreading quickly, fueled by the air in the open building and eating up the dust, cardboard boxes, and gasoline.

"Can you move? We have to get out of here!" Abigail said. "That way!" She pointed toward the doors JP had gone through, but a large metal beam fell, sending sparks flying and blocking the way.

She looked behind her, and the fire was licking its way up the rope to the platform.

Tony struggled to a sitting position. "Tool bag," he said. She slid it over to him, and he grabbed his other rope. She saw the muscles in his fingers trying to fight their way back to working.

He stood, shakily, and threw it upwards. He was weak, and it missed its mark.

He grabbed a clip from his bag and clipped it onto the rope, adding some weight. He threw it again, and it landed, hooking expertly over the platform rail. He gave a little tug and locked it. The flames were moving closer, and the heat was making it hard to breathe.

Grabbing Abigail around the waist, he hooked her to the new rope and wrapped his arms around her. They ascended up to the platform.

"Don't touch the metal," he yelled above the noise of the fire. "It'll be hot."

"I'm barefoot!" she said.

He swooped her up in his arms. While carrying Abigail, Tony unhooked the clip and reattached it to the ladder outside of the window. Abigail climbed out, slipping on the ladder. Her nylons were torn, leaving her feet bare. Her numb fingers couldn't get a grip on the icy ladder rungs. She hung there, suspended far above the ground, and waited for him to climb through. He didn't have a harness on. He slipped, and she grabbed him. She waited until he wrapped his arms around her securely before she pushed the button and lowered them to the ground.

221

trusting the cat burglar

When they landed, cops surrounded them.

Abigail was grateful for the wool blanket they had wrapped around her. She sat next to Tony in one of the fire trucks as the paramedics checked her out. Then they checked Tony out too. He was hooked up to a mobile monitor to check his heart since he had been tasered, but he seemed okay. An ambulance was there too and was getting ready to take JP to the hospital for treatment. He and Karl had both been caught by the police, while they were running up the road, trying to escape.

Johnson, the driver, was sitting in the police cruiser warming up. He had handcuffs on.

Outside, Abigail could see the fire truck battling the blaze. The whole building, and whatever was in it, was engulfed in flames. The place, being so old and neglected for so long, was burning like dried kindling.

Assured that Tony was okay, the paramedics unhooked him and wrapped another blanket around his shoulders. Neither she nor Tony could quit shivering.

"I'm so sorry," Tony said when they finally had a chance to speak alone.

She turned to look at him. His face was creased with worry, his eyes tired. She smiled. "No. I'm sorry for pushing you away. I love you, Tony."

Tears filled his eyes. "I thought I had lost you," Tony said.

"Do you think Jean-Pierre would really have killed me?"

"I don't know. But I mean before that. I lost you before that."

Abigail remembered the look in his eyes when she had sent him to his apartment to sleep and sent him away from the premiere.

"You never lost me. I was just focusing on the wrong things."

He leaned his head against hers, and she closed her eyes, drinking in his touch. "I was *trusting* in the wrong things," she said.

The paramedic knocked on the side of the truck. "The cops want a statement from both of you."

Afterward, a policeman drove them home in his cruiser. Jimmy, Tony's grandma, and Pauline were all waiting for them at their house. And so was Cocoa, Abigail saw with relief.

Jimmy engulfed Abigail in his arms, holding her close to him. "You scared me to death," he whispered. She heard something like a sob escape him, but when he pulled back, he had his cop face on. His eyes grazed over Tony and then dismissed him.

"Oh, Abigail, thank God," Pauline said, pulling her into a big hug. Then she turned to hug Tony. "Thank God you are both okay. But you're freezing. I'll go make some hot tea."

Tony went over and hugged his grandma.

Jimmy's phone rang, and he went into the kitchen to talk, pacing back and forth. There were two other cops with him. Abigail recognized them from the station.

"You two get into some dry clothes," Grandma said.

"That sounds good. I want to shower and warm up," Abigail said to Tony.

"Me too."

He followed her into the bedroom. As soon as the bedroom door closed, she turned and threw her arms around him, burying her face in his chest. She breathed in his smell and thought of how close she had come to losing him. The events of the night came crashing back into her memory. Her panic attack at the library. Running outside in the freezing weather without her coat. Jean-Pierre grabbing her. All of it came back to her vividly.

She clung harder to Tony.

She remembered how scared she was when she knew Jean-Pierre had Tony under surveillance and when Vivian Danes pulled a gun on him. Somehow, he was still able to come to her rescue. And he almost died again freeing her.

Then adrenaline took over, and she had shot Jean-Pierre. *She shot Jean-Pierre.* The image of his wrist shattering flashed through her mind.

"We almost died today," she said, her voice muffled in Tony's shirt.

"But we didn't," he said quietly, stroking the back of her hair with his hand.

"Seven years ago today was the beginning of the worst day of my life," Abigail said. Tears came to her eyes, and she pressed her face harder into Tony's chest. She felt him respond by wrapping his arms tighter around her. "And I thought today was going to top that. I almost lost you too." She started to cry then, the tears falling down her cheeks. The crying turned to sobbing as the memories of today came at her, one after the other. Tony held her and let her cry, and she emptied all of the grief out of her. How could she have ever pushed this man away?

When she was finally spent, she turned her face up to him.

"What are we going to do now?" she asked.

"We're going to stick together," Tony said.

His eyes looked tired. She lifted her hand and reached up to place it on his cheek. He was so dear to her.

"I said some terrible things to you," she said, drinking in his gaze. "How can you still love me?"

He smiled, and a mischievous glint returned to his eyes. They were tired, but Tony was still in there.

"Doubt that the stars are fire, Doubt that the sun doth move, Doubt truth to be a liar, But never doubt I love," he said.

She reached up and kissed him. "Why don't you shower first, Shakespeare? You're faster than I am."

She sat on her bed and pulled her wet clothes off. Her nylons were torn to shreds, and she had no idea where her shoes were. Probably burnt up in the fire. She went to her drawer to look for comfy clothes.

In less than ten minutes, she heard the water shut off. When Tony came out, he was freshly shaven. His dark hair was damp and curly. He was wearing jeans and a long-sleeved shirt.

She let the hot water run over her for a long time, washing the last few hours off, and then changed in to some sweat pants and a baggy sweatshirt. She put on her fluffiest socks and went back out to the living room. Tony was sitting on the couch with a steaming cup of tea in his hand. Someone had built a fire in the fireplace.

She sat down next to him and took his other hand. His finger absently stroked her ring. Pauline brought her a cup of tea.

"It's decaf," Pauline said.

Abigail looked at the clock. "It's nearly morning. You should be with your kids."

"Drew has them. We were terrified that something awful had happened to you."

"It's because of Pauline that we knew where to start looking," said Grandma. "She told us what you said about that awful man with the maps."

"Thank you," Abigail said to her friend. She glanced toward the kitchen at Jimmy. He was still on the phone, and he kept glancing at her and Tony. She had an uneasy feeling in the pit of her stomach.

Chapter Thirty-Eight

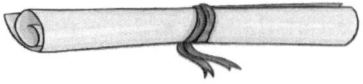

Tony sat on the couch between his grandma and his wife. He was bone tired, and every part of his body ached. Pauline had brought him some aspirin, which was starting to kick in. He had finally warmed up, and he would be feeling sleepy, except he couldn't figure what was going to happen next. Jimmy hadn't said a word to him since their return, and he kept giving Tony looks from the kitchen. Abigail's house had been searched, so he imagined his apartment had too.

He wondered how long it would take for JP to confess everything and show the police the video.

Jimmy held his hand over the phone receiver and came into the living room.

"Jean-Pierre Mauvais is claiming the Vesconte is stolen," he said to Tony without preamble. "And that *you* stole it. He says he has a lot more than that on you."

Tony wearily looked up at Jimmy. "He probably does."

Jimmy grunted and went back into the kitchen. Abigail gave Tony's hand a squeeze. "Trust," she said.

Jimmy hung up and motioned his officers over. They huddled together in the kitchen.

Tony watched them warily. Jimmy pulled something out of his pocket and brought it over. It was Abigail's phone.

"We found this in the parking lot across the street from the library," he said, handing it to her. "My tech guy cracked the password, but there was nothing on it that told us what had happened to you. I did find some photos taken recently of *him* in the arms of another woman."

"Tony! Is this true?" Grandma said.

"It's not what you think," Abigail said, reaching over to pat Grandma on the hand. Tony kept his unwavering gaze on Jimmy.

"Is that woman tied into this somehow? Where was this picture taken? I want her name."

Tony remained silent.

"It's a work thing," Abigail said. "It was just business."

Tony squeezed her hand. "You don't have to defend me."

"I'd like her name so I can check that out for myself," Jimmy said.

"No." Tony figured Jimmy already knew who Charlotte was. Any good cop could use facial recognition software to find her. Because of all of her many businesses, Charlotte's face was all over the internet.

"You're *protecting* her?" Jimmy said.

"Yes. I'm protecting her."

Jimmy's eyes flashed with anger. He looked like he was ready to kill. "You're under arrest. Get up."

"No," Abigail said, her hand tightening on Tony's.

"You're wanted for breaking and entering in to Vivian Danes' house. You drugged her dogs. You *stole her gun,* and you're also wanted for assault. She said you knocked her over. She's a 72-year-old woman!"

"Tony? Is this true?" Grandma said.

Tony glanced at his grandma, and her eyes were wide with fear. He gave Abigail's hand a squeeze and stood. "Can we please not do this in front of my grandma?"

Jimmy looked at Grandma. "I'm sorry, Rosalind."

Abigail still hadn't let go of Tony's hand.

"No," she said. "Jimmy, do you have any idea what today is?"

By the look on his face, Tony could tell he did. "I'm sorry, Abigail. I really am. Martha is home resting, but she'll be over later to sit with you. I know this is bad timing, but your husband here is in big trouble. We even found Danes' necklace on him. How can you continue to defend him?"

For a moment, Tony thought about running. He didn't think Jimmy would shoot him, not here in front of Abigail. And the other two officers...well, he would be fleeing unarmed, so they probably wouldn't shoot either. If he could get past Jimmy, he could run upstairs. A third-story window was loose, and he could slip out onto the roof, jump over into the neighbor's yard, and be gone without a trace.

Then he glanced down at Abigail. He couldn't disappear. He could never leave her like that.

But he was going to jail.

Abigail stood up next to him. "I'm going with him," she said, still clinging to his hand.

"Very well," Jimmy said. He turned to one of his officers. "Read him his rights."

Tony tried not to look at his grandma while Jimmy put the handcuffs on him. He also avoided Pauline's eyes as Jimmy led him past her and to the front door. Abigail grabbed them some coats out of the closet and draped one across Tony's shoulders.

Cocoa came over and twined around his legs. He glanced down at the cat. She wanted him to scratch her behind the ears, but he couldn't. Then he looked over at the table where the roses still sat. They were starting to wither.

Abigail pushed the cat back.

"Let's go," Jimmy said, and Tony walked out of his home, maybe for the last time.

The lights were bright in the police station. Tony and Abigail sat side by side in metal chairs beside Jimmy's desk. Tony was still wearing the handcuffs, which he knew was overkill. He wasn't a flight risk here. Jimmy was just making a statement. He saw Vivian Danes sitting across the room at another officer's desk. She kept darting angry glances at Tony.

Jimmy opened up a folder on his desk and then closed it again and tossed it aside. "You burnt down an entire warehouse."

"*I* burnt down the warehouse," Abigail said. Jimmy looked at her.

"*You* did?"

Abigail nodded. "Read the statement I gave to the police." She was sitting as close to Tony as the chairs would allow.

When she turned her head, her hair brushed against his cheek, and he could smell her lavender shampoo. He closed his eyes.

"Jean-Pierre claims he has a video that will put you away for life," said Jimmy. "I can't wait to see that."

Abigail reached her hand behind the chair and entwined her fingers in his. Her skin was so soft and smooth. He tried to concentrate on her touch. The cuffs were cutting into his wrists.

"Jimmy, don't be mean," Abigail said.

Tony's eyes were still closed. He thought of his life one week ago. Even with community service, things had been good. He still had his new job. And his friends.

"I lost George," Tony said in a quiet voice.

"What?" Abigail said.

He opened his eyes. "I lost George. I told him about my past, and he couldn't handle all the years of deception. He won't speak to me."

Abigail put her hand to his face. "I'm so sorry. When I told Pauline, she handled it well. She doesn't hate you."

Jimmy cleared his throat.

"That's her," Tony nodded toward Vivian Danes. "That's Vivian Danes."

Abigail looked over at her and stood. "I need a drink of water," she said to Jimmy. She walked in the direction of Vivian.

"You nearly got Abigail killed," Jimmy said to Tony after she was out of earshot. "All of this is because of you."

"I know," Tony said. He couldn't argue with that. If JP had never recognized him, none of this would probably have ever happened.

An officer came over to get some information. They moved him to another area and took some mug shots and got his fingerprints.

Then Jimmy came back and grabbed him roughly by the arm. He led him back through a hallway toward the jail cells. Tony craned his neck to get one last look at Abigail. Her back was turned, and she was still talking to Vivian Danes.

Jimmy pushed him into the cell and unlocked his handcuffs. He slammed the cell door. He stood there, watching Tony. It seemed like he was struggling for words. "You have more to say to me?" Tony asked. "Go ahead. Say it." He could see the anger in Jimmy's eyes. But there was something else too. Sadness.

"Okay," Jimmy said. "I will." His jaw worked for a moment, and Tony saw him take a deep breath, calming himself before he spoke.

"I trusted you," he said, his voice low with repressed anger. "I put my job on the line for you, told the guys here that you were okay. Heck, Tony, I even found you jobs to help start your security company! You've been running around town installing security for *friends* of mine! What were you planning to do? Go back in later and steal something? That would be easy, wouldn't it?"

"It would also be bad for business," Tony said. It hurt him to see Jimmy looking at him this way.

"When I brought you in here two months ago on charges at the jewelry store, I got you community service instead of jail time. I *knew* that you were the one who broke in to the library, yet I chose to look the other way. I also know there are a lot of crimes in your past, but I haven't dug hard to uncover them. I'm ashamed of how I've conducted myself. The law is the law, but I let you turn my head. I've never, ever, in my life been tempted to do that before. But when I saw how happy you made Abigail..." He choked on the words. It took him a moment to regain himself. "I trusted you once. I won't make that mistake again."

He turned and left.

Tony sat down on the bed. It sagged in the middle. He was so tired. After a while, he lay down. He thought about all of the things he had lost. Was losing. He thought of their home, and how the two of them were a family now. And Cocoa rubbing against his legs. Would he ever get to pet her again? What about Abigail? She was going to lose another husband. He figured she'd be okay. She was strong, and she had the Stouts and Pauline. His thoughts started to drift and the exhaustion of the past week finally won over. Soon he was asleep.

He awoke to Jimmy tapping on the bars. Tony sat up and looked unsuccessfully for a clock. He had no idea how long he had been sleeping.

"Luck follows you," Jimmy said. "Vivian Danes has decided not to press charges after her little chat with Abigail. She says you were acting under duress. Those charges probably wouldn't hold anyway because of that. And she's happy to have her necklace back." He moved his face closer to the bars. "But I will get you on something," Jimmy said. "And I will lock you away where you can't hurt Abigail again. I promise you that."

Jimmy turned and briskly walked out. Tony sat there for a moment, but he was too tired to think. There was a loose wire hanging from the light above him. In the back of his mind, he realized he could probably pick the lock with it. But then what? Wearily, he lay back down on the bed and closed his eyes.

Chapter Thirty-Nine

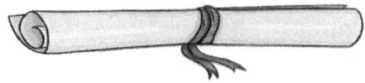

Abigail was allowed back to see him, but they sent a guard with her. Tony was lying on the bed with his eyes closed.

"Tony!"

He rolled over and smiled at her. Then he got up off the bed and came over to the bars, putting his hands through to grasp hers. He looked terrible.

"I called our lawyer."

"We have a lawyer?"

"We do now. Jonathan Stewart agreed to take your case." He was the city attorney that had "found" their painting *The Laurel*. "And I talked Vivian out of pressing charges," she said brightly. She wanted to share all of the good news with him.

"I heard. What did you have to give her in return?"

Tony was too smart. She hadn't planned to tell him that part.

"I had to promise her that you'd update her security system for free, which I realize will cost us a lot in time and money." Abigail knew there was a chance Tony wasn't going to be out of jail to update Danes' or anyone else's system, but didn't say that. She'd keep it positive.

"And the laptop burnt up in the fire. So far, they can't find a backup of the video. Apparently, it was only on the laptop, and Jean-Pierre is having a fit and talking about the flash drive he gave you."

Tony nodded. He glanced at the guard. Abigail looked over at the man. "Can we have a bit of privacy?" she asked.

The guard nodded and stepped back a few feet, politely pretending he was out of earshot.

"Abigail," Tony said, touching her hair. He ran his fingers through it. Then he touched her cheek and traced her lips with his fingers. His eyes looked very sad. It scared her.

"What's wrong?" she asked.

"I'm going away for a long time," he said.

"No, you're not!" she said. Her heart started racing.

"Shhh," he said softly and put his finger on her lips. "Listen for a minute. I've been thinking. We haven't been married for that long. You can probably get an annulment. Then maybe none of this will touch you. Maybe you won't lose your job or your tenure. You can tell people you didn't know I was like this. That you thought I had changed."

She shook her head. "No. No. I won't do that. An annulment? Don't you want to be married to me anymore?"

Tony's eyes filled with tears. "Yes, I do!" he said. They started to spill down his cheeks. "More than anything. But I can't be a husband to you while I'm in here. You know that. Abigail, you need to move on."

He was really scaring her now. "No. I won't. I can't live without you. I will come visit you. They won't put you away forever. Maybe just a few months?"

"More like years," Tony said. "Grand larceny carries up to fifteen years."

"Or minimum of probation," Abigail said. "I looked it up."

She reached through the bars and pulled his head close to hers. She kissed him on the lips. She kept her forehead against his.

"You'll be okay," he said.

"No. I won't."

"Remember what we learned in church?" Tony said. "About trusting in God? Jeremiah 29:11. *He has plans for you... plans to give you hope and a future.* It's not about trusting in this system, Abigail. Or me trusting in you or you trusting in me. We just do the best we can. God is the one Who we must really trust. Trust *Him*, Abigail. No matter what happens to me, you'll be okay."

A feeling of overwhelming panic filled her. What if he didn't even get out on bail? What if he never got to come home? "I won't be okay at all if you're not with me."

Tony looked at her with steady eyes. "You will," he said.

Jimmy walked in then.

"We brought someone in for questioning, and now I want Tony in there too. Abigail, honey, I'm sorry. Go home. Get some rest. We'll take good care of him." He unlocked Tony's cell. "Come on."

Jimmy didn't cuff him, and Tony followed him into a room at the back of the precinct. There was a table with some chairs around it, and another police officer stood guard at the door. The blinds were pulled. Jimmy motioned for Tony to take a seat. He left the room, and in a few minutes, he came back with Abigail.

"She insisted. Maybe this will be good for her to see." Jimmy sat across from him. He made Abigail take a seat on his side of the table, so she was also across from Tony. Their eyes met briefly, and Abigail shrugged. She didn't know what this was about either.

"I have someone I want you to meet," Jimmy said.

Tony looked toward the door, and Charlotte was led through by a policewoman. As usual, she was impeccably dressed. She had on tweed pants and a cream-colored blouse. Her hair was brushed, even though it was the wee hours of the morning.

They had brought her in for questioning. Who else's life had Tony ruined?

Charlotte glanced at him but didn't react. She was playing it cool. Tony looked across the table. Abigail looked terrified. Jimmy was watching the three of them very carefully. So this was a game.

Tony decided to play. He leaned back in his chair, taking on a relaxed position, and let a big smile cross his face.

"Charlotte!"

She gave him a nod, and let a small smile play at her lips now that she knew the rules. She had even put lipstick on. They must have dragged her out of bed. Tony could imagine her making the officers wait. Apparently, they didn't have enough on her for charges. Just questioning.

"How are you?" he asked.

"I'm tired, Tony, and I'm cranky, because these officers got me out of bed. They showed me some unflattering photos of us. Well, *you* looked good in them, as always, but do you think that dress made my butt look big?"

Tony chuckled. He could always count on Charlotte.

"I think you looked fine."

Charlotte glanced at Abigail. Neither woman reacted.

"So where were you that night the photos were taken?" Jimmy asked.

"Have they asked you that already?" Charlotte said to Tony. "Because they keep asking me. I haven't said. I'm down here on my own accord. They have nothing on me, but your wife's *father* here wants to take us down. He thinks you and I have a thing."

"It's strictly business," Tony said.

Charlotte looked at Jimmy. "Told you."

Tony scrutinized the room. Abigail was playing with her fingernails. It was probably best she and Charlotte didn't acknowledge they knew each other. He had one last thing to do.

"Jimmy, is my house still a crime scene?" Tony asked.

"We got in and got what we wanted."

"Please don't hurt my computers. I need them for my security business. My *very legit* security business." He knew they'd never be able to crack his passwords and security. He wasn't worried about them finding anything. Jimmy might have good tech guys, but Tony was better.

Tony crossed his arms and let some angry fire come in to his eyes. When he spoke, his voice was serious and had an edge

"You've messed up my life long enough," he said to Charlotte. "I'm with Abigail now. On your way home, stop by my apartment and get your things. Especially your toothbrush." He put a slight emphasis on the word toothbrush. "I don't want to see it there when I get back. We're through." He had no idea how she'd actually get inside his apartment.

Charlotte's eyes flashed at his tone, uncertain, and for a moment Tony was afraid she hadn't read him. But then he saw it dawn on her. She glanced shyly at Jimmy. (When had

Charlotte ever been shy?) To her credit, she was even able to produce a slight blush.

"I'm sorry," she said. Another first. Charlotte never apologized. She looked back at Tony, her gaze lingering for a moment, a lover getting one last glimpse before she lost him forever. She was a pro. Then she pushed back her chair and stood.

"I'm finished here," she said to Jimmy in a curt voice. "If you need me again, call my lawyers."

And she left.

Abigail sat frozen in the chair for a moment, until she caught Tony's eye. He raised an eyebrow ever so slightly. She suddenly knew what he wanted.

For Jimmy's benefit, she glared at Tony. "You pig," she said and ran out of the room.

She pulled her coat on, digging in her pocket for her keys. She raced to the door and grabbed Charlotte by the arm. The blond woman spun around.

"Don't ever go near my husband again," Abigail said, loud enough for others' benefit. As she spoke, she slid her hand down Charlotte's wrist and palmed her the key to Tony's apartment. She felt Charlotte's fingers close around it.

"Like I said, it was just business," Charlotte hissed loudly. Then she leaned in close, so only Abigail could hear. "Nothing happened."

"I never thought it did," Abigail whispered back.

Charlotte stepped back and jerked her arm out of Abigail's grasp. She plowed through the doors.

Abigail glanced over her shoulder. Jimmy was watching her from the hallway. She saw another officer taking Tony back to his cell.

She watched the two men she loved until Tony was out of sight. Jimmy walked back inside the room, so she turned to go home.

Chapter Forty

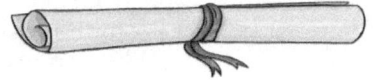

Abigail slept all day Saturday. When she woke, she laid there for a moment, stretching out in the soft sheets. The late afternoon sunlight was coming in through a crack in her shade, filtering across her bed.

Cocoa saw that she was awake and jumped up on the bed, purring. Abigail rubbed her cat on the head. She turned over to look at the clock and saw the huge pile of tissue from all the crying she did before she finally fell asleep.

Tony had saved her. And he had hopefully saved Charlotte and also managed to get the flash drive out of his apartment.

She wondered how he was, and if he had gotten any sleep.

She got up and fed the cat dinner. It was 4 p.m., and she half expected Tony to show up at her front door, having been freed from jail. She even opened the front door once to check. He wasn't there, but his apartment key was lying on her doormat. A sticky note with a smiley face was attached. Charlotte had done her job.

She showered and dressed in jeans and a sweatshirt. She was starved. She hadn't eaten in almost twenty-four hours. She made herself an omelet and a salad and ate alone, looking at the vase of roses on the table. Some of them were already dying. Sitting next to it was the vase with the yellow daisies she had bought to put on Nick's grave. Pauline must have brought them from the library.

Around 6 p.m., Martha called. Abigail talked to her briefly, telling her she wanted to be alone. Then Pauline called to see if she still wanted to go to the cemetery. Abigail told her no. She was just too tired. She called the police station, but they told her she wasn't allowed to visit Tony today. Jimmy's orders.

She hung up and wondered why Jimmy was being so mean. It wasn't like him. She tried his cell, but he didn't pick up. She knew she had hurt him once before when she had lied to him about how she met Tony. Now, she had hurt him again by defending Tony, even though the evidence was against him. But couldn't he see how much she loved Tony? She smiled at the thought of Charlotte calling Jimmy Abigail's father. How true it was. He and Martha were like parents to her. Maybe parents and kids didn't always have to get along.

She tried calling the lawyer, but it went to voice mail, so she went over to the couch and tried to read. She looked at the clock again. It was almost 9 p.m.

She thought about Nick. Seven years seemed like a lifetime. Seven years ago, she had lost one husband. Today, she had lost another.

She called the police station again. She explained that she needed to know if Tony was okay. They said he was, but he wasn't allowed visitors right now. He was being questioned.

Abigail hung up the phone. She went back into the bedroom, undressed and crawled back into bed. She curled up into a fetal position and felt a familiar darkness coming down on her. She needed to fight. She needed to drive over to the police station and demand to see her husband. She needed to make sure the lawyer was doing his job.

But she was so tired. So very tired. She lay there for a long time staring into the darkness, and she finally fell asleep.

She awoke to someone pounding on her door and then heard the doorbell. Her heart started pounding. That was how they came to tell her Nick had died. *Tony!* She reached for her phone but realized she had left it in the kitchen. She jumped up and wrapped her robe around her. She peeked outside the living room window and saw a police car sitting at the curb. Her mind was still cloudy with sleep. She couldn't figure out what was happening.

There was more knocking. She opened the door. It was Jimmy.

"I didn't think you were going to let me in. Where's your phone?"

"I, um..." She looked at it. There were several texts from Jimmy saying he was stopping by.

"Can I come in?"

"Um, yes." She opened the door, and he walked in.

"I'm sorry to bother you at this time of morning, but it has been twenty-four hours. I know you two are up to something, but I have no idea what. Right now though, I have nothing on Tony. Mauvais' apartment in Paris is being searched for that video, but so far, we have no connections to Tony or you, other than that you invited him here to store his maps. And you started that before you even met Tony."

"That's all I wanted, just his maps. I had no idea..." Abigail said and sat down on the couch, fresh tears coming to her eyes. She was beginning to suspect what Jimmy had come for.

"I know. And there are no charges against you, of course. You were defending yourself." Jimmy looked at her for a long while. She could see him fighting some emotions. Finally, he said, "Abigail, I was so afraid I had lost you."

"I'm here. Safe," she said. "It was Tony who saved me."

"It was Tony who got you in to this in the first place."

Abigail was silent.

Jimmy put his hands in his pockets. "I know this is a tough day for you. And I hope you know that I only want what is best for you. I'm giving you something, but I want you to be very careful." He paused. "Martha and I love you."

The tears were running down Abigail's cheeks now. "Thank you," she whispered.

"Don't thank me. If it were up to *me*, he'd still be in jail. You have no idea what you've put me through since you met him. I'm constantly conflicted between my heart and my job. I want you to be happy, but I also have an obligation to my badge. I will do what I have to do to protect you and the other innocent people he has hurt. Your safety comes before your happiness."

She didn't know what to say. She knew Jimmy would protect her at any cost. That was the way he was made.

"It hurts me that you've lied to me," Jimmy said. "And to Martha."

"I haven't lied to you. I just haven't told you everything," Abigail said. "I believe there's a law that protects me from incriminating my husband. Please don't dig, Jimmy. Just let it go."

239

"There are others out there who Tony has hurt. They will come after him. I'm afraid this isn't over, Abigail."

"I'm sorry," she whispered.

Jimmy pushed the com button on his walkie-talkie. "Bring him in," he said.

An officer came through the door with Tony. He looked exhausted. His dark, curly hair was all rumply, and his shirt was wrinkled. He had huge bags under his eyes, but he was smiling. And he was alive.

"Hi, beautiful," he said softly.

Abigail jumped up and threw her arms around him. As she clung to him and wept, Jimmy and the officer quietly made their way outside and closed the door. She never heard them leave.

"I'm home," he said.

Chapter Forty-One

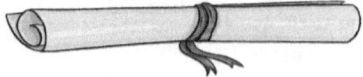

Tony slept for most of Sunday, and Abigail watched him. His long lashes fluttered now and then, and sometimes she saw a small smile on his lips as he dreamed. She lay close to him and felt the rise and fall of his chest with each breath. He was alive. And he was home.

He got up late that afternoon and showered. She made a big dinner, and they ate together quietly. There would be plenty of time to talk later. Right now, they were adjusting to being safe and together.

As they were cleaning up the dishes, the doorbell rang. It was Ms. Scott. Abigail let her in and offered her a seat at the kitchen table.

Lulu Scott had her hair down. It was quite pretty. Black, with touches of gray at the temples, it was full and draped across her shoulders like a silk sheet. She was dressed casually, in jeans and a two-piece brown sweater set.

She cleared her throat and looked at the two of them.

"Paris has been canceled," she said. "Jean-Pierre was the head of it, so of course it has. But the good news is the panel has decided to move it a few months out and still wants you to speak. The library board has decided to pay your way, because it will bring us world-wide recognition."

Abigail reached over and took Tony's hand. "Really?"

"What this means is that you may still have a chance at tenure," Ms. Scott said. "And you have not been fired. Not yet. I figured you have been through enough. Later, after you have recovered, we will discuss all of the secrets you have kept from me and why."

Abigail nodded.

Ms. Scott looked at the flowers on the table. She seemed about to say something else and then thought better of it. She glanced at Tony and picked up her keys and phone. "That is all."

The visit lasted maybe five minutes. That was Ms. Scott, straight and to the point. Abigail let her out and walked back to the table. Tony wrapped his arms around her. She was so excited she felt like bursting.

"Well, there's still Paris," he said.

"We'll always have Paris," Abigail quoted.

"I forgot to tell you," Tony said. "About an hour after Charlotte left the station, it dawned on Jimmy what we were talking about. He dispatched someone to go look through my apartment again. But he was too late. The incriminating toothbrush was gone."

Abigail laughed.

"Jimmy hates me," Tony said, a bit of sadness to his voice.

"But he loves *me*. He'll come around."

Tony kissed the top of her head. "Who are the daisies from?"

"I bought those with Pauline. I was planning to put them on Nick's grave yesterday."

Tony was silent for a moment. Then he asked tentatively, "Would you like me to go with you?"

Abigail's head was on Tony's shoulder, her arms around his neck. She looked through the window. It was a clear day, and there was still a little bit of sunlight left.

"I'd love that."

Chapter Forty-Two

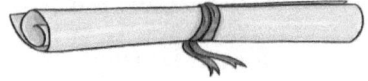

Nick had a beautiful headstone, purchased by his parents at the time of his death. Abigail told Tony this was the first time she had seen it. There were birds and vines carved into the stone around the edges of it. Below the dates of his birth and death were the words *Beloved son and husband.* Tony stood and watched as Abigail knelt and traced the word *husband* with her finger.

There were already some flowers there, probably left yesterday by Nick's parents. Abigail laid her bouquet of yellow daisies down next to them.

Tony put his hands in the pockets of his coat. The weather was warm, in the forties today, but the air was still a little chilly, especially as the sun was setting. A ray of sunlight cut through some trees above them and highlighted Abigail's hair, turning it to a flaming red.

After a few minutes of silence, she stood. She turned, took Tony's hand, and together they walked back to the car.

He put the keys in the ignition, but she put her hand on his, stopping him from putting it in drive. He looked over at her. She was looking at him intently.

"In the police station, you were talking about annulments and stuff. That scared me. I don't want to lose you, too."

Tony took her hand and squeezed it. "I was thinking of you. One of these days, Abigail, my past is going to catch up with me."

"Maybe not. And even if it does, I want to be there. Remember, we're trusting in a Higher Power. None of us knows when our last moment is on this earth. God is in charge of that. Let's enjoy the time we *do* have."

Tony smiled over at her. "Maybe we need a vacation. I only have a few more weeks of community service, and it looks like I'm not going to jail. Not this time, anyway…"

Abigail's eyes brightened as she got where his thinking was headed.

"So let's go to Paris for our honeymoon! We can combine it with the symposium!"

Tony laughed and put the car in gear. He had always wanted to go to Paris, which is where his great-grandmother had met the famous painter, Antonio Russo. Where Tony's past had begun. He thought about the Eiffel Tower, walks along the river Seine, and a trip up to Montmartre to see the plein air painters. Oh, how he could romance Abigail there!

"What's past is prologue." he quoted. "Here's to our new story. Carpe diem and all that!"

Together, they quite literally drove off into the sunset.

THE END

Follow Tony and Abigail in their adventure in Paris in *Romancing the Cat Burglar: A Russo Romantic Mystery: Book 3.*

Acknowledgments

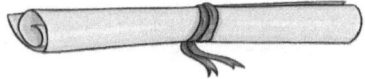

Writing is a solitary job, but publishing a book takes a team. I am forever grateful for mine.

First of all, I am thankful to God. It is my hope that His glory is reflected in all that I do. Without Him, I am nothing.

To Xanthe and Other Pam, my critique partners. Thank you for your continuing support. You read my work in its rawest form and you still love me.

To my beta readers: my sister-in-law Peggy and my Dad, Floyd. I really appreciate your willingness to read and comment. Your insight is immeasurably valuable!

To my incredible publishing team: Erin my editor, Dallas my formatter, and Lyndsey my cover artist. You bring professionalism to the table and are so fun to work with!

And, of course, to those who stand by me no matter what: Duane, Zack, Logan, Mom and Dad. I love you all!

About the Author

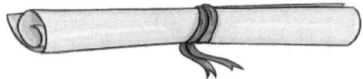

Pamela Gossiaux is the author of *Mrs. Chartwell and the Cat Burglar* and the romantic comedy *Good Enough,* as well as the inspirational books, *Why Is There a Lemon in My Fruit Salad? How to Stay Sweet When Life Turns Sour,* and *A Kid at Heart.* She is also a Christian speaker, writing instructor, and freelancer. She lives and writes in Michigan near a wonderful university town with her husband, two sons, and three cats. Visit her website at PamelaGossiaux.com.

Other Books by
Pamela Gossiaux

Meet Amy Summers, a big-hearted heroine whose simple life gets turned upside down when she finds a winning lottery ticket worth millions...but should she cash it?

Amy Summers has it all: the world's best job, an awesome boyfriend, and a happily-ever-after in sight. Then, in one very bad day that involves burnt toast and a police arrest, she loses everything – except for a winning lottery ticket her ex left behind.

Afraid to cash it, she decides to give up men and become a Bohemian novelist. She takes her laptop to Starbucks and literally bumps into caffeine-free, easy-going Josh Gray, a life coach and very handsome man. (Not that she's noticing.) When he offers to help Amy get back on her feet, she decides to hire him.

Her heart is telling her that he's the man for her, but Josh is big on honesty and Amy has a huge secret that could push him away if he ever finds out.

"Richly meaningful while wildly entertaining, GOOD ENOUGH is a major new book by an exceptionally talented author."
– Grady Harp, Amazon Hall of Fame Top 100 Reviewer

"This story is such a fun read, it is impossible once you have opened it not to be thoroughly captivated by Amy's escapades."
– Susan Keefe, *Midwest Book Review*

"GOOD ENOUGH touches a nerve every woman faces. Are we ever going to be good enough? Gossiaux has written a funny, revenge romance that will have you cheering on the heroine, Amy, until the very end."
—Diana Lesire Brandmeyer, author of CBA Best Seller *Mind of Her Own*

Available at PamelaGossiaux.com